POWER OF FATE

MYSTIC HARBOR BOOK ONE

SUKI WILLIAMS
JARICA JAMES

Thank you to our amazing Betas, Danyelle and Tosha for making sure our final book is perfect, we appreciate you! Thank you to Polly, our editor. Your thirst comments give us life.

WELCOME TO MYSTIC HARBOR

Welcome to Mystic Harbor, a paranormal small town on the coast. This is an omegaverse world, meaning that everyone, including humans, are either Alphas, Betas, or Omegas. If Omegaverse, knotting, and omegas with heat are not your thing, this book may not be for you.

Alpha, Beta, Omegas (ABO)

Dominant, possessive, and protective, **alphas** tend to be leaders. The **betas** are the level-headed caregivers that defer to their alpha for guidance (or at least in most cases). They're the glue that binds a family unit and can help bridge the gap between overbearing alphas and the headstrong omegas. During heats, the betas are generally the ones ensuring everyone stays fed, hydrated, and safe. **Omega males**, while they cannot bear children, still have heats and produce slick. They have the same nurturing, softer natures that help in raising children and creating a family. **Omega females** also experience heats, which is their most fertile time. They bear the children and are the piece that completes the unit. Only alphas can get omega females pregnant, and only omega females can become pregnant in this world.

TRIGGER WARNING

This is an ABO omegaverse Reverse Harem Romance. Despite the main character's background, the story will be a lighter/steamy omegaverse. The main character does experience on-page mental health trauma - hospitalization - and abuse by her medical staff.

CHAPTER 1

Ella

"Sammy, if you don't sit your ass down in your seat, by god I will tan your backside for everyone to see!" The worn-out mother's yell rang throughout the Greyhound bus. It wasn't exactly surprising since her kid had been pushing her buttons for the last sixty miles. Everything from shouting out about how bored he was to fidgeting enough the man sitting in front of them was about to blow a gasket. Probably longer than that but that's when he started getting loud enough for everyone to hear. Mumbles rang out from the passengers but I only grinned at the duo in front of me, finding them amusing and a welcome distraction from the long bus ride.

A stale breeze wafted through the bus, the driver kicking up the air which I appreciated, at least in theory. My hair was sticking to my sweaty forehead, as it has for the last several hundred miles, but the AC only stirred up the smells on the bus... which weren't exactly pleasant.

As the smell of cigarettes and body odor surrounded me, I coughed into my elbow before trying my best to focus on typing out a new story idea in the Notes app on my phone. Anything to tune out the chaos that was my current existence.

"But, Mama! This lady is pretty. She doesn't look grumpy like you do." My eyes widened at his words and I looked up to find the little boy staring down at me with curious wide eyes. His blond hair was a mess and his toothy grin adorable as he studied me. "Hi. I'm Sammy! What's your name?"

"Uhhh—" I was tongue-tied as his mother huffed and reached over to tug his shirt. All while whispering that he would get it when they got home. Little Sammy, who didn't look a day older than four, dramatically rolled his brown eyes and turned to flop down in his seat. *His mom is going to have her hands full with that one.*

The bus stopped for what felt like the millionth time and let on another wave of people. We barely have room and the seat next to me is one of the last empty ones. I cringe as a burly alpha starts heading my way, sighing in relief as he passes me up. Between his deep scowl and scraggly beard, he didn't look like someone I wanted to get to know. At least he had no intention of intimidating an omega like me. *Good.*

The bus was heading up Interstate 95 and right now we were in New Hampshire, but my final destination was another three hours away in Maine. *Mystic Harbor.* An unknown little town I had literally found by accident as I was frantically trying to plan an escape from my family. If you listen to the gossiping ladies around you out in public, you hear about the coolest things. Of course, then I had to look it up and I was sold by the first picture I saw. Plus it was far enough away I knew they couldn't follow.

I had overheard my parents talking a week ago about having me committed to the mental hospital in Atlanta yet again. Honestly, it hurt, I hadn't done anything out of the ordinary either. I'd learned to not mention the supernatural a long time ago. My first stay was enough to teach me that particular lesson. But I also had no filter whatsoever, so who knows if I let something slip out recently and can't recall it. Sometimes things got a bit fuzzy around the edges and I was never quite sure what I did during those times... It got exhausting trying to be their perfect idea of a daughter. To be the Stepford child that smiled and waved and charmed all their friends, went to the right schools, and didn't cause problems. But I didn't have it in me, not that they gave me a real chance anyway.

But one thing I knew for damn sure... there was no way I was going into the asylum. Well, not again at least. My parents had put me in for random stints whenever I talked about the things I saw, but the older I got, the more I kept my mouth shut. At least around them. Apparently, my best friend wasn't to be trusted either because she was at my house as a "concerned friend" and they were planning an intervention. It happened yesterday and I still couldn't shake it.

Just thinking about that conversation filled me with rage all over again. They had no right to take my freedom away. The worst part was that my best friend was the only one I thought I could trust, yet there she was talking to my parents like she'd suffered greatly just being exposed to me. I watched my parents reassuring her as she sobbed on, and from their words, this time it sounded more... permanent, not a few weeks or two months stint.

SUKI WILLIAMS & JARICA JAMES

No, thank you.

Being there for just a week was torture. There was no freedom, and I was constantly watched by the staff, not even getting a moment of peace. And I've heard stories that talked about the conditions on the 'lifers' side, those the court, doctors, or families decided were too insane to be among the public. I hardly qualified, but that never stopped them. Money talked, and they had enough to make anyone listen.

So I came up with a plan, which included raiding my money stash and buying a bus ticket. Thank god I'd tucked away money any time they gave me some or left it lying around. It was of no consequence to them, but to me, every dollar added up.

It all worked out because using cash was the best option as to not leave a paper trail that they could follow. I'd even picked an obscure town I'd never heard of before, all the way up the coast. There was a small bed and breakfast that looked quirky, adorable, and like something my snobby parents would *never* step foot in. They only stayed at the most prestigious hotels and resorts. No room service? No way.

It was perfect.

Shoutout to the couple in the bookstore chatting about Mystic Harbor. They were talking about going to their marina every year as they browsed the travel section. The name alone had me pausing, but the more they gossiped, the more sold I became. I mean, who wouldn't want to live in a town that reminded them of fairytales and sat right on the coast?

When I did some research, it only solidified this was the right choice. The pictures spoke to my soul. Small town life, adorable businesses, a small harbor, and people who didn't know a fucking thing about me. Plus they had a three-month-long tourist season each year, but thankfully that season is ending this week, meaning I'll blend in and be settled before the tourists disappear. It was the perfect plan.

Mystic Harbor was my chance at a new me and I couldn't be more excited. There wasn't even an ounce of sadness for leaving my supposed friends and family behind. And hopefully, I would never have to face them again. I was doing everything in my power to stay under the radar. They'd never been on my side, I was just a burden... an embarrassment. It was time to live my life for me.

Do I use a fake name? The thought had me frowning and wishing I had some top secret connections in the mafia so I could get myself some papers forged, and have a whole new identity. Ella Harper was dead to me and I wanted nothing to do with her. Well, I did love the nickname of my first name, something my parents loathed. But I couldn't risk my parents finding me because of some slip-up. It wasn't like my family didn't have the funds to hire someone to track me down. Nope, the less of a paper trail, the better.

Any step that didn't include an asylum was okay by me.

The thought of the asylum had my stomach clenching painfully. It was a mindfuck for anyone but especially for someone like me. I could hide the things I saw in my everyday life. It was easy enough to not tell people the homeless man on Sixth street was a wraith, but not exactly easy to keep it to myself in a place *full* of supernatural beings. In fact, nearly the whole staff was some form of supernatural, though they hid it well from the other humans. How was I not supposed to stare at the sharp fangs and winding horns of the doctors and staff?

My mind drifted to my first stay as I zoned out.

The plain white walls and floors of the ward were like an omen to me. My parents were sending me here to learn how to fit in their perfect lives, to lose everything that made me unique, to be the trophy daughter they always wanted. Not the mentally ill child they had been cursed with, or so they told me at every opportunity.

"Through here, Miss Harper," the nurse said, her voice raspy. I had a feeling it had to do with the snakes she had for hair. When she took me to the nurse's station, my eyes went wide. Between the dragon, the harpy, the vampire, and the elf sitting behind the desk, I wasn't sure who to look at first. The only consolation was that they were all betas, who were a lot less intimidating than alphas.

"Wow... did you eat the human nurses or what?"

They all turned to me slowly, eyes narrowed as they studied me. The nurse leading me clicked her tongue before ushering me down the hall.

"Talk like that will keep you here," she chided, shoving me unceremoniously into my room. She had been right, though. Every mention or stare got me a few more days until I learned to look down, keep my mouth shut, and pretend everything was fine.

The sound of the brakes squealing as the bus lurched to a stop had me snapping out of my wandering thoughts. I looked up in time to see the sign welcoming us to Mystic Harbor. The sight of the wooden sign had my entire body relaxing. I'm here. *Wait, how in the hell did three hours go by?!* It took about twenty minutes before I had my one large suitcase in hand and was walking away from the bus station.

The town was just as idyllic as those ladies in the bookstore back home had promised it to be. From the adorable, brightly colored main street, to the backdrop of the ocean behind us. The air smelled of salty sea and sweet pastries. My stomach growled and my nose tried to lead me away, but I had to find the bed and breakfast before I gave in and explored.

"You look a bit lost, may I be of assistance?" The smooth, flirty voice had me looking up at a handsome alpha. The scent of cinnamon and spice slammed into me and I had to take a moment to gain my composure before I started panting in the middle of the street. It was like the best thing I'd ever scented and I wanted to wrap it around myself like a blanket. Which was, in fact, crazy as hell. Sure, everyone had a scent, but why was his so intense? My eyes drifted up and I blinked slowly at the curious fae who was studying me, his eyes various shades of green with gold sparks in them like stars. He was much taller than my short five-foot four-inch frame and it took every ounce of willpower not to blurt out why a fae was singling me out of the entire group of tourists getting off the bus. "Oh, so rude of me not to introduce myself, I'm Leif, the Mayor of Mystic Harbor." He didn't offer a hand to shake or anything, just studied me for my next reaction. I didn't miss the way he seemed to be taking measured breaths, like I was affecting him just as much.

My mouth opened and closed a few times, my brain sending warning signals at the fact that he offered a name so freely to me. *Must be his public name if he is actually the mayor and not his real one. No way would a fae just hand out his* true *name, much less an alpha at that.* As he tilted his head, I realized that I needed to say something, any response at all. *As long as it included a damn filter.*

"Oh, yes— Ummm, I'm staying at the Beds and Broomsticks, Bed and Breakfast. I have a horrible sense of direction though." As I spoke, my free hand twisted in the hem of my shirt. I really needed to work on my social skills... *or lack thereof.*

Fae didn't like you to ask them direct questions, it was considered rude. Something I learned as a child from a young fae who actually talked and played with me. I could never remember his name, but he and his nanny were always nice to me. That was before we moved away because my dad got some big job promotion and we ended up down in Georgia.

Keen interest sparked in his eyes as a small smile curled his lips and instant heat filled me as he gestured toward the other end of the street we were standing at. "Head that direction and once you arrive at the end of Main, turn right onto Blue Jay. It's right in the middle of the strip of buildings across from the park, you can't miss it."

Don't thank fae either, dearie. The younger ones might not mind, but the older ones... Well, best to just remember this warning.

"I'll do that." I smiled at him, hiking my purse over my shoulder before setting off. I could feel the weight of his gaze as I walked through the cute coastal town.

I tried not to stare but besides the obvious tourists there, everyone was a supe. *Everyone.* How did I pick a small town out of the entire United States that was flooded with creatures I shouldn't know exist. Maybe this means they would accept me... That my new me can actually be the *real* me. Of course, for that to happen I just had to deal with, overcome, and cope with years of gaslighting, verbal and emotional abuse by my parents.

No big deal.

A slightly hysterical laugh bubbled out of me before I could stop it. And as everyone turned to look at me, I couldn't find it in myself to care. I already felt more at home here than I had anywhere else. And some staring was the least of my problems.

The hint of cinnamon wafting from the coffee shop I was passing, had me biting my lip as I thought of the fae alpha that had greeted me and given me directions as I got off the bus. Yeah, a few stares were nothing compared to catching his interest, even if only for a little while.

The mayor's directions were fairly cut and dry. I turned right down Blue Jay and spotted Beds and Broomsticks right away. I'd never seen a gothic style Victorian painted black, but it was absolutely perfect. My grin only grew as I approached, loving the deep red roses that were growing out front and the old bell-shaped doorbell she had hanging over the door. They'd accented the entire house with white trim, which only made the black pop more. A mix of red and white flowers grew below each window and in the front landscaping. It beckoned me in and I took that as a sign that I'd love it.

The bell rang as I pushed open the door, the smell of incense and herbs hitting me the moment I stepped inside. A gorgeous woman with brunette hair and a bright smile stepped up behind the counter.

"Welcome to Beds and Broomsticks, do you have a reservation?" Her voice had a slight rasp to it. When she smiled I could see sharp teeth, and her eyes glowed a neon blue that caught me off guard. Everything about her screamed alpha, though her scent wasn't as potent as the fae's.

A wolf running a witches' bed and breakfast? Her

smile fell and she narrowed her eyes, meaning I hadn't been so quick to keep my generic pleasant expression in place. I winced and hid it with a cough.

"I love your inn, the aesthetic is fantastic!" I beamed, coming right up to the desk. She visibly relaxed, pride shining clearly in her eyes as she looked around the beautiful place. If this town had this many supernaturals I was going to have to work on my poker face. "And yes, I have a reservation for Ella." I froze, realizing I'd used a fake last name, but I couldn't for the life of me remember what it was. She was already glancing at her computer screen though, saving me from stumbling.

"Ella Reed?" she asked, looking up. Ah yes, I'd used my childhood friend's name. I was high-fiving past me until she asked the next question. "I just need an ID on file and my notes have your reservation as standing, do you want to do weekly fees or monthly?"

"Uh," I bit my lip, panic building up inside as I tried to figure out what to do next. I couldn't just hand over my ID. She frowned at the terrified look in my eyes. It felt like she could see through my soul and I didn't know what to say. Eventually, I grabbed my ID out and handed it over. "Can you just not share this if anyone asks for my real name?" It was definitely the time for blunt questions, or I may as well pack up and leave now.

Her scrutinizing look turned to sympathy as she caught the hint of panic in my voice and the slight tremble of my hands that I couldn't quite hide fast enough and she nodded, pushing my ID back to me. "Ella Reed it is," she agreed and I felt my entire body slump in relief, the tension running out. How readily she agreed made me think that she understood the desperation in my question. *Maybe I'm not the only one running from some-*

thing here. That or her alpha side could see an omega in need.

"Then monthly would be great for now," I said. She gave me another one of her glowing-eyed stares, showing I had apparently passed some unspoken test.

I shifted uncomfortably and waited for my total before handing over the amount she asked for in cash. When I tried to tip her, she insisted I keep it for myself.

"Come on, Ella," she said instead, handing over a key and coming around the counter. She took my bag, not listening to my protests, and walked over to the staircase. I followed her up, staring at the art lining the walls as I went. It was the typical things you'd expect from a place called Beds and Broomsticks, like the full moon and tarot images, but they were gorgeous.

The hall was long with doors on either side and one at the very end, facing the staircase we'd come up. She walked all the way to the end and pushed the door open.

"This is our biggest room and it has the best view. If you're going to be here for a while we may as well make it comfortable." She grinned, looking proud of her bed and breakfast, and she should have been. It was beautiful.

"Thank you," I said, practically knocking her over as I rushed in and explored the room, not able to contain my excitement. There was an adjoining bathroom with a vintage clawfoot tub and a floor-length mirror. The bedroom itself stuck to the black and white theme, from the white walls and black bedding to the black brick fireplace and plush white rug in front of it. "This is amazing."

She pushed open the curtains and raised an eyebrow. "You haven't even seen the best part yet." My cheeks hurt from smiling, but it grew impossibly wider at how nice she was being. Moving toward her, I glanced out the window, gasping audibly at the view. I could see her back gardens, which were even more beautiful than the front landscaping. Back here she wasn't shy with colors and a path wound its way through them. A fountain sat in the center, spraying water upward, lifting a glass orb so it shined beautifully in the sun.

But beyond that was the coast itself, the waves crashing against the shore and an island just in the distance. A bright white aura surrounded it and I couldn't peel my eyes away. She must have noticed my gaze, so she gave me a bit of the history behind it.

"That's our town's namesake. Mystic Island," she explained. "It's the center of many local legends, but the truth is the island is dangerous so we don't explore it. Instead, we let it keep its mystery."

Her words were an obvious warning, but I didn't mind. I was definitely okay with letting things keep their magic.

Before she could say anything else, the bell downstairs rang and she sighed. "Better go see who that is. If you need maps, directions, or anything I'll be downstairs. Coffee and snacks are available at all times of day, except overnight, and we serve breakfast, lunch, and dinner. It's included in your price of staying here, but if you bring anyone there's a paid menu. Oh, by the way, my name is Violet. Don't hesitate to reach out to me if you need help with anything. And if you want a first night in town dinner date, make sure you come back by six. That's when I sit down and I can give you the rundown of this place." She rattled off the information so quickly that I stood there stunned, processing it still as I watched her hurry away. But my heart warmed at the invitation and I made a mental note to keep an eye on the time.

Now that I was alone in my room, I walked over and closed the door before going to my suitcase that Violet had placed on my bed. I unpacked everything on the bed first before finding semi-permanent places for them. It would be temporary, sure, but I'd be here long enough to want everything to have a place.

Flitting around the room, I put my clothes in the drawers and closet, and products in the bathroom, until all I had left was the cash I saved up. I'd spotted a safe in the closet and went to check it out, finding the key on top. I counted out enough for exploring before putting the rest inside and locking it. I'd need to be careful with my funds. It wouldn't last long and I'd need to find a job, something I never had before... but that was a problem for another day. The key was small, so I pulled out my necklace and looped it onto the chain.

Now that all the tasks were taken care of, I felt a sense of unease. I'd really done it, I had left my life behind and claimed my own future. But no matter how relieved I felt, I couldn't shake the feelings of doubt and fear that lingered there. I'd never run away before, instead, letting them dictate my life and lock me away at will, but now that I was gone... Would they find me again? Could they let go of the one pawn they'd used as an outlet for their hate and control issues? And beyond that, freedom in itself was kind of terrifying. My options were open, I could be anyone I wanted to be here, no one knew me. But I had been silenced for so long that I didn't even know who I was anymore, and that was unsettling as fuck.

"Okay, Ella," I said out loud, giving myself a pep talk. "First things first, get your bearings. Learn the town and maybe make a few friends. The rest can come next week."

Nodding to my own words, I went to the closet and

picked out a new outfit. The last thing I wanted was to stand out, so I chose some simple skinny jeans, knee-high boots, and a loose tee that hung off one shoulder. My long blonde hair was a bit wild from being on the bus all day, so I brushed it out and braided it to the side. Satisfied, I grabbed the room key and locked the door behind me.

Time to see what Mystic Harbor is all about.

CHAPTER 2

Ella

Hurrying down the stairs, I waved at Violet as I passed through the foyer and she shot me a quick smile while talking with an older woman at the counter. I breathed in the brisk air signaling the beginning of fall as I ran outside, a huge grin spreading across my face. I was determined to push my anxiety to the back of my mind. There was no way those controlling jerks were going to ruin my first taste of freedom.

It probably should have worried me that I was a lone omega in a town full of alphas, but I couldn't find it in me to worry. So far I'd seen enough supernaturals to know this wasn't the average town. And at least my heat wouldn't be coming for another five months or so, I'd rode out my last one with heat suppressants but I didn't have any left to bring with me. But that was a concern for another day. Right now, I was facing my new town and I wanted to see it all.

But where to start?

Tracing my previous steps I looked around and passed the small diner that was beside Beds and Broomsticks, Quick Bite, which looked like one of those hole-in-the-wall places that always have great food. Note to self, I'll check that out some night before I run out of money. My interest piqued when I crossed the street, a row of shops with plenty of tourists milling in and out. I was trying to figure out what I would do first when the smell of coffee hit me. The lifeblood of a writer. I followed my nose to a beautiful coffee shop, The Enchanted Mug.

I stood outside just staring at it, breathless at the beauty of the small shop. It was a light sage green with a huge glass window that allowed you to see right inside the cozy place. Groupings of cushioned chairs and small tables, sofas, and a coffee table, along with a few small cafe tables outside made the place seem comfortable and not crowded. To most, it might seem chaotically decorated with mismatched styles, but I could see the consistent palette of earth tones that made it all work together. The pops of color came from the plants and flowers that were carefully arranged outside and inside the shop, and a wall of plants along the back wall near a small sign pointing to where the restrooms were located.

A body hitting my shoulder pulled me from my wandering thoughts. As I stumbled back, the older man who knocked into me reached out and apologized. I smiled and told him it was my fault, getting lost in my thoughts. Walking into the shop I felt immediately at home and got in line behind two families so I could place my order. I looked up at the neat menu on the wall behind the counter, trying to figure out what I wanted to try. There was French press coffee, drip coffee, regular, cold brew, even some organic teas that looked interesting. I chewed on my lip, almost overwhelmed at the choices.

"Welcome to the Enchanted Mug," a harried, tired voice greeted me. Blinking, I tried really hard to consciously keep my expression blank. The man in front of me was inhumanly handsome, if not for his eyes and ears I would have thought he was fae like the mayor. But this guy, Drystan according to his nametag, had rich brown eyes with small rings of green and gray on the outside accenting the deep color. His ears were pointed similar to the mayor as well, though his weren't as long. But, it was the scent that really struck me. Just like Leif, his hit me like a ton of bricks, knocking the breath from my lungs for a moment. The fact he smelled just like Earl Grey tea was fitting for his workplace, but I shouldn't have been able to smell it over all the coffee and tea swirling around the shop. *What the heck is going on here?* "Are you going to order?"

Hell, I really needed to get my thoughts under control. I felt my cheeks heat and blurted out before I could stop myself, "I love your eyes."

Drystan leveled me with an incredulous stare. "My eyes are brown."

"Brown is beautiful—"

"Like shit?" he deadpanned, making me burst out in laughter.

"Like the dirt of the earth helping plants grow." I gestured at the plants around us. "Trees, the warmth of hot chocolate, and of course, coffee," I sang out the last word, my bubbly personality apparently too much for him.

He blinked slowly, his full attention focusing on me as he listened to my comparisons and I swore I saw a slight twitch of his lips. "Well, lover of shitty brown, what do you want to order?"

I bit my lip, glancing up at the giant menu again. Then it hit me exactly what I wanted to do, new experiences are exactly what I needed. "Make me your favorite coffee, whatever that is. Hot or cold, I'll take it."

His head tilted at that, his earlier exasperation nowhere to be seen as he studied me. "Are you allergic to anything?" I shook my head and he nodded sharply. "I'll make you a large."

"How much?" I asked as he turned to start making the drink, but he ignored my question.

I shifted from foot to foot, unsure what to do with his silence until he came back with my large mug. "It's on the house. Welcome to Mystic Harbor..." He looked at me with a question in his eyes before I realized that he was probably waiting for my name.

"Ella." I grinned up at him as he slid the drink carefully to me. My heart clenched at the way he studied me, something about him just pulled me in. Maybe it was the excitement of a new town and my freedom, but yet again I found myself enthralled with someone new.

"Ella." He nodded, warmth filling his eyes before he abruptly turned to help the next customer in line. One point for me! I melted the surly barista, even if only a little.

Quickly I moved out of the way, walking around tables and chairs until I found the perfect place to sit and people watch in the back. I was hoping to get a feel for the place while I drank my heavenly treat. Holding the mug with both hands I carefully lifted it to my lips to take my first sip. The bitter, earthy taste of the coffee hit my tongue first, then it was followed by the slight sweetness of vanilla and the smokiness of cloves complementing it perfectly.

I sighed at the perfect concoction and licked my lips as I settled back in the armchair, my writer's mind instantly creating stories about the customers flitting in and out of the cafe. Reaching into my bag, I tried to find my notebook and frowned, realizing that my old notebook had been confiscated by my parents. They always said all these imaginings for my stories were damaging my brain even more. *Assholes.* I really needed to find another notebook soon. From the shops lining the square, I knew it wouldn't be a hard task to complete.

I took my time, drinking the coffee slowly and enjoying fully relaxing for the first time in my life, not worrying about what my parents were thinking or what doctors were writing in their notepads. Every movement, word, and silence weighed and judged to be used against me later.

About half an hour later, I finished off the drink and took it to one of the bins put out for dirty drinkware. Drystan was outside when I walked out, his expression shifted from annoyed to curious as I approached him. "Thank you for the coffee. It might be one of my favorites now."

He smiled then, just a small curl of his lips, but it was real, the warmth sparkling in his eyes too. "Come back anytime, Ella. I'll make sure to expand your horizons."

"I do love coffee!" A shop out of the corner of my eye made me gasp, grabbing my attention. "Ohhh I need to go check that out. I'll be back tomorrow for sure."

I waved absently at Drystan as I skipped past him and hurried to the store next door that had caught my attention. A sex shop called Kinkubus that couldn't be more aesthetically different from the warm cafe next door. But it called to my curious nature all the same and I whipped the door open, a small twinkle of a bell going off as I entered.

The outside had been simplistic but classy, and the inside was more of the same. The white walls had black and white art and pictures strategically placed. The shining marble floors inlaid with glitter and industrial-style ceiling shouldn't have worked, but they did, giving the place an upscale, modern vibe. If there weren't rows and rows of sex toys and lingerie, I'd have thought it more of a boutique.

"Welcome to Kinkubus, let me know if you need help finding something." The rich baritone caught me off guard and I blinked up at the man behind the counter. He was also a supernatural, the sleek black horns poking out of his hair curled backward, his eyes dark as night and just as captivating. *Incubus.* If I looked hard enough, his human disguise fell over him and I could see the adorable, timid man who was running the sex shop. It was kind of funny considering it was a shop where shyness didn't really fit, but shy betas could be kinky too. Even as the shift between supernatural and human changed again, I could see he had the same shyness about him.

"Thanks!" I called out, ripping my eyes away from the intriguing man behind the counter. He nodded once and glanced away, a hint of a blush on his cheeks at my lingering stare. Smiling to myself I started going through the shop. The lingerie could wait, I didn't exactly have anyone to wear it for, so I started with the toys.

Story ideas sparked in my head as I casually walked the aisles. Romance hadn't been my usual choice, the idea of fantasy worlds and leading females who weren't afraid to raze her kingdom to eradicate evil always calling to me more. But now that I was free of my own evil, took the world into my hands and escaped a terrible fate... Now I wanted more out of life for me and my characters that lived inside my head.

Living the life I had didn't give me a lot of life experiences, which meant I was in over my head in here. Sure I knew what vibrators were for, but some of these toys had me tilting my head in confusion.

Grabbing what looked like mini jumper cables off the display, I went up to the man behind the counter and held them up so they dangled off of my index finger and raised an eyebrow.

"Can I ask a question?" I asked. He looked from me to the dangling chain and back again, clearly not sure where this was going to go, but at least he wasn't annoyed. The warmth of sweet honey surrounded me, making me tongue-tied for a minute waiting for him to speak.

"Sure..." he mused, waiting patiently for what words tumbled out of my mouth next.

"Why do you have tiny jumper cables?" He let out a slow chuckle at my words, then startled when he realized I was serious.

"Uh, this is our french line, but the words on the package say that they're nipple clamps. Some people like a little pain with their sex," he said bluntly. I felt my eyes go wide at the idea of clamping them to my own nipples.

"Interesting," was all I said before walking back and putting them on the display I found them on. Not wanting to leave empty-handed, I grabbed a glitter infused vibrator and went up to the front.

"Is this it?" he teased. "No jumper cables for you?"

"Nah, but don't be surprised if I drop in and ask more random questions." I grinned.

"Well, this place is fairly slow after tourist season, outside of our shipped orders, so feel free to come brighten my day," he said, his tone a bit flirtier than before.

I bet your horns give your partner a nice place to hold on to during sex, I thought to myself as I gave him a wide smile. His eyes went wide before he started to cough. *Oh god, did I just say that out loud?! At least I said that to a beta who didn't look like he'd repeat it, and not a fucking alpha. I didn't need that kind of trouble.*

"Uh, here," I handed over the cash he needed and he didn't comment further as he finished the transaction and handed me a bag.

"I hope to see you again soon," he offered, not looking the least bit startled by my lack of filter and inability to keep thoughts to myself. That was good, because usually it got me in trouble.

"You will," I promised, turning before I could make an ass of myself further. His low laughter followed me out of the shop and I reminded myself I wouldn't let my embarrassing moment keep me away. Something about the shy incubus drew me in and I wanted to hear more of that rich tone of his. For now, I needed to get back to Violet for dinner.

The moment I stepped back into Beds and Broomsticks, the smell had my mouth watering. I wasn't sure what it was, but it seemed the cook here knew their way around a spice cabinet, the fragrant aroma amazing. Rushing upstairs, I dropped my stuff off and used the bathroom before heading down just in time for dinner. Violet's face lit up as she spotted me.

"There you are, I have a table for us in the back," she called out. I grinned and went to the small table she pointed to, only pausing momentarily at the sight of three place settings.

The dining room was just as cute as the rest of her place. The same gothic, witchy aesthetic extended in here. And it wasn't the Halloween style making a mockery of witches, but it felt like you were genuinely eating in a witch's kitchen. A string of herbs hung over each window. The walls were black but the trim and ceiling were white, keeping it from being too dark. Each table had a centerpiece that was either a crystal assortment or a pretty jar of dried flowers and herbs. The art was minimal, but just as pretty, the colors coming through and bringing another element of brightness to the room. A large fireplace was in the back, and the large polished stones fit her aesthetic perfectly. It was still weird to me that a wolf ran a witch's inn, but she was obviously killing it.

"How was exploring the town?" Violet asked as she sat down, flipping her wavy dark brown hair over her shoulder. Her bright blue wolf eyes flashed at me before I saw the guise of honey brown take over. This was really disconcerting to see two versions of people... I almost wanted to ask if they could take it off because if this kept happening for too much longer, I'd start to think I was as crazy as everyone in my family said I was. "Ella?"

I felt my cheeks heat, realizing I had just been staring at her. "Sorry. It was a lot of fun. I checked out the Enchanted Mug and a random store then decided I'd head back. Didn't want to do too much the first day after traveling for hours."

"That makes sense," she nodded slowly, a grin curling

her red lips. "You went to Kinkubus next door, didn't you?"

A nervous laugh escaped as I rubbed my face with one of my hands. "Is it that obvious?"

Violet gave me an almost predatory smirk, her eyes lighting up with laughter at my expense. But unlike my family laughing *at* me she was laughing *with* me. "I have no idea what almost all of the stuff in there is. I thought one of the items were jumper cables, so I asked the cute guy what they were..." A hissing sound came from the woman at the table with me, her eyes watering as I tried to keep going. "Hey, the packaging was in French! How was I supposed to know what it said?"

She threw her head back and lost it. Loud laughter and tears ran down her face at my story. Before I knew it I was joining her and we both had to stop looking at each other because every time we did we started laughing hysterically again. It was strange becoming friends with an alpha, but Violet wasn't all intimidation and posses-siveness that most alphas projected. She was down to earth, genuine, but could kick some ass. Definitely the type of friend I needed.

A ding sounded from the kitchen and Violet stood up, motioning for me to stay seated as she wiped the tears off her face. She hurried back to the kitchen and came back a few minutes later with three big plates.

The plates were filled with green beans, fresh fish, and potatoes. She set everything down and rushed back into the kitchen only to emerge a minute later with three bowls of clam chowder. My stomach rumbled loudly as all the smells hit me at once, making Violet smile.

"This all looks amazing! Did you make it yourself?"

"I cooked most of it. But I had some help with the

fish." She turned and yelled out. "Come and join us, Tanniv!"

There were some light footsteps, then a man, unlike anyone I had ever seen, sauntered into the dining room. I had to consciously keep my jaw from hitting the ground as the sexy alpha approached. Dark gray, almost black eyes, were wide as he blinked looking me over just like I was him. His skin was tan with a hint of black and blue underneath that matched the peek of scales I saw along the gills on his neck. The man pushed his long dark hair behind his ear and I saw they finned and pointed with a touch of the black and blue that matched his scales on the edges. I had no idea what kind of supernatural he was... but he was mesmerizing.

And once again I was lost in a new scent. That alpha swagger was only accented by the strong scent of the sea that followed him. And not that salty, briny scent from spending the day on the docks, but a fresh sea air type of scent that wrapped around me and calmed my soul.

"I hate to interrupt the intense staring going on between you two," Violet's voice cut through my trance, her voice making me jump. "Tanniv, this is Ella. Ella, Tanniv. He is the harbormaster and he brought the fresh seafood for dinner tonight."

"It was no problem at all." His voice was husky and warm and he sat down in the seat across from me while Violet took the seat next to me. The smell of salty seawater and leather surrounded me as the alpha looked between the two of us with a wicked gleam in his dark eyes. I had a feeling he was just as affected as I was. "It sounded like I was interrupting an interesting conversation earlier."

"Oh gods." I covered my face but I'm sure they saw the crimson tint to my cheeks.

Violet chuckled. "Ella met Orion." I peeked out from behind my fingers, gauging if I should pack up and leave or go with it.

A lazy smile filled Tanniv's face, dark eyes glittering with laughter. "Orion himself or his store?"

"Both." I managed behind my hands before I let them fall away and looked up at them both with narrowed eyes. "Can you both tease me while we eat though? I'm starving and this smells amazing."

"I am an excellent multitasker," Tanniv purred, the sound sending a wave of heat through me. This alpha was too sultry for his own good. Violet rolled her eyes and smacked his chest before we all dived into our food.

Violet and Tanniv talked about things going on in town and some small-town gossip, though his eyes flickered to me often, like he just couldn't help himself. I didn't really listen, instead, focusing on slowly enjoying the food and not rushing through it. It was better than the usual psych ward food I was used to. Each bite of the fresh food brought about a feeling of warmth and home, both things I'd never really felt before.

I looked up at them, the magic momentarily in place to show me Tanniv's appearance to humans. Copper skin, long black hair, a goatee, and mustache that only he could pull off were all paired with his worn blue jeans and black button-up shirt that had the top three undone to show off a dusting of chest hair. He was every sexy and devil-may-care pirate character that I had ever fantasized about come to life. *That glitter vibrator might get used sooner than I thought.*

"Did you want to come with us, Ella?" I blinked

slowly at Violet, trying to rein in my wandering thoughts and recall what they were talking about. "You weren't listening at all, were you?"

I shot her a sheepish grin, belatedly realizing I had my spoon paused midway to my mouth. "Half listening."

"There is a town meeting tonight," Tanniv spoke up smoothly, his dark eyes glittered with enough heat that I had the sudden worry he could read my horny thoughts. "You want to come with us? It is the best entertainment around. Some of our residents are... colorful."

Bright laughter bubbled up at that. *It was the understatement of the century recalling all the people I had met so far.* "I'm in."

"Awesome." Violet pushed away from the table. "I'll just clean up and we can walk over together. We have our town meetings in the park across the street. It's the biggest place and the easiest location for most of the residents to comfortably set up."

"I'll do that." Tanniv stood up and grabbed all the plates, clearing the table faster than I thought possible. With the skill of a fine dining waiter, he carried them back into the kitchen all by himself.

"I'm going to get a small basket of snacks together. It really is the best entertainment to see the small squabbles break out amongst everyone. And you'll get to meet everyone without having to talk with them all at once."

I nodded. "Perfect! I'm just going to run up to my room really quick. I'll meet you at the front door in a few?"

She waved in acknowledgement as she walked to the kitchen to get the snacks together. Rushing upstairs I went to the bathroom and checked myself over in the mirror, worried about my looks since Tanniv came over to eat with us. *What was wrong with me? I'd never cared about that kind of thing before. Though I'd never met an alpha or supernatural like Tanniv. Time to focus, this is going to be story inspiration gold. A small town where everyone knows everyone's business and a town meeting... Was this Gilmore Girls or what?*

I couldn't wait.

CHAPTER 3

Ella

"There should be a standard ordinance on lawn decorations. When is too much, too much?!" a minotaur roared. It should have been a terrifying growl but his disguise was a middle-aged white dude with dad socks and a polo. The beta definitely thought himself scarier than he was.

"I know you're talking about me!" A woman that couldn't be anything other than an Amazon stood up and crossed her arms. She towered over the man by several feet and his eyes went wide as he looked up at her. He sputtered over his next words, clearly intimidated now.

"This is better than I thought it'd be," Violet hissed excitedly, offering me some of her popcorn. I took a handful and turned back to the show.

The minotaur was now standing on his chair so he wouldn't be overshadowed by the alpha. "We can put it to a vote then. Ten pink flamingos, twenty gaudy gnomes, and those creepy cherubs are too much!"

"Oh, it's a lot better than your yard, *Harold*," she spit out, saying his name like a curse. "I didn't realize uneven mow lines and dead flowers were a thing to brag about."

"Oh, shots fired." Tanniv laughed. His eyes bounced from one to the other excitedly. Before it could get better, Leif was stepping up and banging his gavel on the podium they'd set up in front. At first, I thought it seemed a bit extra, but now I see the benefits of using it.

"Enough!" His voice was final. Both parties sat down with a huff, looking no less annoyed. "If the lawn is well maintained, then there is no reason to put an ordinance in place. Now, moving on. Anyone else have a grievance worthy of discussion?" His eyes flared for a moment, a show of power to get everyone to behave. "Might I remind everyone that tourist season is still among us, let's not scare away our *guests*."

A short man stood up next. He couldn't have been more than five feet and from under his human disguise, I could see his broad shoulders and a thick, long beard. I wanted to ask what kind of supe he was, but I shoved down my curiosity.

"My clan is having issues at the Dwarven Beard," he said. His gruff voice echoed over the crowd and it seemed he commanded a lot of respect. *Well, guess that answered my question.* Honestly, dwarf made sense now with his build and height.

"What issues?" Leif asked. He leaned forward on the podium to listen, but it put him right under the streetlight. His image wavered, showing a dusting of iridescence that glimmered in the low lighting, glimmering over his cheeks and the tips of his pointed ears. It wasn't a bright and colorful glow, but deep jewel tones that looked amazing against his olive toned skin. His eyes were a deep, emerald green, flecks of gold dancing with amusement as they locked on me. I startled, not realizing he'd even noticed me. He winked at me before giving the dwarf his full attention as my cheeks flushed from his unexpected attention.

"Someone is getting into the storage room. I've noticed it for a while but after rechecking inventory, we're missing several small kegs. We don't want to make a big stink over it but we wanted to say that we're watching now."

"We'll do a few more rounds after dark," an officer said as he stood. The dwarf nodded in thanks before they sat down, the issue resolved for now.

But my attention was stolen away yet again by someone whispering in front of me. A shifter and another supe sat a few rows ahead of us. Their attention was on each other but I couldn't look away. The smaller man was definitely a supernatural, though I couldn't tell what. He had a stoic face and tattoos lining his skin, his handsome face showcasing a jawline that could cut glass. His eyes were sharp but adoring as they stared at his partner. The shifter's blunt fangs poked out of his smile as he chuckled softly at something the other said, a hand resting on his thigh.

"Who are they?" I asked before I could stop myself. Violet and Tanniv both followed my gaze.

"Spencer and Hunter. They're dating and absolutely adorable together," Violet answered, nudging me. "Girl, you've set your sights on some of the hottest men in town."

"A girl after my own heart," Tanniv teased, giving me a wink.

"I didn't say I was interested in them, I was just asking," I feigned innocence. They both shook their heads and grinned at each other.

"Those two definitely prefer men. However, *I* could be persuaded to spend the night in the company of a woman," Tanniv said, matching my innocent stare from before. Violet snorted and shoved him away. My body reacted to that statement, a surge of warmth pooling between my thighs at the thought of being wrapped in his scent, being worshiped by him. They both gave me a knowing look and my cheeks heated, part of me worried they could scent how aroused I was.

"Don't scare this one away, Tanniv, I like her," Violet grumbled before the gavel was banging again. I didn't miss that Leif's eyes were locked onto mine again. He couldn't have missed how close Tanniv was sitting next to me or how he threw an arm around the back of my chair while laughing off Violet's warning.

"Alright," Leif called out, a slight strain to his voice. "Our last order of business is a reminder that our next meeting starts the talk about our annual festival. Volunteers for that committee will work closely with me." The last part he seemed to be saying directly to me, his eyes once again studying me so intensely that I had to look away. But even looking around at the quaint town did nothing to distract me.

"Well, it seems you have competition, Tanniv," Violet teased. She didn't miss the tension between me and the mayor.

Tanniv for his part just shrugged and gave her a lazy

grin, "I'm the one sitting next to Ella, aren't I? I'd say I'm already ahead in the competition."

Leif gave one last bang of his gavel. "Dismissed until next week."

Violet and Tanniv stood up, talking to themselves about the meeting and something about getting more lawn ornaments to annoy Harold. But I wasn't quite ready to go back to the bed and breakfast just yet.

"I think I'm going to go for a walk," I said. "It's been too long since I've seen the night sky." I turned before they could stop me, that all too familiar claustrophobic feeling starting to creep up my spine. All I knew was that I needed to be away from all these people and the buildings. I couldn't tell what triggered me but I knew that I had to move... now. Giving Violet a quick smile that I hoped was reassuring, I hurried off down the sidewalk. I didn't pay attention to where I was going or which direction I went, but by the time my feet ached the sound of waves splashing the shore filled the air.

A smile spread across my face. I'd never seen the ocean, all my life I had missed out on family vacations and instead was sent to psych wards and institutions. But that wasn't important anymore, I pushed off those gloomy thoughts, it was time to experience it for the first time. Salt air was sharp on the cool breeze and I rubbed my arms, wishing I had a jacket with me. But the lure of something new and unknown was too strong a pull to ignore so I kept going excited when I saw the dock and boats tied up. I'll just sit down and enjoy the view and enjoy the vastness of the night sky.

Tanniv

After wrapping up small talk with Violet, I hurried after Ella, curious to see where she was going. My interest piqued even more when I realized she was down at the docks. I made sure my steps were loud as I approached, letting her and the other sirens nearby know I was approaching. No need to scare the little omega by having an alpha try to sneak up on you. Especially one as interesting as Ella. I didn't want her to run away before I got a taste. I had lived here for a few hundred years and have been the harbormaster for the past fifty. In all my life I've never met anyone like Ella. Hell, I'd never been drawn to anyone quite so intensely. Her vanilla and coffee scent was delicious, making me want to pull her close and mix her scent with mine, to warn off all the other alphas, which was insane, I wasn't usually the possessive type. But the moment I smelled how turned on she was by my simple flirting, I knew I had to have a taste. Though I wasn't distracted enough to realize how skittish she could be, this one would take a delicate approach. Good thing I was a patient man.

Just hearing her voice in the bed and breakfast had captured my attention, her bright and warm tone bringing a smile to my face. She could have been a siren given how much that sound alone called to me. When I rounded the corner, I saw her big blue eyes and wavy blonde hair. My alpha side hated seeing her alone, but the sight of her had me moving toward her.

She sat at the end of the dock, feet hanging off the side. I saw the hint of a blissful smile on her face as she stared out at the waves and the sky as I approached. Ella glanced over as I got close and her smile widened, face lighting up when her eyes landed on me and she patted the space beside her, inviting me to join. I glided over and slowly sat down beside her, my stare focused on Ella and not the view in front of me.

"It's beautiful." She sighed, the sound happy as she looked around. "You know I've never seen the ocean before. It might be one of my favorite things though."

I blinked slowly, my brain unable to process the idea of anyone never seeing the ocean before. "You've never seen the ocean before? Where are you visiting from?"

Ella bit her lower lip, avoiding my gaze and I narrowed my eyes at that. *She's going to lie.* "I don't want to talk about it. It's complicated." *Ah, an evasion and not a lie. Interesting.* But I'd let it go... for now.

"Fair enough." I nodded, leaning back on my elbows, trying to resist the seductive call of Ella's scent and the ocean. My body aching for the touch of both. "If you want to explore, I am the harbormaster. I'd be happy to show you around."

"Around the water or one of these boats you probably live on?" She snorted, eyes dancing with laughter as she looked over at me. She was brave, teasing me like that and it only intrigued me more. She was an enigma, a puzzle. Something told me if I tried to unravel it I'd get swept along with her... The thought should have concerned me, but really it just made her more appealing.

"Hey! I'll have you know my houseboat is beautiful." I placed a hand on my chest playing up my mock offended response. She giggled at my antics and I grinned back at her. Needing to be closer, I sat up and leaned in, taking in her scent as subtly as possible. "But to answer your question, I'd be happy to show you around both. I'm an expert in both of those things *and* I'm a great teacher."

Her face heated and it was easy for me to see the red on her cheeks as she studiously stared up at the stars, refusing to look at me. Though I didn't miss how her body instinctively scooted closer to me, leaving just a few inches of space between us. "I don't think I'm ready for any of that."

"Says the woman who went to the sex shop earlier today," I teased her gently, but let it go. I didn't want to scare her off, her nonfiltered self a refreshing change to the usual people who passed through town. I'd enjoy her company, in any capacity, until she left when tourist season ended. The thought sent a pang of unease through me and I was surprised that I didn't want her to leave.

"Do you know about stars?" Her soft voice pulled me from my musings and I cleared my throat.

"Yeah, I do."

"What constellation is that?"

I looked up to where she was pointing. "It's the Aries constellation." Taking her hand gently, I moved it around pointing out the different stars and constellations and telling the stories behind them.

Her eyes were bright with wonder and excitement at every bit of information I had to share. *How long had it been since someone wanted to just be with me and talk? No expectations on my end.* I couldn't remember a time to be honest, and her hanging on to every word I said was intoxicating. For a moment, I had to stop and think if my siren's allure was slipping past the glamour we had to wear during tourist season. It couldn't take away our powers, but it dampened it. I couldn't sense any of my powers being used on her at all and that was maybe the most fascinating thing of all. Ella shivered and I looked at her then checked my watch, letting out a sad sigh when I saw that it was already close to midnight. Her eyes were heavy and I could tell that she needed rest.

"You should go back to the bed and breakfast, little stargazer." She looked surprised at my suggestion then checked the time on her phone, cursing softly when she saw how late it was.

"Oh no, I'm so sorry. I didn't mean to take up all your time." She scrambled to her feet and I pushed myself up to standing as well.

"Don't apologize. Not many people want to hear all my stories, it's nice to be able to share."

Her eyes widened, whirling to face me. "I love stories! I always wanted to be a writer, but... " She waved her hands, pushing away the shadows that had entered her eyes. "But I'm always up to listen to more."

"I'd like that," I murmured. My eyes flicked down to her pouty lips then back to her beautiful blue eyes that were studying me closely, the heady scent of her intensifying as she continued to watch me. I tilted my head, watching her, realizing that she wasn't as unaffected by me as she seemed. "Ella—"

"I've never—" She licked her lips, her gaze moving down to my lips and staying there.

"Been with someone?" I asked, teasing her gently.

"That." Her cheeks heated, but I watched as she fought her instincts and kept her blue eyes on me. "That... kissing... all of it."

All of it? How? How could this gorgeous, sweet omega have no experience? Not even a kiss? Then a wave of satisfaction and possessiveness took over as I thought of that. Untouched, completely innocent, and wonderful. A temptation I couldn't bring myself to resist. The alpha side of me practically salivated at the prospect. She would have my scent, if only temporary for now, and it would be the first to mingle with hers. A rumble of satisfaction went through me at that thought alone.

I stepped toward her, bringing a hand up to cup the back of her hair, moving slow enough that she could move away at any time. Her eyes snapped up to meet my gaze then studied me, curiosity clear and I wondered just what she was thinking. Ella didn't move away or say anything, just licked her lips, and I took that for the silent invitation it was.

Moving slowly so she could stop me at any point, I leaned down and claimed her lips in a searing kiss. If I was going to be her first, I was going to be fucking memorable. The moment her tongue flicked against mine, responding to me, fire consumed me. She tasted like warmth and honey. A sweet summer's day that could warm and welcome you home.

Magic filled the air as my other hand gripped her hip and I deepened the kiss, groaning into her mouth as she whimpered against me. In the midst of all the sparks flying, a coolness covered my wrists. We broke apart a moment later and stared at each other before she took a few backward steps out of my arms and back toward land.

She raised a hand to her lips and sent me a shaky, happy smile. "Goodnight, Tanniv."

"Until next time, my Ella," I told her softly and she took off, running down the pier to get back to her room, before I could offer to accompany her. I lurched forward as she slipped on a wet board, but miraculously she managed to catch herself before falling into the dark water.

"I'm fine! I'm fine!" she yelled back to me and continued running back into town.

I found myself shaking my head, still breathless from that kiss when I looked down and saw the marking on my wrist. Shock filled me as I tried to process what I was seeing. *A mating mark.* A new moon was clearly visible on the inside of my right wrist and I stared after the woman who just ran away from me.

The *human* woman.

The thought of her walking alone was unsettling, especially after she nearly tumbled into the sea. I needed a moment to process the mark, so I kept my distance, simply ensuring she made it safe. She looked back as she opened the door to the bed and breakfast, her blue eyes shining under the porch light.

There was something about her I just couldn't put my finger on, but there was one thing for certain now. She was *mine.*

CHAPTER 4

Ella

Walking through Mystic Harbor was one of the most soothing experiences of my life. With the soft, sea breeze and the sound of gentle chatter surrounding me I felt completely at ease. Not many would find the beauty in such a common thing, but to me it was everything.

The only issue was that I lost track of time so easily here. Violet might kill me if I was late to another meal. But every time I walked, I saw something new. From the small little art studio to the adorable bakery.

Just as I passed the coffee shop, my phone started to ring and I smirked as I saw Violet's name lighting up. I answered on the second ring, picking up my pace before she could gripe at me.

"I'm on the way, I promise," I say in lieu of an answer. She let out a string of laughter, knowing damn well I was rushing now.

"Is that why you sound like you're running?" she teased. Then as I went to pass an antique shop it was like I slammed into an invisible wall. I let out an audible oof as the air was sucked from my lungs. It took several seconds before I could regain my composure and I deserved a gold star for not falling onto my ass. "Ella?!"

"Shit, sorry. I nearly fell. I uh, got to go. I'll be there in a second," I said before pulling my phone away. I could hear her protesting but I ended the call anyway, staring into the window of the shop. Lost Relics was emblazoned on the glass and a display in front showed an array of gorgeous antique mirrors. Each one was polished to a shine and glinting in the afternoon sun.

But the mirrors weren't what I was after. It was like a magical tug was pulling me forward and I was unable to stop it. My feet carried me inside the shop. I was immediately hit with the smell of pipe tobacco and spearmint. It was a particularly comforting scent that made me feel safe and protected.

"Can I help you?" I turned at the raspy, weathered voice. An old man hobbled out from behind the counter. His back was bent and his face covered in wrinkles. But when the magical disguise was lifted I saw that he held his age well. Through the magic, I could also see his glowing eyes and wolf-like features, angular and sharp, but mostly dangerous. He must have lived many years to show his age like this, that or was turned later in life.

This old alpha felt just as safe as some of the other residents I met, though his demeanor was more subtle, like an uncle welcoming you home with a weathered smile and corny joke.

"Uh, no?" I didn't mean to answer with a question, it was just that I couldn't explain why I walked in here.

"Something in here seemed to call to me." The last part was muttered, but he heard it if his ears twitching slightly and his amused smile crossing his face was any indication.

"That's the way about antiques," he agreed despite my low tone. I blinked up at him, unsure if I should worry that I gave myself away or pretend I didn't say it. "They hold a history, a story, and sometimes those tales are meant for new ears." He turned like he didn't give me a cryptic answer and walked back behind the counter. Mystic Harbor definitely had its fair share of colorful citizens.

"Thanks?" I offered, sounding like a question yet again. He chuckled low and encouraged me to find him when I finished browsing. Properly dismissed, I turned to the store. Before I knew it I was heading past a row of creepy porcelain clowns and into a section holding vintage books. The smell of dusty pages and leather covers hit me and a smile tugged at my lips. Books were some of my only escape when I was inside the ward, and I was eager to see what I'd find here. As my fingers brushed against the first cover, something on the table to my right caught my eye. My hand fell away as I turned, a gorgeous journal practically screaming at me to buy it. Fuck, if I didn't think I was crazy before, this might solidify it, but I was too far in to ignore the strange magic here. The whole town seemed to be covered in it. Not just from the people themselves, but the land held an ancient aura to it. There was definitely more to Mystic Harbor than what meets the eye.

A small breath rushed out of my parted lips as my heart pounded in my chest. The moment felt so momentous for such a simple task. The leather of the cover felt warm to the touch as my finger traced the intricate design.

It was a depiction of the sea and cliffs, birds in the leather clad sky, and crashing waves below. The detailing was impressive and the moment I had it in my hands, the magic all came to an abrupt halt. I felt breathless and dizzy for a moment, clutching the journal in my hands as I took in exaggerated breaths of tobacco-filled air to calm myself.

"Did you find your tale?" the shop owner asked. He was so quiet I didn't hear him come over to me and I let out a completely undignified squeak.

"I did," I answered in such a quiet voice I was surprised he could hear me. "I'd like to buy this."

His eyes dropped to the journal in my hands and his eyebrow raised at how closely I clutched it. No more words were spoken as he turned and meandered through the cluttered shop with more grace than I'd expect from an ancient wolf. But it seemed this shop was full of surprises.

"There's magic in history, you know. Maybe you'll write your own version of it in these pages," he said as he settled on a stool right behind the cash register. "That'll be five dollars."

"What? That's it?" I questioned without thought. He let out a rumbling laugh that didn't hold any judgment, just friendly teasing.

"I couldn't charge more for something that was obviously meant to be with you," he promised. He reached to a display of pens and selected an aqua blue encased one, putting it on top of the journal with a wink. Not sure what to say to the generous man, I handed over a five-dollar bill and thanked him profusely. He waved it off, his face holding a knowing smile as I hurriedly grabbed my purchase and rushed from the shop. The magic was strong in there and I wasn't ready to out myself yet. They didn't need to know that this human could see their magic, that I was potentially a threat to them all. But something told me that the wolf wouldn't spill my secret if he caught on. He was kind and mysterious, not untrusting.

With my purchase in hand, I rushed the rest of the way to the bed and breakfast to enjoy lunch with my new friend. She'd probably call me out on making yet another stop, but I couldn't find it in me to regret the strange encounter and lucky purchase I'd made.

I made it to lunch barely and playfully shrugged off her amused and exasperated expression as she served me a fresh lobster roll. Taking a bite I hummed, doing a small dance in my seat loving the flavors as they hit my tongue. Violet just shook her head at my antics.

"Do you have any plans tonight?" Violet asked as I finished off the sandwich and stood up with a yawn ready for a nap.

"Nope. Just going with the flow at the moment. Why?" I tilted my head as I waited for my new friend to keep going.

"I was thinking it was a wine kind of night. You want to join us?" My surprise and insecurity must have been plain on my face because Violet shot me an understanding smile. "We can just eat, have some wine, and talk about all the newest craziness in town. Nothing too crazy."

"So like our own town meeting?"

She laughed at that, blue eyes flashing through. "Yes, yes. Very much like our own town meeting. Don't tell Leif, but I know more than he does about what's happening in this town." A laugh bubbled out of me at that and her eyes sparkled. "I have some things to wrap up here, but meet me down here at seven?"

"Sure!" I offered, excited to have some actual friend time, not just a quick meal or chat here and there.

"And I get together with my three close friends at least once a month, we have brunch planned this weekend if you want to join? No pressure," she offered before walking away. I blinked after her and nodded a few times like she could still see me. The idea caught me so off guard that I had to force myself to grab my bag with my new notebook and ran upstairs.

Violet was super nice, as was everyone I had met so far in Mystic Harbor, but in my experience, everyone was friendly until they got to know me. *Did I want to try again here? That's the whole point of me getting out from under my parents' thumb was to be my own person... but if I am honest, I'm scared they will think I'm crazy just like my family does. Would they just gaslight me and tell me that what I see through the magical cover up isn't real or would they tell me the truth?*

When I made it back to my room, I tossed my purse on the dresser and kicked off my shoes. I wanted to take a nap and a shower, but a shower would have to wait, I was exhausted. No sooner had I dropped onto the bed then I was asleep.

A loud knock on my door had me jolting up in my bed. Disoriented and disheveled, I stumbled over to the door and pulled it open. The hall light flooded into the room and I shielded my eyes, groaning as Violet started laughing at me.

"Damn, rough nap?" I flipped her off half-heartedly and stretched out my sore body.

"Sorry, is it already seven?" She quirked up an

eyebrow and I snatched my phone off of my bed to check myself. I was already thirty minutes later and felt awful. "Shit, sorry. Give me five and I'll be good." She closed the door and went downstairs with only a small chuckle in answer. Not wanting to keep her longer I decided to skip the shower and just change as fast as I could. After combing my long blonde hair into a bun, I rushed downstairs to her room.

"I'm here!" I called out as I knocked and pushed the door open. She was already pouring two glasses of red wine and passed one my way.

"Perfect timing. Here. It's the best that the Dwarven Beard has to offer," she said. I lifted it to my lips and took a slow sip. It had a hint of tartness but it was cut by the sweet burst of flavors. It was the best wine I'd ever tasted. I mean, I hadn't had many options to drink in the past, but my parents loved to serve fancy wines with dinner so I'd had my share of glasses full of wine older than me.

"This is amazing." I hummed, taking a bigger gulp this time.

"They really do have the best," she agreed, pulling me over to her couch to sit. "Now, tell me why you were late today. What distracted you?" Her eyes sparkled with amusement.

"It was the craziest thing. I was talking to you and trying to rush back. But when I passed the antique shop it was like I couldn't pass it up. So I went inside and ended up finding this amazing notebook for my stories. I was just thinking I needed one, then bam, found it."

"That's awesome. What kind of stories?" I used my wine glass to give me a moment to answer, gauging her question but all I could detect was genuine curiosity. My entire body relaxed at that.

"Whatever comes to me. Sometimes they're silly little kid books, other times they're complicated worlds and dashing knights," I explained. "I've always had them swirling around in my head and now I can get them on paper at least."

"That's amazing," she agreed, smiling softly before her grin turned wicked. "So, did anything exciting happen after the meeting? Don't think I missed Tanniv heading after you."

"We may have kissed." I shrugged. But of course, I gave myself away with a wine infused giggle, the potent alcohol already swirling through my head.

"Not even in town that long and already caught the attention of our local playboy pirate," she teased as she stood up. "How about we move this to the hot tub?"

"Oh! I've always wanted to get into a hot tub," I gushed. She frowned at the comment but I was already rambling on. "Wait, I don't own a swimsuit."

"You came to a beachfront town and didn't bring a swimsuit?" She snorted, but was already walking off into her bedroom, coming out with two bikinis. "Both of these are new, pick one and I'll wear the other."

I opened my mouth to protest but her glare shut me right up. I considered the two options she was giving me trying to figure out which one to pick. One was a dark green and the other a bright pink. Both were beautiful but I knew exactly which one I wanted to wear.

"The pink one," I said, reaching for the brightly colored garment. I'd never worn anything so revealing but I'd survived years of communal bathrooms, I wasn't too worried.

"Good, I don't even know why I bought such a bright color, I've never worn bubblegum pink in my life."

"It was for me, you just didn't know it yet." I laughed, rushing off to the bathroom to change. I swore I heard her whisper, 'it might be' but I couldn't be sure.

After dropping my own clothes unceremoniously into a pile on the floor, I pulled on the small pink bikini. Turning to the floor-length mirror, my jaw dropped. I blinked once, twice, my mouth hanging open at what I saw in the mirror. Somehow I had a tattoo, *a fucking tattoo*, under my breasts. Delicate line work that reminded me of mandala designs, but it didn't look complete. There was a new moon under one of the points on my left side, but all the other dips didn't have a moon under it. Where the hell did that come from?!

Freaking out, I rushed out into the living room to find Violet. She was already changed and waiting, startling at my panicked yell.

"Violet, help!"

"What's wrong?!"

"This is what's wrong! What the hell is this? Some kind of joke about me falling asleep for so long?"

Violet moved forward and ran her fingertips over the design, my panic fueling her alpha protectiveness. Shock, surprise, and curiosity all flickered across her face before forced amusement took over. "When did you get a tattoo? Did you get it here in town?"

"That's my point." I shook my head vehemently. "I *didn't* get a tattoo! What is going on here?!"

"Ella, I have no idea. I'll try to see if one of our guests was trying to play a bad prank. If they did, rest assured they won't be here long. We can figure this out. Just try to take a deep breath and relax. I'll take care of everything." I had a feeling she wasn't telling me everything. Something in my gut and her face before she spun the tale about a guest playing pranks hinted that she was making things up. "I promise to figure it out, Ella. Don't you worry. I'll ask around now, if they do this to other guests my business will go to hell. Sorry to cut girls' night short. We will have to do it another day. And I promise we can actually get to the hot tub next time." She all but ushered me from the room, grabbing my clothes from the bathroom floor and shoving them in my hand before pushing me through the door. I stood on the other side, stunned as she closed it on me.

It was an abrupt end to girl's night and I couldn't make sense of the shift in mood. What was she hiding from me?

With my head still swirling, I headed back to my room, hoping I didn't run into any guests on the way given I was still in the borrowed bathing suit. I stood in my doorway for several minutes before letting out a sigh and heading for the shower. My buzz had worn off and all I felt now was confusion and exhaustion.

Glancing down at my half-finished, unexplained tattoo, I tried to scrub it away but it wasn't budging. I let out a growl of frustration and slammed my hand into the tile walls. I knew I wouldn't be finding out answers today, but I vowed to get Violet to talk tomorrow.

After drying myself off and pulling on pajamas, I crawled back into bed. I'd find some answers tomorrow but for now, exhaustion was quickly pulling me under.

Leif

Settling back into an armchair in my study I let out a long sigh, happy that the day was finally over. If I had to hear one more word from Harold about lawn ornaments I'd buy some myself just so he would leave me alone. The town meeting was a mess, but at least all the glamours held throughout. No need to scare the tourists off when the season was so close to being finished. Bright blue eyes, blonde hair, and sweet coffee and vanilla filled my mind, making me growl.

Ella.

Violet told me her name at the town meeting when I was making the rounds to talk to everyone. I couldn't get her out of my mind ever since she walked off the bus looking so excited and nervous at the same time. At first, I thought it was just my alpha instincts kicking in to protect her, but then I caught her scent. It was *intoxicating.* Then seeing her with Tanniv at the town meeting... I wished she had been next to me instead.

Groaning, I pushed myself up to standing trying to refocus my thoughts. Tourist season was over in two weeks and then she would be out of Mystic Harbor. The wards from the island made sure that they all left when tourist time was up then we all got to drop our glamour so we all appeared how we actually looked instead of this human face. I let mine fade as I made myself a cup of chamomile tea to relax.

Ring!

So much for relaxing. I grabbed my cell phone, brow furrowing at Violet's name on the screen. "Violet?"

"Leif! Thank the moon you answered." Violet let out a shuddering breath, my concern rising as she struggled to calm herself. "We have a situation."

I sat back down in my armchair and put the tea on the

side table, letting the leaves steep. "Please, don't tell me you want to put a collection of flamingos or garden gnomes in your yard, Violet. I swear, I'll ban the damn things if I have to hear about them anymore." Completely ignoring my earlier thought of getting some for myself to be left alone.

"No, no. This doesn't have anything to do with the flamingos." Violet's voice was tight, showing just how anxious she really was. Anything that was making the alpha wolf feel this way can't be good. "It's Ella. The human staying here, remember her?"

I was taken aback by her direct question, the abruptness showing just how off Violet must be because she was better than most about that. It wasn't the smartest to ask the fae direct questions, but lucky for her... I wasn't most fae. I licked my lips, "Yes, I remember the human. Blonde, blue eyes."

"She has a fated mate marking, Leif." All the air was knocked out of me as I tried to comprehend what she was saying. *A human... with a fated mate mark?* Fated mates were rare among supernaturals but humans didn't even have fated mates, just chosen. I licked my lips, my mind racing trying to figure out what this means. In the end, I dropped any pretense of propriety in favor of getting answers quickly.

"Who?"

"If I had to guess? Tanniv. They kissed yesterday after the town meeting. We were having a girls' night and when she was changing she saw the marking and freaked out. She has no idea what's going on, Leif. I played it off as a prank from another guest but I don't think Ella bought it." Violet took a deep breath before continuing, "There's more."

"More?"

"It's the *beginning* of a marking." I hummed, running a hand through my black hair, not surprised that it would be multiple mates. Only humans stuck to one or two mates, supernaturals were known for more. "Leif. The design is big. It covers her entire sternum."

"We need to figure out more about her."

Violet was quiet for a minute. "She is running from something, but I have no details and I won't ask. Not even for this. The fear and pain in her eyes... I recognize that pain, Leif. What I will say is that I truly believe she has no idea what's going on and this is just the beginning."

"Fuck." She burst into laughter and I smiled slightly even as possessiveness filled me. Everything in me screamed to go to this omega, protect her with everything I had. But that wouldn't be fitting for a mayor or a stranger. But I did vow to 'run into' her more often, to keep tabs on the mysterious omega. It seemed she wasn't a marvel to just me and it was my job to ensure it was nothing that could affect us all.

"That's a good summary."

"In two weeks the magic of the island will force her to leave town."

"If she leaves we will lose at least our harbormaster," Violet replied softly. "And a lot of others."

"But if she has a mating mark, maybe she isn't human?"

Thoughtful silence filled the line. "Maybe I can bring Birdie around. She has a knack for puzzles and maybe she will have some insight after meeting her."

"I'll keep an eye on her as well. And talk to Tanniv," I tacked on with a grumble.

"Try to keep your jealousy under control," Violet

teased lightly. "I'll check on Ella. I rushed her out to call you. I need to make sure she's okay."

"May the moon bless you, wolf."

"May the elements bless you, Leif."

Click.

I dropped my phone onto my lap and leaned my head back, a pounding headache forming behind my eyes. Nothing was ever simple in Mystic Harbor, but this? This was going to be pure chaos. Loneliness pricked at the thought wishing that I could be part of it, though if her scent was any indication, maybe I would be.

CHAPTER 5

Tanniv

I ambled up the bed and breakfast and with a smile, opened the door. I had stayed away for an entire day, coordinating the morning off so I could have breakfast with Ella. The trials and tribulations of being a harbormaster during damn tourist season. And my soul was aching for the water so I spent most of the evening in the dark depths, swimming and seeing family, giving myself a chance to connect with my true home. Especially my twin, Asra, who avoided the humans and the chaos of town like the plague. He much preferred the water.

Violet called out a greeting and when she saw it was me her eyes turned serious, neon blue flashing. I quirked an eyebrow, curious what that was about but before she could say anything Ella hurried down the stairs talking a mile a minute to Violet about going out for coffee and that she wanted to check out the library. My smile grew to a grin as Ella's eyes landed on me and they lit up. Satisfaction and happiness warmed my chest at the spark and the scent of coffee, vanilla, and a hint of my saltwater hit my nose.

"Hey, Tanniv! What are you doing here?"

"I was hoping you'd let me take you out for breakfast."

"Oh... really?" Her cheeks flushed with a beautiful pink that made me want to groan aloud, but I suppressed it. *Barely.* She was gorgeous. And beyond that, she didn't even realize she was. The omega was oblivious to her charisma and the effect she had on alphas like me.

The fact that she was my fated mate was mind-blowing. I'd waited so many years to find a match, expecting to find no more than a chosen mate someday. But the issue was, this omega was very much human, and I very much was not. We had laws against outing ourselves, I didn't know what it meant for us. The idea of living a life without her was painful, but a life of suppressing my siren side was even worse. And I couldn't look at Ella and lie to her for the rest of my life, that was no foundation for a solid relationship. The alpha side of me wouldn't allow it.

"Is that a yes?" I prompted when she seemed to not be sure how to answer. She blushed even worse and squeaked out her answer.

"Oh, yes!" She turned to Violet and whispered something, Violet's eyes flashing again as she turned away. I gave Violet a look of my own, a warning that I'd be asking about that later. I had a feeling something happened to Ella and the thought of anything being wrong with her set me on edge. I barely knew her yet I'd raze the world for her, it was a feeling that was foreign. Sure, alphas cared about those they loved, but what I felt for Ella was so much more intense, which warred with my otherwise laid-back outlook on life.

Ella waved and walked closer, her intoxicating scent filled my senses and I had to hold myself back from leaning close and taking in a full breath of her. Instead, I offered my arm. She grinned up at me and slipped her arm through mine.

"A gentleman," she noted. "What a pleasant surprise." Her pleased smile had me wanting to puff out my chest. Making her happy, even in small ways, was everything to me right now.

I feigned hurt. "You're surprised? Did I strike you differently?" She ducked her head and seemed to be fighting with herself on whether to answer or not but the words spilled out anyway. She seemed to lack a filter in general so I wasn't even fazed.

"You struck me as a sexy pirate who ravages women any chance he gets," she responded with a thread of amusement in her voice. I barked out a laugh at her depiction.

"I'll give you the pirate part, and I've had my share of seaside escapades, but I hardly ravage women in the night... have you seen how small this town is?"

"Good," she teased, giving me a mischievous grin. "Where are we going for breakfast?" Her eyebrows furrowed as we passed the diner, but she mentioned wanting coffee so I figured Drystan's shop was the better choice.

"The Enchanted Mug," I explained. Her eyes lit up.

"Oh good! Drystan makes the best drinks!" she gushed, then her smile fell. "Wait... they have food?"

"They do," I promised. "You'd be surprised how fancy it is too."

"I love surprises," she said happily. Her enthusiasm over everything was refreshing, I had a feeling she was one of those who could find the positive in anything. That wasn't a quality you found often in people. Hell, everything about her stood out to me, though being my fated mate might have had a bit to do with that.

The Enchanted Mug was fairly empty when we walked in, but it was in between the busy times. Drystan looked up at us as the bell chimed, his stoic face transforming ever so slightly at the sight of my omega. Shockingly, I didn't feel possessive, in fact, it was amusing to see him affected by her so easily. He never lost his impassive mask, so it stood out. It seems she's enchanted the whole town, even our grumpy barista. And the fact my alpha was allowing it likely meant she had more than one mate waiting for her. His acceptance made it a lot easier to handle that thought, but we'd have to see how it played out.

"Let's snag a seat so you can look at the menu," I offered, leading her to my favorite table. It was nestled between two trees, vines wrapping around their thin trunks and weaving through the branches, giving it a natural gazebo effect. They'd even hung twinkle lights in the leaves to give it an extra whimsical feel.

"Oh my gosh, this is so cute! How did I miss this last time?!" she asked, mouth wide as she gaped at the table. I pulled out a seat for her and she sat, barely looking away from the foliage.

"If it was busy, that was likely why. This place gets packed wall to wall a few times a day," I said with a shrug. Before I could even slide a menu her way, Drystan was walking up with a latte mug, the foam art on top depicting a little grove of trees.

"We didn't order anything," I said, confused. He

turned his eyes on me, expression hard and I swore there was a bit of anger and jealousy behind it.

"I know you didn't, it's for her," he said before turning to her. She grinned excitedly and clapped her hands before going on about his skills. It was a bold move for a beta, but Drystan had the fire of ten alphas in his beta body.

"That's so pretty! How did you do that? What kind of drink is it this time?" she asked. Her sole focus was on him now. She had a way of giving the person she talked to her full attention, but honestly, I liked that about her. Her reactions were genuine and she actually seemed interested in the people around her. It was a change from me who'd rather throw the annoying tourists in the sea.

"It's a crème brûlée latte with a hint of lemon, sounds crazy, but try it," he said. In fact, there was more happiness in his voice than I'd heard in all the years I'd known him... combined.

We both watched as she put the drink to her lips, eyes closing and a moan escaping her as she drank, a sound that was far too sinful for being in public. I refused to look at Drystan, not wanting to have to kill him for lusting after my omega, so I watched as she came back to earth. Apparently, my alpha wasn't so 'go with the flow' as I thought.

"Holy hell, that's like heaven in a mug! You're amazing!" Drystan's cheeks tinted the slightest pink and he grunted out an indecipherable answer before rushing to help the customers coming in the door. "You should try this!" Her attention was back on me, oblivious to nearly killing me with her noises and the fact she'd ignored me for a time. I wasn't upset that she had, I was quickly learning that it was just Ella in a nutshell.

"No thanks, I prefer my coffee bitter," I said, handing over the menu finally. Her nose wrinkled adorably and she chuckled before opening it up, eyes going wide at all the selections.

"They do have a lot of options. How does he cook it while running the coffee bar?" She glanced over at the bar, likely noting how small it was.

"There's a kitchen and he prepares it all ahead of time then heats it in those ovens and sandwich presses," I said, pointing out the food prep station. "No one minds the wait."

"Well, I know what I want." She grins, folding the menu. "How can a girl say no to a cheesy breakfast sandwich and a good coffee?" The way her blue eyes locked on mine had my heart pounding in my chest. How could one person change my life so completely? She flooded my thoughts and even my dreams and it's only been two days. If I was in this far and barely knew her, I'd hate to see the gooey, lovey-dovey mess I'd be in months.

If she's here that long, I reminded myself. The thought killed me. She was human, though the fated part didn't make sense. If the wards kicked her out after tourist season... would I follow? *Could* I even follow her? A shiver of apprehension filled me, what if she lived away from the water? I don't know why humans even attempted it... or any race for that matter. I couldn't imagine that life.

"Tanniv?" Electricity shot through me as she placed her hand on top of mine. She sounded concerned. My gaze flicked to her and I was happy to see she wasn't unaffected, her cheeks flushed and lips parted as she stared at me. *Keep it down, boy. You're over a thousand years old, self-fucking-control.*

Smiling widely, I flipped my hand over so I was holding hers. "Sorry, just lost in thought. Cheesy breakfast and coffee does sound amazing."

"Is something wrong? Did I—" Her brow furrowed. My heart clenched at the slightly broken expression that peaked through. Her past was a mystery to me. Hell, everything about her was, but from the small moments in between her cheerful exterior, I knew it couldn't have all been sunshine and rainbows.

I waved my free hand immediately, cutting her off. "No, no. Just my thoughts wandering. How are you liking your stay at Mystic Harbor so far?"

She searched my face intently and I saw the flip side of having her full attention. I felt like she could see right through me, even my small evasion. Then she relaxed, lips tilting up slightly, hinting at a smile. "I'm loving it! I've explored a few shops and I come by here every day. The first day I came here..." She waved to indicate the Enchanted Mug. "I was so overwhelmed by all the options, so I just told Drystan to make me his favorite drink. It was amazing. So it's kind of become a thing."

They have a thing. For a moment I wanted to growl out my displeasure at that, but the reminder of her smile while talking to him had me backing down for her sake.

Ella reached over with her free hand and took a sip of her drink, the entire time keeping her other hand in mine. It took every ounce of restraint to keep myself from holding tight and not letting her go. I nodded slowly. "He does come up with some interesting concoctions."

"I'm sorry I haven't made it down to the docks again." She shifted in her seat. "There's just so much to see here."

I grinned at that. "Whenever you want to come down,

just let me know. I'd be happy to show you around anytime. We had fun last time."

A loud, irritated cough made both of us turn to see Drystan standing there with a glare directed at me. "Sorry to *interrupt*, but what would you like to eat?"

There was enough bite in his words that my brows raised. *A very bold move for a beta.* He stepped back immediately, clearly backing down with his challenge but not leaving either. *Interesting.* "Ella wants one of the cheese breakfast sandwiches. I'll take a black coffee and one of the smoked salmon sandwiches."

"Do you two not like each other?" Ella blurted out, looking between the two of us, confusion clear on her face.

Drystan's face heated as I chuckled. Before either of us could respond though, the door opened and in walked none other than Leif. He searched the place and he tensed as soon as he saw the three of us together. Given the flash of jealousy that crossed his face, I could tell he could sense that I had bonded with Ella. His face smoothed out to a welcoming expression as he got closer.

"Ella! I see you've made quite the impression on the people in this town." He smiled at her. "Everyone is being kind to you I hope." He froze though when he saw that her hand was still in mine on the table. If I was another kind of alpha I'd flip her on the table just so I could fuck her to let everyone know she was mine. But, in truth, it was amusing how many people were drawn to her. That didn't mean I couldn't have my fun though. I brushed my thumb across the back of her hand, enjoying the slight catch of her breath and the flares of anger from the other two men. *This was going to be fun.*

"Everyone has been wonderful," Ella replied, biting her lip. "This town is so beautiful."

"I'll go get that food," Drystan commented stiffly, brushing past Leif with a none too gentle nudge, which just made Leif roll his eyes. Ella's eyes were wide, staring at the mayor then back to Drystan, then back to Leif, disbelief bright in her blue eyes.

"Any plans for the day after this?" I asked, trying to help Ella feel more at ease. This was amusing at first, but now I was getting annoyed that they were making her worry. My protective side wanted to put them in their place, but I'd stand down. This time.

"I'm going to go check out the library." She lit up again, smiling at me and Leif. "Need to do some research for one of my stories. Plus, I love libraries, so many books everywhere."

"You do love stories." I smirked, warmth filling me as I remembered telling her about the stars out on the docks before our kiss. "They have a lot of fascinating books there. The brothers that run it are very helpful if you need anything. The boys can act like frat brothers amongst themselves sometimes, but don't let that fool you. They're brilliant under that facade."

"Like the pirate being a gentleman?" Ella replied with a mischievous wink.

Leif snorted and I placed a hand over my heart to give him a mock affronted expression. "I am a perfect gentleman, the lady herself even said it."

"Gentleman is not a word I've heard applied to you once, Tanniv," Leif replied dryly, making Ella giggle before she tried to cover up the sound by sipping her coffee.

"Maybe it just takes the right person to bring it out of

me." We might have sounded playful to an outsider, but in reality, we were two alphas getting territorial. He could feel how he wanted, but this wasn't a fight I was about to lose.

"Your food," Drystan interrupted in a clipped tone. Ella pulled her hand out of mine so we could make room for our plates. It all smelled and looked delicious. I thanked him with a nod, sipping my coffee first as I settled back in my seat to watch Ella dig in. The fact she already had a crowd had my hands clenched into fists, but I couldn't look away quite yet.

The moan at her first bite made my cock throb, the sound going straight through me. *Middle of the coffee shop. We're in the middle of a damn coffee shop.* I can't just fuck her here... plus there was an innocence about her that made me want to savor the first time. That inkling had me restraining myself and focusing on the other two men watching her. Leif was completely focused on Ella, the tic in his jaw hinted at how much he was fighting for control. Drystan for his part was a mixture of pride and lust watching her eat the food he provided for her. Providing for an omega was one of those things that spoke to the primal side of us and she was, unintentionally, putting on a good show of just how much she appreciated Drystan's efforts.

Leif offered his goodbyes, as did Drystan, leaving us to our food a few moments later. We finished up in relative silence, outside of the happy noises and little dance she did as she ate. It was downright adorable.

"Do you want something to go?" Drystan asked as he cleared our plates after I signaled to him that we were finished. Wanting to mess with him just a little bit more, I couldn't help but put in my own request.

"I'll have a black coffee to go, and whatever you want to impress her with," I mused. "One check, of course."

"Of course," he said bitterly before flashing Ella a warm small smile. "Craving any certain type of coffee?"

"Oh! Something iced this time!" she said excitedly. It was crazy how even the smallest gestures seemed to mean the world to her and dammit if I didn't want to present her with the world just to keep that look of excitement and wonder firmly in place. It also made me curious as to what was so bad in her past she never got to enjoy the simple things in life. If a simple coffee is so significant, then something must have kept her from living her life. The question was what... and if there was anything I could do to fix it. As an alpha, especially one bonded to her, it was my duty to make sure that nothing causes her harm. That made the debacle of staying or going even harder. I wouldn't stay and send her back to whatever unknown hell she was running from, but how could I leave Mystic Harbor behind?

CHAPTER 6

Ella

anniv is such an interesting man. Not only was he sweet and observant, but he didn't seem to mind the fact I was so easily distracted. And our breakfast was full of interruptions. Though I was still trying to figure out why all three of them seemed so interested in... me.

"To the library?" Tanniv asked when I didn't say anything as we slowly ambled down the sidewalk. Sometimes it was still hard to get used to people actually speaking to me and not over me.

"Sorry, yes," I agreed, finally taking a sip of the iced coffee in my hands. "How does he do it?"

Tanniv looked amused at my reaction. "What is it this time?"

"I don't know other than heavenly. It kind of tastes like what I would imagine crème brûlée to taste like. But I don't have a comparison," I said, taking another long drink and sighing happily.

"I'm telling Violet, she'll be horrified and make you some. I'd say I'd make some for you, but it wouldn't be edible. Need me to filet a fish, I'm your guy, but my culinary skills end there. I've got delivery on speed dial and live on Violet's cooking."

"I imagine when tourist season is over she appreciates that," I laughed. "I'm sure you don't get many visitors outside of it. Though that's crazy, this town is gorgeous."

"We don't," he added, something dark flashing over his eyes before it was gone again. "But she still cooks dinner for us locals."

"Good. I'd hate to starve when everyone else leaves," I added absently. We'd just stopped in front of the library and my head fell back as I studied the structure looming in front of us. It had a classic, old library feel with stone griffins guarding the door. The tone of the exterior was weathered and had a green tint from the sea air. "Wow."

"Impressive isn't it," he agreed, studying me more than the building he's likely seen a million times before now.

"It is. The last library I was in had a few shelves of outdated books, almost all of them chosen to placate and not allow for free thought," I said bitterly before realizing how ominous it sounded. I put my smile back in place and turned to him. "Thanks for walking me! I'm going to head in so I don't keep you from the docks for too long. You're the harbormaster after all."

He winced at the reminder. "Shit, yeah, you're right. We have a huge charter going out today. Thanks for coming with me, I had a great time." He stepped closer and I swallowed hard, the scent of him washing over me until I felt like I wanted to strip right here and let him fuck me on the sidewalk. Which was insane... I'd never even had sex before and hc was making me willing to go all out for a public claiming. How one person had such an effect on me was crazy. He leaned down and brushed his lips over mine, the touch light and leaving a slight tingle in its wake. I was dazed, my fingers going up to touch my lip as he turned around and walked away from me.

"Are you okay?" The gravelly tone startled me from my trance and when I blinked, I realized Tanniv was completely out of sight and I was standing here like a complete weirdo.

"Y–y–yeah," I stuttered out the answer, blushing furiously as I glanced at the man standing next to me. There was an innocence in his face that rivaled the hard lines of his strong features. He was obviously an alpha, but unlike any alpha I'd encountered. He made me feel safe right away. The gentle scent of fresh snow wrapped around me and I could imagine curling up and soaking it in. *A safe space, something I've never had before.* This man... he wasn't like anyone I'd ever met before, not that anyone in this town had been so far. Every inch of him seemed to be chiseled, muscular but it was more than that. There was a gray-blue tint to his skin that made me immediately think of stone. What could he be? Then I couldn't hold back my question.

"How do you smell like snow?"

He let out a startled laugh, cheeks flushing pink. "What?"

"You smell like snow... but not like the midday flurries, more like the stillness of snow in the middle of the night," I rambled on. His eyebrows rose higher with each word I said. Apparently, I was hellbent on making an ass of myself. Great.

"That's a first," he mused, clearing his throat as he

rubbed the back of his neck. "Must be my cologne." His tone was off but he sounded amused. "You going in or standing on the steps?"

"Definitely going in," I said, glad to have a distraction as I turned and ran inside, hoping the ground would open up and swallow me whole.

"An unsuspecting tourist?" someone called out the moment I stepped into the lobby. The smell of old books and ink permeated the air and I took a deep breath of what I imagine heaven smells like.

I glanced to the circulation desk where several hulking men were playfully arguing. Their disguise fell for a moment, the sight of wings and dark gray skin made it click for me, they were gargoyles. This was a first for me, I'd never been face to face with them before. At least I assumed that's what they were. It's not as if I know every supernatural creature in existence, especially given I was always told I was crazy to believe such a thing anyway. *A memory lane trip I don't want to take any time soon.*

"I've got dibs!" another yelled from the second floor balcony, drawing my attention up there. The room was circular, with three levels, the balconies above showcasing more books than I'd ever seen in my life.

"No way!" the first one called out before an arm wrapped around my shoulder.

"I found her first and she doesn't need you all over-whelming her," the guy I met outside called out. They all let out a loud 'aww' in defeat.

"Baby brother thinks he's got game today," one of them teased, and the youngest but definitely not the smallest gargoyle groaned.

"Ignore my brothers. I swear they were taught manners, they just forget them sometimes," he said with a sigh. "I'm Maddox. If you need anything, just let me know."

"Thanks." I laugh, loving the energy the guys have. I'm also glad it's not the strict librarian at the ward. She would send us to our rooms for a damn sneeze and here they were yelling in the library. The brothers went back to joking around, laughing loudly as I walked away, my curiosity becoming stronger than my earlier embarrassment.

Books were always my getaway, my escape from the insanity of my life. No one believed me when I told them about the people I could see. And then when I kept pushing my parents, insisting that I was right, they committed me. The first time I was eleven years old. I bit my lip before letting out a shaky breath. Never again, this was my new beginning. They would never find me here. Time to focus on me and the present.

I ran my hands along the books on the shelves looking for anything that caught my interest. A story was calling to me but I had all day and I loved getting to know every inch of this small town, that included this library too.

Non-fiction, literary fiction, travel, kids' books, teens, and romances. They had so many options! A few things caught my eye and I pulled them off the shelf to flip through before sadly putting them back. I didn't have a library card so I wouldn't be able to check anything out. I pulled out my phone and wrote down the names, maybe I could plan a day with some coffee from Drystan, and then I could spend the day curled up here reading through some of these. The perfect day, plus cheap since I was *very* aware of my limited funds sitting back in my room at the bed and breakfast.

Then something caught my attention, a section of the

library that almost seemed to call to me. Not bothering to question it I walked right over, exploring the shelves until I saw it. A giant, leatherbound book on the top shelf. There was a design on the spine that was very worn, but it reminded me of the design on my sternum. *A bad prank.* My gut was telling me that Violet wasn't telling me more and now that I saw this I *had* to read it. But of fucking course it was on the top shelf, way out of reach.

"Do you need help?" A deep voice made me jump and whirl around with a hand over my heart. "Sorry, I didn't mean to scare you." Maddox held up both hands with an apologetic expression.

I tried to calm my racing heart as I gave him a timid smile. "No, I was just lost in thought. Not your fault. Umm... I do, actually. Can you get that book for me? The one with the design on the spine." I tried to point up at the book that I wanted.

Maddox's brow furrowed as he walked over and easily grabbed the book, checking it over before handing it to me slowly. "Here you go."

"Do you know what it's about?" I asked, taking it from him. There was no title on the front which was strange.

He didn't respond right away, making me look up at him as he studied me curiously before he answered me. "It's a book on mating marks. Different designs and... uh, things like that."

A loud crash from the first floor had us both jumping and Maddox let out a loud sigh as two men started arguing. I swear I heard something about pink flamingos and garden gnomes on sale. The two of us looked at each other before we approached the railing to see two of his brothers carrying in what looked to be an army of lawn ornaments. There was a new gargoyle behind the circulation desk, messy blond hair, glasses, and a look of amused frustration clear on his face as he watched all of these things being brought into the library.

"What are they doing?" I asked, unable to help myself.

"Were you at the last town meeting?" I nodded in answer and Maddox laughed softly. "Some of my brothers have a friendly rivalry with Harold. So in solidarity, I think they went to three surrounding towns to buy all of this to decorate this place."

I threw my head back as laughter bubbled out of me, unable to hold it in. The others stopped talking, looking up at me as I lost it again. I held up the book, trying to cover my face as I attempted to get myself under control. Maddox was grinning at me, dimples clear as he stared and I handed the book back to him. "Mind holding this for me? Do you guys need help setting those up?"

"Oh, baby bro, I like her!" A giant redheaded guy in a flannel shirt and jeans called out as the blond behind the desk watched me run downstairs with a small smile on his face.

"We have a plan." A dark-haired guy with glasses and bright blue eyes came out of the back hall with a large piece of paper. He laid it out on the circulation desk and I swear I was smiling so big that my cheeks were starting to hurt. They had a full battle plan at this point, a full-scale battle depiction of flamingos and garden gnomes at war. It was shown in grand scale too, taking up the full front lawn of the library and it almost looked like a recreation of the battle of Helm's Deep with the garden gnomes trying to take down the flamingos. I was freaking here for it.

"Do you have anything to represent the Ents?"

"You love Tolkein?" The dark-haired guy's eyes snapped up to study me as the redhead sighed.

"Of course I do!" I put on a mock affronted tone. "Now, there is no way you did all of this and ignored the Ents, did you?"

"Of course not." Maddox walked up slowly to stand beside me and he still had the book in his hands. "I bet we could use the Christmas trees in storage for this and some of the decorations we have stored away for Tolkein's birthday every year."

"I have so many questions." I looked around at all the brothers around me.

"Don't worry, you'll have plenty more before this is over." Maddox handed me the book again with a small smile tugging at his lips. "Here, why don't you look this over and I'll help them get the trees out? This is going to be an all-day staging process."

"Which you've volunteered for!" one of his brothers yelled back.

"No way am I missing this epic recreation." I smiled and held the book tight to my chest.

"You clearly were an only child," the blond brother joked as he rounded the desk to join in the fray. "No one gets this excited about being included unless they lived a sheltered life."

"You have no idea," I muttered, moving out of the way as they brought in more boxes of lawn ornaments. Figuring I'd let them do the heavy lifting, I found a comfy chair to sit in while I watched them work. When they disappeared to the basement, dragging Maddox along with them, I finally cracked open the leather bound book.

It felt like I was holding history in my hands, the book almost bubbling with energy I couldn't see but I could definitely feel. Maybe it was a sign that I was looking in the right place, just like I'd found the journal when I needed it.

Fated Mates are rare, and nothing like the tales suggest. It's not an insta-love at first sight. In fact, with most supernaturals, the connection has to be made either by touch, or it depends on one moment. A moment that is significant enough to spark the bond to life. From a kiss to a brush of hands, to a mutual understanding. There are many ways for it to present itself, but a fated mate is always identified by the matching mark on their skin.

Wait. My tattoo showed up after kissing Tanniv... could that be what it is? I've thought about the fact that it looks incomplete, what the hell would that mean? Could I even get one as a human? Fated mates were unheard of for us. Does the fact that I recognize supernaturals mean that I am one somehow? No... that's crazy.

As I read through the section, more and more started falling into place. How quickly he drew me in, how this town felt like fate led me to it. There were far more than mere coincidences happening here. And as I read on, it got even more interesting... or terrifying, depending on how you looked at it.

Even more interestingly, mates aren't always monoga-mous. In fact, the largest recorded fated mate group was twelve mates in total.

Twelve.

My brain broke at that sentence and as the book went on to explain further about the mark itself, I knew mine wasn't complete. In fact, I'd already figured out it was some intricate pattern around moon phases. Did that mean I'd end up with a mate for every phase of the moon?

Before that thought could fully process, the brigade of

alpha gargoyles lumbered up the stairs with no less than ten Christmas trees in tow.

"You ready?" they called out. I grinned and tried to hand over the book, but Maddox shook his head.

"That book isn't even cataloged, I think it belongs to you," he said mysteriously, and who was I to argue with that logic. Instead, I tucked it right into my messenger bag and rubbed my hands together conspiratorially.

"Where do we start?"

The front lawn of the library looked like the lawn and garden section of a store threw up on it. There wasn't a free spot left, except for under the giant oak tree which I'd claimed as my spot. The shade controlled the sun from blinding me as I cracked open my journal and got to work weaving a story of an old woman enchanting her lawn ornaments to life to defend her home. The evil villain was a rich man intent on buying up the land to create a shopping mall. As far as stories went, it was chaotic and a bit cliché, but what better way to get back into writing than a crazy short story?

Needing a flat surface to really get to work, I said a hasty goodbye as I packed up and ran off toward the bed and breakfast. I barely noticed the hello from Violet in my quest to get to my desk.

As soon as I sat in my chair, pen poised over the paper, it was like the words flew onto the page. The flamingos and gnomes banded together, defending their home from the evil frogs and garden faeries sent in by the evil millionaire.

I probably looked like a psycho, laughing maniacally

as I wrote the ridiculous story, the lawn ornament war reaching new heights as new characters joined in to defend the town. They gained power under the moonlight, but as the sun rose again, they fell lifeless onto the grass, the aftermath rivaling that of a tornado.

Satisfied with my ability to write and finish the silly short story, I had confidence I could find inspiration to write an actual novel like I'd always dreamed of. This town was already giving me so much, but the fact I managed to find a way to get my words out meant everything.

Now if I can just get a job without giving away my real identity, then I'll be golden.

CHAPTER 7

Maddox

E ver since she left the library, I couldn't stop thinking about the blonde-haired goddess that had even won over my brothers. The entire afternoon was as chaotic and crazy as it always was, but having her there made it so much more bearable. Not that I didn't love my brothers, but they could be a lot.

She was an anomaly of sorts. Her scent was so strong I couldn't ignore it, the warm scent of coffee and vanilla enticing. Yet she was human? A tourist that was only here until the glamour was up, but something about her screamed that she was different. She was important and even now, hours later, she haunted my thoughts.

"Shit, Maddox! Sterling! Carver!" Jonah's voice echoed up the stairs of the library, the sheer panic in his tone had me flying out of the chair and down the stairs. We were all night owls so we never left until it was well into the early morning hours.

"What's wrong?" Sterling, our oldest brother and the most serious, asked as he came to a stop behind me.

"They came to life. All the lawn ornaments in town, and we set up a literal army today," Jonah choked out before bolting out of the door.

"If this is a joke your ass is getting kicked," Sterling rumbled as we followed him out. My jaw dropped as I took in the army defending our library with sticks and anything else they could find, brandishing them like tiny weapons. The creepiest part was the glowing eyes on the gnomes as they turned their stiff bodies our way.

What the actual fuck.

"Spread out, I'll stay here and oversee these little assholes," Sterling ordered. Jonah and I took off since he had the rest of our brothers defending our library. The flamingos, trees, and gnomes were everywhere. The battle was spreading across the entire town. As we ran down the streets we saw others outside trying to defend their homes and businesses from the lawn ornaments. What was even crazier was the other lawn ornaments coming to life as the ones moving approached.

"Shit, Drystan," I said, getting Jonah's attention. The elven barista had a huge broom and was batting away plaster frogs, launching them in the air so they hit the ground in an explosion of shattered pieces.

He was quickly getting outnumbered so I grabbed an umbrella I spotted left on a nearby bench and joined in to protect the coffee house. The last thing this town needed was no caffeine after a night like this.

"I'm going ahead," Jonah called out as he ran past, the sounds of a scuffle coming from further down the street.

"They've taken the whole town," Drystan huffed as

he launched another frog into the brick wall. "What the fuck."

"This is nuts," I agreed, spearing one of them with the pointed tip of the umbrella before smashing it into the concrete.

"We are never going to hear the end of this from Harold," Drystan managed dryly as he pushed back a few more. I let out a triumphant laugh as we demolished the last of the frogs, at least for now. We took a breath and then I turned when I heard running to find Leif approaching with Jonah right behind him. Leif looked on with disbelief as he stopped, the glamour falling slightly for a moment to reveal his pointed ears and emerald, gold-flecked eyes. A grimace flickered across his face as he glanced over at us.

"Harold might be the least of our problems."

"The least of yours," Drystan commented dryly. Leif didn't bother to comment, too busy taking in the destruction around us. But it was almost comforting that the usual tension and bite between the two frenemies was still there in the middle of all of this. Some things didn't change.

"What the hell is going on in this town?!" Tanniv yelled out across the square. The siren was wading through the gnomes and flamingos with ease, flinging them away from him as he walked toward us. Under the streetlights, the blue hint of scales and black eyes wavered before his glamour snapped back into place. The fae in charge of glamouring the entire town must be fighting her own battle and losing given this was the second time I saw it slip. If that happened with the tourists awake we'd be in big trouble. Leif must have had the same thought because he rubbed his face with his hands.

"I have no idea, but right now that doesn't matter. This needs to be dealt with and contained without the humans knowing what's going on. Something to cover this so the humans don't notice or question the damage that will be left in the morning."

Tanniv nodded as he stopped next to us, though I didn't miss the way his gaze kept straying to the bed and breakfast where Violet, in wolf form, was defending the building. The siren took a steady breath, running a hand through his long hair and I caught a glimpse of a new moon on his wrist, the moon shaded and detailed so it wasn't just a dark circle. My mind immediately went to Ella today with the mating mark book. *No, no I'm just jumping to conclusions.*

"Ella will be fine," Leif told Tanniv softly. "Violet won't let anyone in there." *Guess I was right.* I tried to push down the pang of disappointment and the overwhelming sense of possessiveness I felt when I imagined her bright blue eyes and blonde hair as she laughed at something stupid one of my brothers said. *She is mine.* My inner alpha wasn't about to just walk away though.

"If there is a way to help, just tell me," Tanniv focused on our mayor.

Leif was about to say something when cursing sounded from the other side of the square. The Dwarven Beard's doors flew open to reveal Hunter and his boyfriend, Spencer, throwing gnomes and flamingos out of the bar. *How the hell did they even get in there?!* Hunter turned to say something to Spencer who nodded before the big alpha jogged over toward us. Apparently, it was just a big conference going on here right now.

"Where the fuck did all these things come from?!"

Hunter growled as he got close. Leave it to the bear shifter to cut right to the chase.

A hint of a smile curled Leif's lips before he grimaced. "No idea."

"A storm," Tanniv spoke up suddenly. "If someone could conjure one it could explain some of this tomorrow morning."

"Birdie?" Drystan proposed, looking at the others. "I bet she could do it. Opal seems to be having a hard enough time holding the usual glamour given everything going on."

"That's perfect." Leif nodded a few times then glanced at the elf. "If you could ask her to do that then I'll help everyone else here." Drystan nodded, tossing the broom at the other man who caught it effortlessly before running off toward the witch's log cabin on the edge of town.

"How could this have happened?" I asked, swinging my umbrella at some of the approaching faeries that were flying our way. *Guess our short respite is over.*

"No idea," Leif and Tanniv answered grimly.

"Let's just hope the storm comes quickly and makes this fight easier, not harder."

As if on cue, the door next door slammed open and faeries flew out, laughing hysterically. I blinked a few times, mouth dropped open in shock as I tried to compute what just happened. "Did they—"

"Fly out of my shop wielding dildos as weapons?" Orion asked, sounding tired but amused as he stepped out of his sex shop."Yes, yes they did."

Thunder so loud it seemed to shake the ground made everyone freeze, even the possessed lawn ornaments. I looked up to find dark clouds rolling in, lightning flashing across the sky, and rain started pouring down. The others started talking about hoping this slowed down the fighting but my gaze caught on movement at the bed and breakfast. They moved quickly, but I didn't miss the glimpse of blonde hair in the window or the pale hand pushing back dark curtains to look at the storm. I didn't want to draw the attention of the others so I stayed silent, but I didn't miss the way her gaze moved from the storm to us and then the lawn ornaments fighting in the town square. Her blue eyes widened, lips parting in surprise before she moved away from the window.

I had a feeling things were going to get very complicated, very soon. And my gut was saying it would center around Ella. The intriguing and beguiling human who waltzed into this town and claimed a mate from none other than Tanniv, a siren who was over a thousand years old. She also called to me, and given how the others kept randomly looking in the direction of where she was staying, they felt her pull too.

Just who was Ella Reed?

Chapter 8

Ella

The ward was quiet tonight, which was unusual enough to snap me from sleep. No wails of upset patients, no guards talking loudly and not caring if it woke us. Nothing.

Stepping out of bed I padded my way on socked feet to the small window in my door. It was little more than a small square, but the lights in the hall were flickering and I could see shadows moving around.

"What's going on?" I muttered to myself, starting to pace as that uneasiness grew.

My door flew open with so much force it slammed into the wall. There was no forewarning, no key creaking in the lock, or the usual quick knock to let me know someone was coming in.

As light spilled in, still flickering, I pressed my body into the corner of the room, heart pounding frantically in my chest until I felt light-headed.

"Ella." The way my mother's biting tone tore through the silence was enough to make me jump, but the feral rage on her face was far more terrifying. "The staff tells me you are refusing to get better, to move past these delusions of yours!"

My mouth opened and closed in frustration. I may have let my gaze linger a few times on the open door behind her but I never once said anything. I'd learned years ago how stupid that was. Not that it kept them from throwing me in here every chance they got. They'd concoct whatever lie they chose to, even using my silly stories as fodder.

"Don't ignore me, Ella!" Her lips curled in a sneer as she stared me down. "Speak up."

"I don't have those delusions, I am better," I pleaded, but her face didn't change.

"Your father and I have decided you're to stay here permanently. It's safer for you and better for us. You won't see the light of day again," she said evenly, her tone almost casual despite the malice on her face.

"You can't do that," I protested, panic clawing up my throat. "They decide if I'm capable of leaving, not you."

She laughed cruelly and walked closer, leaning down so we were nose to nose. "Oh, but that's not how it works when money is involved, Ella. You'll stay here whether you're crazy or not." The slam of the door was like a crack of lightning. Betas are supposed to be calming... my mother never got that memo. Sometimes she was even more terrifying than my ever watchful father.

I jolted from sleep, body covered in sweat and panic flaring through me. A flash of lightning outside lit up the room for a moment and it helped calm my racing heart, explaining some of the noises in my dream.

A rumble of thunder practically shook the room and I frowned. When I went to bed the sky was clear and there was no call for rain. Padding across the room I had a brief sense of déjà-vu, but at least this time I knew my parents wouldn't come bursting in.

When I pushed aside the curtain, my jaw dropped. The storm was brewing, but it looked fake, distorted somehow... almost magical. There were flashes of the starry sky underneath just like the glimpses I saw of supernaturals in the human world. But that was nothing compared to what was going on in the streets below. Flamingos, garden gnomes, faeries, and frogs were engaged in what could only be called an all-out war. *What — How— Lawn ornaments?*

The street below was busy for it being the middle of the night, and I noticed a few familiar faces as they battled with living lawn ornaments. What the actual fuck? It was so strange but vivid that I knew I wasn't dreaming. When Maddox's eyes turned my way, I ducked back behind the curtain. That familiar sense of fear hit me, knowing I couldn't let them know what I'd seen.

I let out a growl of frustration because here I was hiding again and I was so fucking tired of hiding who I was. Seeing through their disguises was something that I did naturally, yet it was the one thing I was judged and punished for as far back as I could remember. And here I was hiding from those I instinctively knew could be my friends.

"You should be used to it by now," I scolded myself as I climbed back into bed. It took hours to fall back asleep, my mind a jumbled mess of frustration and anger. The sun was peeking out of the curtains before I finally drifted off.

The sound of yelling outside shook me from sleep and it took a few seconds to shake off the grogginess, but not the lingering anger from last night. Flashes of the nightmare and the storm replayed in my mind as I walked to the window, peeking carefully through the curtains this time, and consciously ignoring the tremble in my hand as I brushed the fabric aside.

This time there was no storm, just the aftermath. Whoever had conjured it had scattered tree limbs and leaves around as well, making it a bit more real, but the shattered lawn ornaments were still mixed in.

I shuddered, my mother's bland voice and the memories of the sterile ward making me break out in a cold sweat as I turned away. My mood darkened and stayed that way while I got dressed, grabbed my bag, and headed downstairs. I'd slept in, so breakfast was over. I needed coffee from Drystan and fast.

"Some storm last night," Violet said as I stepped past her desk. I hadn't even noticed her at first, but the question filled me with annoyance. I wasn't the only one hiding here and I was tired of it. *Would I always be rejected and ostracized?*

"Yeah, almost like it came out of nowhere," I snapped, ducking out of the front door before I could get myself in more trouble. It seemed my normally filtered self was officially without one completely today. It might be best to get my coffee and find a patch of beach somewhere out of the way, away from people. I had my notebook in my bag and I was in desperate need of an escape.

As I walked through town, everyone was outside, cleaning up their yards and streets. I spotted Leif ordering a few men around down the road, pointing to the town square and all the debris covering it.

"Crazy night, huh?" I was startled by Sterling's stoic voice. "Destroyed every one of our trees, gnomes, and flamingos." I hadn't even noticed him standing next to me, but I just blinked twice and shook my head sadly, walking on not wanting to upset the man who I had spent hours setting up the Helm's Deep recreation with yesterday. Nothing I could have said would have been kind or productive, the lies working their way under my skin until I felt like I might scream.

Drystan's shop was blessedly cleared of debris and the line was nonexistent. His smile lit up when he saw me but I didn't return it. I didn't want us to talk about the fake storm and ruin our forming friendship. At this point, every sound and movement felt like nails on a chalkboard. Desperately, I hoped he understood that one more thing would send me to my breaking point.

"Caramel coffee with whole milk and sweetener, two shots of espresso," I ordered. He blinked back at me, his smile falling at my order. This was the first time I hadn't greeted him with my usual bubbly 'good morning' and I hadn't ordered for myself before.

"Sure," he said, giving me the side-eye the entire time he stepped away and I couldn't find it in me to care. Not today. "Here you go," he offered, sliding my cup over. I paid in silence before stalking out of the shop, still needing to be alone.

The streets were full of tourists when I stepped outside. Everyone was talking about the storm from last night, the thunder that shook the ground, and crazy lightning that had lit up the sky out of nowhere. Every word was like glass shards along my skin as my nightmare mixed with the memories of last night and the flashes of the normal night behind the storm. These people were just like my parents, lying to everyone because they thought it was for the best. Like I was a fucking child. It was always 'what was better' for me, what I could 'handle.'

I didn't realize I was shaking until searing pain shot through my hand. Hissing, I cursed softly when I realized I had crushed the to-go cup of coffee in my hand. Tears of frustration and embarrassment pricked my eyes as others around me whispered. Walking over to the trash can, I tossed the cup and untouched coffee into it.

"Ella! Are you— What's wrong?" Drystan's voice called out behind me.

I shook my head, refusing to turn his way, not wanting him to see the tears and question them. *My lack of filter isn't going to do me any favors right now. I need to get away from these people.* Ignoring him calling out my name, I pushed through the crowd and practically ran towards the harbor. *At least he didn't chase after me.* I pushed aside the slight twinge of hurt that accompanied that thought, it's not like I wanted him to follow me anyway.

It was the last day of the tourist season and the harbor looked insanely busy. Glancing around, I instinctively tried to see if I could spot Tanniv but I couldn't see him anywhere nearby. I was bordering on a panic attack and I just needed my alpha.

Someone brushed by me, murmuring a quick apology as I whimpered at the fresh wave of pain. Cradling my hand close to my chest, I bit my lip when I saw just how red my skin was from the hot coffee spilling all over me. I knew I should get someone to look at my hand, but I needed to calm down first. And honestly, the pain was keeping me grounded.

Walking away from the docks, I headed toward a small strip of beach that was nearby and carefully walked over the rocks until I settled on a small stretch of sand, not caring that wet sand was getting all over my clothes. They already had coffee on them anyway.

My anger and frustration slowly calmed as I listened to the waves crashing along the shore, the salt air surrounding me. Taking measured breaths, I tried to center myself. A few minutes later I released the last bit of my stewing anger as the scent and sound of the ocean soothed me. In my heart, I knew that I shouldn't blame the supernaturals. They were protecting themselves, but after becoming friends with them all, this betrayal just cut a bit deeper. I could never hold onto a grudge or anger for very long though, my parents being the only exception.

I had tried for years to be who they wanted, the perfect daughter, even with all the times they institution-alized me. Every time I came home from the mental ward, I'd attempt to act like I was 'fixed,' but as I grew up I could feel the malice and disgust every time they saw me. If anything they were always on the lookout for anything that they could use as an excuse to lock me up again. Their latest attempt to throw me into the hospital was the last straw. I couldn't do *anything* without their approval. I shuddered as the ghost of my mother haunted me, saying they were going to lock me away forever.

My hand throbbed, pulling me from my wandering thoughts. Chewing on my bottom lip I considered the ocean water, trying to figure out if it would help with my hand or not.

"I wouldn't if I were you," an unknown voice made me gasp. Whirling around I tried to figure out where it was coming from but I didn't see anyone nearby. My brows furrowed in confusion as I turned to face the ocean again and I froze. There in the water, maybe six or seven feet away from me was someone watching me. A male, from the feel of him he seemed like an alpha, looked as if he was treading water, watching me with eyes that were completely black, no hint of white in sight. *Siren.* Black hair hung loose around their face, the hint of pointy, webbed ears stuck out from some of the wet strands. Gills were dusted along his neck along with a purple tinge to his skin and as he moved, I noticed scales along his body.

"Wouldn't what?" I asked hoarsely, clearing my throat at the horrible sound as I used my uninjured hand to wipe my face, as if that would erase the tears on my cheeks.

He was silent for a few moments, considering me before slowly getting a little bit closer. "Put your hand in the water. The salt won't be good for the burn."

I blinked, looking down at my hand then at the ocean again. "Really?" He nodded slightly, studying me like he was trying to figure me out. "Thanks."

"You're welcome," he replied slowly, moving a bit closer. As he walked out of the water he shifted, almost as if a distorted second layer wrapped around him. I could see the siren underneath, but it was overlaid with another person. He looked so much like Tanniv, but with a bit more muscle and a harsher face. The swim trunks he was wearing were a bright orange, something else that differed from Tanniv, who was a bit more subtle in his clothing choices. I smelled the salt of the ocean that clung to him, but underneath that was a wonderful hint of sage and rosewood that had my cheeks flushing as he sat down next to me. "We haven't met before."

I shook my head slightly, very aware of how close he was sitting next to me. "No. I think I'd remember that."

His answering smirk had me blushing even more. If it was possible for a blush to set someone on fire, it would happen right about now. "I'm Ella. You look like Tanniv."

The man cocked his head to the side, studying me intently, "You're Ella?" I nodded, unsure why it sounded like he had heard my name before when I still had no idea who he was. "Tanniv is my twin brother, I'm Asra. What happened to your hand?"

A self-conscious laugh escaped me as I waved my hand, trying to make it seem like it was not a big deal. "Just spilled some coffee. It hasn't been the best day so far."

He grabbed my wrist gently, stopping my movement, and pulled it toward him. My heart raced and I found myself instinctively finding comfort in him.

Turning my wrist over slightly in his hands, he carefully examined my burn. "It might be tender, but nothing serious." He looked up, eyes narrowing as he caught me studying him intently. "What is it?"

"I liked you better in the water," my words spilled out of my mouth, and instantly, I wished I had bitten my tongue. Asra froze, his hold on my hand was still gentle but he looked as if he was carved from stone.

"What do you—"

"Not the human disguise or whatever this is." I waved my free hand, indicating his human form. Apparently, I had hit my breaking point of being lied to, and this stranger, Tanniv's brother, was going to be the tipping point for me. *Will he lie to me like everyone else I have met in my life? Or will he be honest?*

"You— You can see through the glamour? That's interesting." He grinned, a hint of excitement sparkling in his dark eyes. "Just what are you, Ella?"

"No one." I laughed and it sounded broken, even to my own ears. "I've never been anyone who mattered."

Before I could register what was happening I found my back against the sand with Asra hovering above me, a challenge and promise of violence clear on his face as he stared down at me. "You could never be no one. Tanniv has talked about you and I didn't expect to meet you without him. Though now... I'm glad that I did."

"Why?" I breathed out, my heart pounding loudly in my ears.

"Because you smell so damn sweet and I don't think I would have been able to stop myself."

"Stop yourself from what?"

"This." He leaned down, slanting his lips over mine in a heated kiss. Maybe it was a siren thing or my lack of experience, but fuck, Asra and Tanniv knew how to kiss. My toes curled as I wound my arms around his neck and pulled him down closer to me, letting my body take over, following his lead. A nip of my bottom lip made me moan and then I moaned as he took the opportunity to deepen the kiss, his tongue teasing mine and hands skimming my body. Slick pooled between my thighs, my body a puddle under him, omega responding to her alpha.

Burning along my rib cage had me gasping and pulling away from Asra to find him staring at me, eyes wide then I saw it. A waxing crescent moon on his wrist and my jaw dropped.

"How can this be possible?" Asra questioned, staring at his wrist in awe. "But Tanniv... Shit. I just thought I'd see what the fuss was, I didn't intend for that..." he trailed off from his rambling and stared back and forth between me and his wrist with wide eyes.

"You sound like me now." I laughed. "How can that

be possible?" Though even I wasn't this dumb. I had a feeling I was collecting mates like baseball cards, I just needed someone to be honest. And Asra's blunt demeanor was my best chance at a real answer.

"Fated mates. Mate markings," he stumbled over the words as he pushed himself up, solidifying my earlier suspicions. "Wait. Where's yours?" he asked, fingers brushing over my wrist and not finding it.

"Thanks for not lying to me," I deflected, not ready to flash him my tattoo and my boobs in the process. It looked unfinished and I knew even with his addition, it wasn't done. Would he be angry? Would Tanniv? I'd kissed him and felt the same thing. *Why is my life so complicated?!*

His expression softened. "They only lied because we aren't allowed to tell the humans what we are. But now that we know you can see through it, that's a different story."

My reply was a shaky whisper, and I hated that I sounded so vulnerable. "It's just been a long life of lies. Of being made to feel like I was crazy, that my mind was playing tricks on me. Even the doctors who weren't human lied." My bitter tone was well earned. Soft fingers brushed away my tears and mortification hit me hard. I didn't know this man at all, yet here I was unloading my emotions on him. "Oh gods, I'm so sorry," I hissed, groaning as I closed my eyes. "I shouldn't have word vomited all of that."

He chuckled at my reaction. "Oversharing comes with the territory. Don't worry." As if he could sense that I needed space to process, he smirked at me. "I'm still waiting to see yours. Please tell me it's somewhere... delicious." His smirk turned downright predatory and I swallowed hard and clenched my thighs together. He took a deep breath and his chuckle told me he could smell just how turned on I was by one simple look.

"I uh... need to go," I finally said, scooting out from under him and standing up, brushing off what sand I could. The abrasive grains rubbed against my tender palm but I ignored it. Asra looked more amused than startled as he stayed seated, watching my every move closely. Good, because I needed time to figure out what the hell just happened. I was trying to escape and find peace, instead, I've found two mates and a gut feeling I wasn't anywhere near done. I turned and rushed off, half wondering if he'd follow. When I glanced back, he hadn't moved from the shoreline, eyes trained on me intently as I walked further into town. With one last forced smile, I turned away and continued walking, praying no one else would stop me along the way.

Asra

Ella. She wasn't what I was expecting, that's for sure. I had been coming up to shore to talk with Tanniv when I saw her coming toward the beach. Anger, pain, sadness... all of those emotions poured off of her as she settled on the sand, but the waves pulled that from her, in turn calming her. I was mesmerized. There was no going to see my brother without seeing who she was. Anyone who found that much comfort in the sea deserved my curiosity.

As I got closer, that intrigue only doubled. She smelled like heaven, her coffee and vanilla scent the only thing better than sea air. But how could a human smell so amazing? Just who was she?

The moment I heard her voice, some part of me knew that she was mine. She was sexy, and in a way that showed she didn't even realize it. She was a mix of alluring yet shy, and it pulled me in like no one ever had. Then confessing she liked how I looked as a siren instead of the horrible human facade we were forced to wear during tourist season... She was perfection. The glamour was the main reason I avoided the shore during these times, I couldn't stand it.

Tanniv had told me about his new mate. I grinned to myself, excited to see my brother's reaction when I tell him we have the same mate. We have been competitive since we were young. Women, wars, and whiskey— we've competed for it all, but there has always been a friendship stronger than anything else underneath all that.

Ella had hurried back to town and I waited a few more minutes before meandering toward the docks in search of my brother. Business was booming, humans hurrying towards a ship at the end of the docks, trying to get in one last boat ride before the town closed tomorrow to humans. A grimace crossed my face thinking of Ella and wondering what was going to happen with her. She was human, but more... She was *ours*. With a deep breath, I tried to focus on anything besides wondering where on her creamy skin was marked with our mate marks.

"Asra!" a familiar voice called out. I spun around, a wide smile on my face as Tanniv pulled me into a tight hug, slapping my back a few times before pulling back. "You were supposed to be here thirty minutes ago!"

"Fate had different ideas." I lifted an eyebrow in challenge as I grabbed his wrist with the marking.

"What are you—" His question trailed off as I smugly showed my marked wrist next to his. The next phase of the moon after his was clearly shown on my wrist and he looked up, eyes narrowed and a flash of possessiveness filled him before he took a deep breath.

"I met Ella and you were right, brother, she is absolutely something else." I licked my lips, still able to taste her on my lips and smell her heady scent of coffee and vanilla. "What happens if she leaves town tomorrow?" My smile fell away at that sobering thought.

"She isn't leaving... *us*," Tanniv sent me a feral smirk. "She's ours."

"Oh, I think she is going to be more than just ours before the end. But I already know she is going to be with me first, Tanniv."

"You wish, Asra," he growled, a spark of good-natured humor shining through in his dark eyes.

I'd feel sorry for Ella, but I was too excited at the prospect of her being mine.

CHAPTER 9

Ella

After wandering around town refusing to go back to the inn yet, I ended up outside of the Dwarven Beard. The brick building looked unassuming and I figured a quiet bar and a drink might just get me through this day. Tomorrow I could be strong, and process all this mate business, but here and now I just wanted to avoid it all.

Inside the bar was a bit livelier than I was expecting, but that was probably because it was the last day of the tourist season. The dark wood walls and floors should have made it feel like a cave, but the red accents and brightly lit bar evened it out enough to be a mix of classy and fun.

The tables were nearly full, but the bar was practically empty which suited me just fine. I rushed forward and claimed a spot at the far corner against the wall. It took a good ten minutes before the bartender came over and I recognized him immediately from my first town meeting. He was with the buff guy wearing a beanie... I think his name is Spencer? But the last thing I could think about was cute guys, I wanted no thoughts of men for the night. I wanted the calmness that's supposed to come with alcohol. But my wandering thoughts weren't easily distracted when he smelled so amazing, the citrus and sage scent enticing. I shook my head, physically ridding my brain of those thoughts and willing my body to calm the hell down. *Not. Tonight.*

"Hey, what can I get you tonight?" Spencer asked with a quick smile. He looked exhausted, his honey blond hair tousled, but his emerald green eyes still held a hint of curiosity as he gave me his full attention.

"Surprise me as long as it doesn't taste like fire," I said, praying he wasn't about to ask me for an ID. Sometimes I looked younger than I was but he didn't even flinch, nodding before turning around and pouring me a drink.

"Here, first one's on the house," he said, sliding it over. He looked like he was going to say more but someone was already waving him down.

I hated to admit that I stared that shot down for longer than I should have, but now that the moment was here, I was a bit intimidated by my first taste of hard alcohol. I've seen the movies, people spitting it out because it tasted so awful and I didn't want to make an ass of myself. *Probably too little too late, why did I have to be so confident to have him surprise me with my first drink?*

"Is it bad?" Spencer asked, coming back over and raising an eyebrow at my expression. Not wanting to be a jerk, I slammed back the shot, fully expecting it to be awful. When it tasted like chocolate cake instead, my eyes went wide.

"Holy shit, it's so good," I gushed. "How does it taste like cake?!" He smiled then, looking proud of himself.

"I'm just that good. I'll get you an actual mixed drink this time. You just looked like you needed a strong drink to start with," he promised, moving away and getting to work. He came back with a red concoction a few minutes later and I slid over my cash. As soon as he slid my change back he was off again, the poor guy didn't look like he got much of a break.

The drink was just as good. It was a mix of tart and fruity and I enjoyed the warmth it gave me as I tried to subtly stare at Spencer. Of all the glamours I'd seen, which was a lot in my lifetime, his was impossible to see through. That immediately made me think he was a type of shifter, power clearly emanating from him, it felt too primal to be a mage or a witch. But I couldn't tell more than that and there was no hint *at all* what was beneath his disguise.

A vibration caught my attention and I frowned as I looked down at my purse. Fishing out my cell phone I sighed when I saw Violet's name fill the screen. Ignoring it, I tossed it back into my bag as I took a long sip of my drink finishing off the last of the cup. I would talk to her, just not right now. I hiccuped and burst out laughing, finding the sound way more funny than it probably was. I fanned myself, looking around the bar, suddenly feeling like it was a million degrees in here. *When did it get so hot in here?!*

"Did you like the— Hey, are you okay?" Spencer's soft voice made me turn to face him, still laughing so hard I would have fallen off the barstool if he hadn't reached across to catch me. *How much alcohol did those drinks have?*

"Do you really want the answer to that question?" I asked, my words slurring slightly at the end after I finally calmed down enough to answer. His eyes widened a bit a that, but apparently, the alcohol made honesty pour from me like a fucking fountain. My cheeks flamed, the logical side of me knowing I should shut the hell up, but I couldn't. Tears pricked at my eyes and I had no control of the tidal wave of emotions overtaking me. "No. No, I'm not okay. I'm being lied to by everyone, every damn person in this town! And I'm supposed to just act like it's all fine, I'm tired of it! I knew that all these supernaturals I've seen my whole life were real, I can see right through the shitty disguises everyone wears! And to top it all off," I yanked my arm from his hold. The world spun as I fell back, but instead of falling onto the floor, I fell back into a wall of muscle. Gentle hands gripped my shoulders, keeping me from falling onto the floor. Even the deliciously attractive man who smelled like wintergreen couldn't stop my tirade. "I'm mated. Mated! To two different men... sirens! I was coming here to escape, find peace and quiet. I'm not getting any of that!"

"Hunter, you need to get her out of here," he whispered harshly, glancing around us. The other patrons weren't paying any attention to us. I don't know what his problem was. "Everyone is going to hear her."

I tilted my head back at the growly voice above me and the smile froze on my face when I saw the uniform he had on. A cop. *A fucking cop.* No, no way. Panic filled me as I attempted to pull myself from his hold. His face filled with concern as I frantically and uselessly tried to get away from him. There was no way I was going to cooperate with him. Memories of the police officers I had run into in the past, their taunting and crass words pushing me closer to a breakdown. I'd never had a good experience with cops and I wasn't going anywhere with him, small town or not, some things never change.

"You're not taking me anywhere!" I yelled, lashing out and somehow managing to slap him across the face.

"Fuck," Hunter rumbled, not physically reacting to my hit besides turning his face away as I lashed out again. "Spence, help me out here."

The blond hurried from behind the bar, reassuring people with ease as he came over. Once they were both there, they got me out of the back of the bar, away from tourist foot traffic along the town square.

"Let me go!" I cried out, annoyed, drunk as fuck, and my sternum felt like it was on fire.

"We can't do that," Hunter said firmly.

"Of course you can't, you're just going to take me against my will, that's what every fucking cop has done so far," I protested, angry tears welling in my eyes as defeat filled me. He was so stunned his hands fell away, sending me toppling into Spencer since I was far from stable.

"Ella," Spencer warned, but that was the last thing I heard as the world spun out of focus and I passed out in his arms.

CHAPTER 10

Ella

The moment I opened my eyes nausea rolled through me making me fight my upset stomach until it settled. My mind was still a little bit foggy, and I had to force myself to keep my eyes open. *What made me think drinking was a good idea? I'm never doing that again, one and fucking done.* After blinking a few times I looked around, realizing that this was *definitely* not my room at Violet's. Glancing down, I let out a sigh of relief at the sight of my clothes still in place under the sheets. With my mind in disarray, I was counting small blessings right now.

The room itself was fairly unremarkable and gave nothing away. It was a calming mix of blues, whites, and grays. Neutral tones that made it look open and airy. The king-sized bed was the centerpiece, two closets flanking it, but no pictures lined the walls.

Where the hell am I?

My gaze stopped on a slightly opened door and I really hoped it was to an attached bathroom. Between my nausea and my bladder screaming at me, I had no choice but to find out. Forcing myself out of the bed, I crept to the door, doing an internal happy dance when I pushed it open to see a small adjoined bathroom. I closed and locked the door behind me, my instincts still on high alert since I was in an unfamiliar house.

After doing my business, I splashed cold water on my face, trying to wake myself up more. I racked my brain trying to remember what happened last night but after that first shot, everything was blank. I'd never had a hangover before, but this was literal hell on earth. My body ached, my stomach churned, my head was pounding, and I just wanted to take some tylenol and pepto then pass the fuck out. I searched the medicine cabinet, but there were no meds to be found, just extra toothbrushes and toothpaste. *How does this person not even have tylenol?* My only saving grace was the bottle of mouthwash on the counter. I grabbed a disposable cup and poured some in before taking the swig and swishing it around my mouth. Having a clean mouth was one step closer to feeling normal. Though that step was small.

Glancing in the mirror, I saw how awful I looked. My makeup had run, giving me raccoon eyes and my hair was a tangled mess. Thankfully I always kept a hair tie on my wrist. Yanking it off, I reached up to throw my hair in a messy bun. My world froze at the sight of the mate marking poking out from under my crop top. With shaking hands, I shifted my shirt up and gasped at the sight of four moons staring back at me. The new moon, the waxing crescent, first quarter, and waxing moon clear along my sternum.

"Wait," I said out loud, grasping onto the marble sink and taking a few deep breaths to calm myself. "Who…" but then the memories slammed back into me. Hunter. Spencer. Me spewing out gibberish about supernaturals, mates, and cops. "Fuck, fuck, fuck," I chanted as I started pacing back and forth in the tiny space, anything to center myself.

I went to the bar to escape the fact I had two mates when as a human I shouldn't have any, and the mindfuck of more lies from everyone in town, and somehow ended with a massive hangover and two *more* mates. To make it all worse, I made an ass of myself to my new mates and almost outed the supernaturals to the other humans celebrating the end of the tourist season. How the hell did I get here? I mean… I was supposed to be having a quiet life but here I was collecting mates like damn Pokémon cards when humans don't even *have* fated mates. And I vividly recall now that Violet mentioned Spencer and Hunter at the town meeting… weren't they fated mates with each other? How the hell do I have a mark from them?

The pacing wasn't helping but I couldn't make myself stop as my thoughts continued to swirl. A shock on my fingers had me finally pausing, eyes widening at the sight of electricity sparking on my fingertips. I had no clue what the fuck was happening, but I was pretty sure it was related to all these mates. All of it had me nearing a full-blown panic attack. Forcing myself to stop moving, I crouched down and wrapped my arms around my knees, resting my head on my knees as I took steady, measured breaths.

Get your shit together, Ella. You have to sneak out before the rest of the house is up.

At this point, I knew it had to be Hunter and

Spencer's place, but that also meant if I wasn't careful, I'd have to face them right now. Facing them wasn't really something I wanted to do at this very moment. I wanted time to process what my life was spiraling into, though I was completely ignoring those sparks because I couldn't even wrap my head around that development. *I wish Tanniv and Asra were here. I didn't know them that well but I felt at ease instantly around them both and desperately needed that right now.*

Once I could breathe again, I stood up, straightened my clothes, then rushed out of the bathroom. I searched the room to realize my shoes and bag weren't in there, but at the moment I didn't care. The house was small enough that I easily found my way to the living room. The lights were all off and it was silent, so I took careful, quiet steps until I reached the front door. Luckily I found my shoes and bag right next to the door so I quickly grabbed both.

The moment my hand wrapped around the knob, someone cleared their throat. I froze, my eyes closing in defeat before I put a fake smile on my face and turned around. Spencer and Hunter stared back at me. Hunter looked concerned, his eyebrows furrowed as he studied me. Spencer studied me, mouth set in a grim line, but I could see the spark of worry in his dark green eyes. Neither man was super inviting and it took everything in me to take one step away from the door to fully face them.

No part of me wanted to face this right now. I'd run from two mates and now I suddenly had four. Call me a runaway mate cause Julia Roberts looked like a damn genius right now.

"Um... Sorry for last night and thanks for taking care of me. I appreciate it, but I really need to go," I said quickly, trying to turn away and grab the doorknob again, but Hunter was quicker.

"Wait. No, we have to talk about this," he said, his voice holding a slight command that had me instinctively freezing. The alpha was coming out to play and I hated that my body responded with a surge of longing. My mind was still firmly in flight mode and wanted no part of this impending conversation.

Spencer stood up and held his hand out as if trying to calm me, gesturing to the kitchen.

"Do you drink coffee?" It was an obvious attempt at diffusing the tension and I was glad for it.

"Yes, I love coffee," I said, my voice sounding small and slightly hysterical, even to my own ears. As he walked by, those hysterics only increased. The smell of citrus and sage filled my senses. It was so strong that it wrapped around me like a cloud, holding me in place yet easing my worries a fraction. My head still spun, but my flight mode dropped a notch or two. Betas, especially ones omegas bonded with, had the ability to calm. I guess us being mates made that a hundred times more effective.

When he was fully out of the room, I turned back to face Hunter. His eyes were glowing a slight amber, giving away that he was a shifter, though my foggy mind couldn't recall what kind of shifter he was. Unlike with Violet, it wasn't as obvious what kind of supernatural he was, but that likely had to do with how guarded I was in front of him. I was mostly relieved to see he wasn't still in uniform, which did help some, but the fact I knew he was a cop still lingered.

He stood, and as he towered over me I flinched away. It didn't go unnoticed by him and he immediately froze then sat back down slowly, the movement sending wintergreen my way. It was a refreshing, crisp scent and my body reacted just like with Spencer, loosening me up even further until I was almost at ease. Everything about him was screaming that he was safe, but trauma never let go that easily. It liked to infiltrate you, body and soul, dig its claws in and not let go.

Needing to look at anything but him before I started going back into a panic, I glanced around the room. It took about two seconds before I spotted his uniform draped over the back of a chair, handcuffs hanging on a loop. The sight alone, along with this feeling of unease had me right back with my family.

It was raining and the night was cold as we walked up the path to the front door. We'd been out to dinner and I was a good girl, hadn't brought up a single supernatural, even though they were everywhere tonight. But I'd apparently not been as subtle as I thought, my parents noticing my pauses and drifting gaze.

When dad excused himself to the bathroom at the restaurant and it took longer than usual, I knew. They were going to send me back again. It hurt, pain lancing through my chest. I felt betrayed and wished I could run away, but I was a kid. Not to mention they were loaded, they'd find me easily.

As my mother pushed open the door and ushered me inside, my heart sank. Two officers were standing in the entry hall, flanking Dr. Sloane. He owned the asylum and was almost always the one to escort me to my prison.

This time I didn't fight them, though inside another piece of my soul was fracturing.

One officer stepped forward, handcuffs dangling from his fingers. "We have to put these on. For your safety and ours, of course," he said with no sincerity. He wasn't gentle as he bound my hands, the cold metal digging into my wrists as I bit back my tears.

Instead, my focus landed on the awful doctor. I'd never quite figured out what he was. His eyes were solid black and a smattering of red scales dusted his hands, forearms, neck, and face. Likely elsewhere, but that was thankfully something I'd never know. Dark horns curled up from his head and tilted back. My guess was dragon, but I couldn't exactly ask.

"Let's go," the other officer said, grabbing my bicep in a bruising grip as he dragged me out the door. I had to jog to keep up and focus to not lose my balance. He was being an asshole and once again, I wished I could run. But it was useless, I was at their mercy and heading into another stint in my own personal hell.

"Hey!" The sharp bark mixed with an alpha command had me snapping from my memory. I blinked a few times before jumping, the alpha standing far too close to me. He backed away once he saw me regain my senses. The concern was obvious in his expression but I wasn't having it, no matter if my omega side was on the same page as my brain or not.

"Sorry," I whispered, tears burning my eyes. I felt vulnerable and exposed and then my flight mode kicked in so hard I couldn't ignore it. "Look, I get it. We're mates. But I'm not dealing with it right now. I need time to process before we talk. I... I just can't. I'm sorry," I said, turning and yanking the door open and sprinting outside. No one followed me and I didn't slow down as I headed into town, hoping I was going in the right direction. I just needed to sleep off this mindfuck and this hangover, then I could deal with it all later.

Deflection... It works every time.

Hunter

"Well, that went well." Spencer snorted as he flopped back on the couch, closing his eyes as his head rested against the back cushion. I was so confused that I didn't even really have the words to say anything. Guess Ella wasn't the only one who needed time to process what the fuck just happened in the last twelve hours.

"I feel like we were just picked up by a tornado and slammed around for a few hours." It was the only way I could summarize everything that had happened from the time I walked into the Dwarven Beard to now.

"Because we were," Spencer snarked back. "But she's definitely our mate." He flashed the moon on his wrist for emphasis and I glanced down at my own. It was right above our matching marks, the large black and white tree with deep roots branching out beneath the soil now had a first quarter moon on Spencer's forearm and a waxing moon on mine.

"How..." I trailed off, trying to make sense of it. My alpha was struggling. Every instinct in me wanted to run after my omega and comfort her, calm her, but it wouldn't do any good. There was *something* I could do though. She was staying with Violet, a good wolf alpha who could help keep an eye on her for me. They were friends already, so it was a perfect solution. I pulled out my cell phone and called the bed and breakfast.

"Thanks for call—" I cut her off before she could utter the rest of her go-to greeting.

"Violet, it's Hunter. Ella is coming your way now," I started and she cut me off right back.

"Oh, thank fuck," she breathed out, obviously relieved. It solidified my choice to trust her with my omega for now. Not that I had many other options.

"She's not in a good place... She's our mate and she knows it," I said, summarizing what I could about last night. She cursed as I wrapped it up.

"Shit. Okay. I've got this," she promised. "Probably not Tanniv when he finds out... but that's between all of you."

Fuck... the siren. It suddenly hit me that she was already mated to someone else, another *alpha*. This was going to be interesting.

"One more thing. She's terrified of me, of cops in general," I said, needing someone else to know, though I was unsure why.

"Give her time. She's..." She trailed off as well, unwilling to spill her friend's secrets and I was glad for that. Ella would open up and tell us herself someday, when and if she was ready.

"I get it," I reassured her. "Just letting you know in case you see her react in the future."

"Noted," she said. "I've got to go, she'll be here soon." She hung up, the call ending.

Taking a deep breath, I pulled up the number for the harbormaster. It wasn't something I was excited to do. It felt like I was admitting I wasn't alpha enough to comfort my omega. It warred with my entire physiology, but it was what was right. And that, I reminded myself, was exactly what an alpha does, takes care of the omega no matter how that presents itself.

"Harbormaster," Tanniv answered on the first ring. He was always quick to answer, and always sounded bored. He had that laid-back attitude that I definitely could never achieve. I guess it made sense since we were both her alphas.

"Hey, it's Hunter. We've got a situation." That had him clearing his throat.

"Oh, and what is it?" He was all business now, the laid-back falling away in lieu of his position.

"Ella. She's heading back to Violet's place and she's upset," I told him quickly. "She mated with both me and Spencer last night. It was just us trying to get her from the bar before she told the entire place about us, but all it took was one touch."

"Uh, wow. That's not what I expected, but we're on our way." He hung up and I cursed, hating that I would be out of the loop now. *Wait... we?*

"She definitely never drank before last night," Spencer started, breaking the silence that fell after that phone call. It was an obvious subject change, but a welcome one from the one we were both avoiding. "I know a first timer when I see one. If I would have just realized that before she had that second drink, I would have made it a whole lot less strong."

"She reacted the same today, drunk or not... She's terrified of me." Saying the words out loud again was like a knife to the chest. I was an alpha, the protector. How was I supposed to protect an omega who wanted nothing to do with me?

Spencer scooted closer, his hand resting on my thigh and my building tension sank back down.

"Look, I don't know anything about her. But I don't think it's you personally."

I shook my head. "It's not, it's the uniform. But it's just a part of me as anything else. This is *what* I do. It's *who* I am. How do I counteract that? She was running on instinct. She's never gonna let me get close."

The bear in me was pacing and clawing to get out, to go after whoever wronged our mate and tear them apart with our teeth and claws. Return the favor for traumatizing our omega because whatever happened in her past... It was dark.

"And to address the elephant in the room. We've got a fated mate. An omega. A third." He sounded vulnerable, which was so unlike him. It had me turning his way, my hand grabbing his jaw so he had to look at me.

"It's crazy, but we knew it was a possibility. No matter what happens with her, it changes nothing between us. We are still fated mates, and we are still the same. Our dynamic may change as a whole, but we're solid and will remain that way. It's been you and me, Spence, for how long?"

"Five years," he said, letting out a soft huff of laughter. His eyes were full of relief at my words and I knew I hit the nail on the head. "I just don't want it to change us. You're all I've got."

Griffins didn't stick together, so he'd been on his own for a long time when we met. I was also alone, my family dead for so long I forgot what it felt like to have someone to rely on. For a bear shifter, that was torture. But our two lost souls found each other and gave each other a home. This wouldn't change that, it was too important. We'd form a new relationship with Ella, over time, and it would have to be its own entity. It might be complicated, but I knew in my heart it would be worth it in the end.

"You feel her call though." I watched him closely as Spence nodded slightly, a hint of heat filling his face.

"Yes," Spencer growled, his soft voice deepening as

his scent grew stronger. His emerald green eyes almost dazed as he pinned me with an intense stare. "She feels... different. I don't know how else to word it right now."

"We found a home in each other." I leaned my forehead against his, needing the feel of his skin against my own. "Seems like we are lucky enough to have space for someone else."

Spencer didn't respond right away, something that wasn't unusual for him. He spoke again a few minutes later. "A family... good thing we both like lots of people because considering the moon marking we got from her and how many phases there are, Ella is coming with plenty of people included." A rumbling laugh escaped despite myself and he pressed a quick kiss to my lips before pulling back. "Why don't we invite her to dinner? After we give her a few days to cool off like she asked, then we can go talk to her. In fact, maybe I should go in alone and invite her? I'll tell her you'll be there with no uniform."

"Agreed," I said quickly. "That's probably for the best." As much as I hated admitting it, or letting my beta handle this one for me, I knew it was for the best.

Spencer leaned forward again, brushing his lips over mine and dousing me in that citrus and spice scent. It covered me like a warm blanket and the world around us disappeared until it was just us. Even if our lives were a mess now and my soul was a bit torn, right here in this moment with him, I was still whole.

"Come on, let's go distract you for a bit," he urged, standing and giving me a wry smile. I stood without thought, happy to follow my beta to our bedroom. His smile transformed into a wide grin before he started to run and I growled, excitement filling me as I ran after him. This wouldn't be an easy transition, we both knew that, but my love for Spence wouldn't change throughout it all and as much as he was offering a distraction I think he needed that reassurance right now. And if I was being honest, I needed it too.

CHAPTER 11

Ella

I don't remember the walk back to the bed and breakfast. My mind was consumed with all the new things going on in my life: the mate mark on my sternum, the fact that I had fucking mates *at all*, my queasy stomach that was ready to spew all over the ground, and not to mention the *cop* I'm now tied to for life. Isn't that how fated mates work? Apparently, fate was a raging bitch or I pissed her off... either way, I didn't find it funny how things have fallen in my lap since getting to this small town.

Briefly the thought of leaving hit me before I pushed it out of my head. I had been looking for space to become my own person and be away from the constant threat of my parents tossing me into the psych ward, but the thought of not being here, never seeing the men who had been tied to me already twisted my heart with pain.

Running up the front porch steps I burst through the front door and, ignoring Violet, hurried up the stairs to my room. Barely making it to the bathroom I managed to throw up in the toilet, but it was way too fucking close. Loud footsteps sounded behind me and skidded to a stop at the bathroom entrance. I rolled my face to the side to see my friend wrinkle her nose at the smell and her gaze was filled with sympathy.

"Ella," her voice was soft but firm. "Oh honey, what did you get yourself into?" I started to laugh, but that was a bit too much for my stomach and I ended up throwing up again. Violet sighed before stepping around me and turning on the shower. "Shower and I'll grab some meds and water. You'll feel a bit more alive after that. Note to you, little lightweight, full bottle of water and tylenol before you pass out."

I flipped her off with a slight smile as she left me alone to clean up. Flushing the toilet I brushed my teeth and did my second round of mouthwash this morning before stripping and stepping under the spray. The warm water felt amazing and I wasted no time washing off the smell of alcohol from my hair and skin. Once I was cleaned up I padded out to the bedroom to find Violet sitting there waiting for me. I took the meds she handed me and dry swallowed them, used to taking way more than that at once before chugging the full bottle.

I slipped into a pair of clean underwear, black leggings, and a large sweater, needing to be comfortable right now more than I needed to look pretty. My friend just watched me silently, not leaving me alone with my thoughts but waiting for me to start talking.

"Sorry I didn't make it back last night," I mumbled,

chewing on my bottom lip as I sat down near her and towel dried my hair.

"You don't have to come back here every night. You *are* an adult." Violet's eyes were full of concern even as she gave me a half smile. "But I'm more concerned about the call I got from Hunter this morning... You mated with him and Spencer?"

The question was gentle but tears still spilled down my cheek. The fluffy towel fell from my hands and I focused on her in confusion, "What am I supposed to do, Violet?"

"You can't control fated mates, Ella," Violet informed me gently and a sob fell from my lips as I wiped at the tears on my face. "I think it's just interesting..."

"What's interesting?"

She opened her mouth to answer me but was cut off by the downstairs door opening and Tanniv calling out my name. My eyes went wide when Violet called down to say where we were. Two sets of footsteps sounded on the stairs and in walked Tanniv and Asra, both immediately focused on me and the tears on my face.

"Asra?!" Violet's jaw dropped slightly before she started to laugh almost hysterically. "No...!"

"Hunter called me," Tanniv told me as Asra and him approached the bed, settling on either side of me as Violet scooted back to give them room. The comforting smells of saltwater, leather, sage, and rosewood instantly made me feel at home, something I desperately needed after last night. Tanniv wrapped an arm around my shoulders as Asra placed a hand on my knee, both staking a hold on me. "It seems you are collecting mates."

"Some very powerful mates at that," Violet tacked on as she watched the three of us.

An indecipherable expression flashed across her face as Asra hummed and clicked his tongue. "And you're still in town."

His brother and my friend looked at him before all three alphas focused on me. My brow furrowed in confusion. "What does that have to do with anything? Of course I'm still here. Why wouldn't I be?"

Tanniv licked his lips. "Because humans leave town today. *All* of them."

"Which means that you are very much *not* human." Asra watched me with a teasing smile.

"Of course I'm human," my voice wavered. "There isn't—"

"You saw me in the water, sweetheart. You even mentioned it."

"So you can see through the glamour... Is it just with Asra?" Violet cut in and I bit my lip, studying all of them trying to see if this was a trap of some kind. No, they aren't my family or friends back in Georgia.

So I took a deep breath and let it out shakily. "No. I've seen through it with everyone, just glimpses, ever since I came to town."

"You never mentioned anything." Violet's blue eyes were wide.

I felt my face drain of blood and cuddled further into Tanniv's side and looked down at the black jeans he was wearing. Slender fingers clasped my chin, gently forcing me to look up and meet Asra's dark gaze. "You can trust us, omega."

I swallowed hard and kept my gaze trained on his serious and calm gaze as I attempted to explain some of my past to them. "I— I've always been able to see through the, what did you call it?"

"A glamour?"

I nodded, not looking away from Asra, using his steady gaze and Tanniv's arms as my anchor points in the storm of my memories. "Even when I was a child, I could see. But no one believed me when I said that supernaturals were real, no matter what. So eventually... my parents had me committed, multiple times, to help me get over my 'affliction.'" The words were bitter and tired as I let out a self-deprecating chuckle. "But all the staff there were supernaturals too. Eventually, I just stopped saying anything. I thought if I pretended hard enough I could be the perfect daughter they wanted instead of the one they got... It never worked though, I always ended up back in that asylum. The supernatural doctors probably found it hilarious... the resident joke. And the other night, I saw through the storm here in Mystic Harbor."

A growl made me jump and I saw Violet push herself away from the bed, pacing with a clipped stride as her body vibrated with violence. Tanniv and Arsa both seemed calm, but I could almost sense the building anger from both alphas.

"Firstly, there is nothing wrong with you, little stargazer. Do you understand me?" Tanniv asked me gently and I nodded slowly, uncertainty clear in my hesitancy but he took it. "Second, you could see through it all your life... are you sure you're human?"

The sparks from this morning choked my automatic yes in my throat and they all noticed it.

"Ella?"

I tried to push away from the sirens, but they held me steady between them, not letting me run this time. "This morning when I woke up at– at Hunter and Spencer's place. I saw the new mate marks and remembered that

Hunter was a cop, he was in uniform last night... I panicked. When I was trying to calm down there were sparks coming from my fingers. Eventually, they stopped as I calmed down, I guess. That's never happened to me before."

"You should talk to Birdie," Violet announced definitively. "She might be able to figure out what is going on?"

"Birdie?" I asked, curious because I haven't met her before.

"A witch who lives here," Tanniv explained.

"And we need to talk to Leif."

"A witch? And Leif?" My gaze jumped between them all trying to keep up with all of them but the pounding in my head wasn't making it easy.

"Tomorrow," Asra and Tanniv declared firmly at the same time. There was silence as Violet froze. "Ella needs some time to process what's going on and she obviously isn't feeling well. She can think over all of this tomorrow."

I wanted to protest them taking over and making decisions for me, but they were right. There was no way I could handle any serious discussion right now. I just hoped I was finished with throwing up for the day.

"I'll call Leif today, he at least needs to know you aren't leaving, Ella. Just in case any other residents freak out when they see you thinking you shouldn't be here given the tourist season is over today."

"Good call," Tanniv agreed, pulling me fully into his arms as he stood up. I groaned, hiding my face into his neck, not bothering to hide how I nuzzled closer to him happy at the warmth he offered.

"The boat might not be a good idea given her stomach," Violet deadpanned, making Asra chuckle.

"We can make do here until you settle a bit, Ella. Then you can come home with me—" Tanniv started.

"*Us*," Asra corrected him with a shit-eating grin.

"And I'll give you that boat tour I promised you."

"We definitely can do that," Asra tacked on.

I let out a breathy laugh, not missing how Tanniv tensed around me and the goosebumps that broke out along his neck.

"I'll leave the three of you alone to figure that out. And, Ella? You are always welcome here, just so you know."

"Thank you," I murmured, not pulling away from Tanniv as my friend left the room.

There was slight shuffling then Tanniv sat back down on the bed, shifting us until we were laying down. Tanniv's lean body was pressed along my back as Asra's more muscular body laid down on my other side. I smiled, happy in this moment between these two men who I barely knew. But I knew enough, they were home and I'd never had one of those before, not really. And more than that, my soul knew them, and for once, I was going to trust myself.

"Thank you. For coming for me," I whispered, sleep already starting to claim me.

"Remember you said that the next time we come barging in," Asra joked gently and Tanniv chuckled. "Now that we have you, we aren't letting you go."

"We will always come for you, Ella. Sleep. We will be here when you wake up." Slender hands combed through my wet hair making me moan.

"Okay."

Between one breath and the next sleep claimed me,

pulling me into blissful dreams of warm fires, the depths of the ocean, and the cool breeze of the wind on my face. Even in my sleep, my mates claimed a part of me... I couldn't find it in me to be mad about it. It was... almost perfect.

CHAPTER 12

Ella

The gentle sway of the ocean and the sound of crashing waves was a soothing way to wake up. I wasn't expecting to be here when I woke up but I was grateful that Asra and Tanniv made the decision for me. The perks of having alphas. I could get used to having someone there to keep me safe and make decisions when I can't. *Thank goodness my hangover had passed fully. Just how long did I sleep?*

"There she is," Asra mumbled sleepily, propping himself up on his elbow and trailing his free hand through my messy hair, smoothing it out of my face. This felt a bit like heaven, wrapped in my alphas' scents, connecting with someone this intimately. I've never had that, hell, I've never even had a real friend. His finger teased over my furrowed brow. "What's this frown about?"

"I was just thinking that I've never experienced this,"

I whispered, hating how vulnerable I felt and sounded. "No one has ever wanted to be this close to me. But this is nice... I feel safe."

"You are safe with us, little stargazer," Tanniv promised. I turned to see him watching me intently.

"And I can promise you, that no one is going to take you from here," Asra added, but I instinctively shook my head.

"I hope you're right, but they have money and influence, it's worked every time before now. Years... that's how long overall I've spent in that place. It's hard to imagine never having to go back."

"I don't think that's something you shake off overnight. But every day here in Mystic Harbor, with us and your other mates, you'll start to realize that it's okay to live," Asra promised.

"Well, this is a good start." I chuckled, cuddling into the soft blankets. It was insane how much better I felt now.

"Nope. You've slept enough," Tanniv teased, nuzzling into my back. It was like he flipped a switch, my body surging with heat. It didn't go unnoticed, both men perking up and taking a deep breath.

"And it seems you've been fantasizing about a twin sandwich," Asra growled. My cheeks flared to life and I curled in on myself a bit, but these men seemed hell-bent on not letting me hide. "Don't worry, Tanniv told me this will be your first time and we'll be gentle."

"If you want this," Tanniv finished, his voice serious now. I swallowed hard, but I didn't even have to ask myself if I was ready. I wanted this.

"I'm sure," I whispered. Both men heard me, moving

in perfect synchrony as they slid my clothes off. Their mouths converged on me at once, tasting, kissing, and licking their way over my skin. Goosebumps erupted in their wake and slick surged between my thighs, a moan escaping my lips.

Slowly I reached out, hesitant at first to touch them afraid I would fuck this up. But once I heard them groan at just a slight graze of my fingertips my confidence grew. My hands explored, ripping at their clothes until they both obliged me. Instinctively, my gaze flickered downward, gasping at the size of Asra's cock. It was huge, not just that but the girth of it had me apologizing internally to my poor pussy. Who knew sirens would be so impressive?

"Oh, we are impressive," Tanniv joked, making me realize I had spoken aloud. My cheeks heated but he didn't let me be embarrassed for long. He pulled me toward him and turned me so I faced him. The moment our lips were close enough, I surged forward, capturing his mouth with a matching passion. I felt needy and desperate now, caught up in the fog of our lust. Between their scents, the warmth of their bodies, and the rocking of the boat, I was more at peace and alive than I'd ever been.

While Tanniv had me distracted, Asra shifted me to my back, Tanniv following. I was so lost in Tanniv's kiss that the first swipe of Asra's tongue over my pussy had me gasping into Tanniv's mouth and bucking my hips up. He chuckled, but held me in place as he ate me out like he had never tasted anything so exquisite.

Pleasure coursed through me, my hands tangled in Tanniv's hair to try to steady myself as I whimpered against the sensitivity. Asra apparently didn't think I was loud enough, sucking hard on my clit as he pumped one then two fingers into my core. The stretch and intensity of his invasion had my orgasm surging through me so quickly I was screaming out.

"One for me," Asra noted, finger fucking me through the orgasm. Just as one started to calm, the next hit, my legs shaking around him as my pussy clenched around his fingers. "Two."

Were they really competing right now? I'd be more upset if I wasn't the winner regardless, but I'd remember this for another time when I wasn't completely overwhelmed with my first time.

"Just wait, brother. I have no intention of losing." Tanniv laughed, rolling onto his back and pulling me away from his brother to situate me on top of him so I straddled his hips. "Take control, Ella. It'll be easier on you."

I swallowed hard and shifted over his cock, realizing he was just as impressive as his brother. Tomorrow I might not be able to walk, but it would be one hundred percent worth it.

And that was without his knot swelling.

Following his gentle instructions, I started to lower myself onto him. Thanks to the slick it wasn't as painful as I anticipated, but he still stretched me enough that I had to go slow. When he was finally fully inside of me, I paused, breathing through the stretch and burn of it. But I was never a patient woman, the urge to move hit me almost immediately and I rocked my hips over Tanniv. But that was about as far as he let me go, grabbing my hips and taking over. I'd have laughed at his need to keep control if it didn't feel so fucking amazing.

Glancing behind me, I groaned at the sight of Asra slowly stroking his own cock, watching me fuck his twin. If it wasn't my first time, I had a feeling that these two would have been a lot more intense. Asra wasn't exactly the sit back and watch type, though he didn't seem too opposed at the moment.

Tanniv's knot started to swell, it wasn't a quick thing, but slow and torturous just like his leisurely pace. It felt amazing, the omega inside of me practically purring as he hit every sensitive spot in my core with every thrust. We couldn't move much, but each thrust pushed his knot deeper.

I whimpered at a particularly deep thrust making Tanniv growl. Dark eyes flashed with possessive need as he started to fuck me harder. I cried out his name, needing more as my arousal built again. *This was heaven... How did I not do this before?* Because it wouldn't have been with these two, my heart whispered to me. I swallowed hard at the emotion so early on behind that realization, however, it was true. Regardless, we would be doing this a lot and often if I had anything to say about it.

Tanniv was right telling Asra to wait, the feel of his knot and the shallow but well-placed movements throwing me into a marathon of orgasms. I was babbling nonsensically now, gasping through the intensity of it all. I was thankful that we only got pregnant during heat, because this wouldn't have been as amazing with a condom.

The knot held us close together as I felt him fill me with his cum. Tanniv held me, pressing kisses along my throat while my body came down to earth again. I whimpered, my hips grinding down on him as he scraped his teeth along my skin making him groan in turn. Cupping his face in my hands I pulled him away from my neck, wanting his lips on mine rather than more teasing, and thankfully, Tanniv was happy to follow my lead with this. My tongue slid along his and I moaned at the taste of him as he easily took control of the kiss. His hands on my back pulled my breasts flush against his pecs making me shudder at the feel of his chest hair against my sensitive nipples.

"Not too bad for a first time, brother," Asra's sly voice sounded behind me, making me jump slightly. "Guess only one of us has stamina."

"You say that now," Tanniv growled at his brother, but there was no real heat behind it. "But you haven't felt how fucking tight she is. You won't last long."

Tanniv grabbed my hips, pulling me off his dick slowly making me realize the knot must have gone down when they were talking. Asra wrapped an arm around my middle, pulling me toward him as his brother moved out of the way, letting Asra and I have our space. He didn't go very far, watching us with flushed cheeks and a glint of possession in his eyes.

"My turn," Asra almost taunted me with a quick grin, and I saw through the glamour for a second. The slight blue of scales, charcoal gray eyes with no whites staring down at me, and webbed fingers running down my arm... He was magnificent and a hint of regret hit me that I hadn't seen through Tanniv's. *How could I see through it? I wonder what they look like without the glamour at all.* A sting had me jerking and a gasp escaped me as my gaze focused on Asra. He growled slightly showing off razor-sharp teeth before the glamour snapped fully back into place. "Your focus better be all on me, Ella, or I'll be throwing you in the deep end of rougher sex sooner than we should."

"I was thinking about you," I tried to explain when he thrust balls deep inside of me without any warning.

My back arched as I cried out and I could feel him chuckle into the crook of my neck, placing a deceptively gentle kiss on my vulnerable throat. "There's a good girl. Just like that."

Unlike his brother, Asra pounded into me like he was going to war. Every thrust and kiss was a battlefield on my body as he roughly claimed me. It was intoxicating how similar and different they were and Tanniv didn't miss the chance to call out commentary as Asra fucked me. My body was sensitive and Asra wrung two orgasms from me before his knot slowed his thrusts and he spilled inside of me, marking his territory. He cursed my name as I raked my nails down his back marking him in return as I climaxed yet again.

We slowly calmed down, held together by his knot, and eventually, we managed to separate. I was covered in cum, slick, and a bit of bright red blood. My cheeks heated but before embarrassment could fully settle in Tanniv scooped me up in his arms and Asra followed behind down the hallway of what must be Tanniv's houseboat.

"No embarrassment, little Ella," Asra's voice was warm. "We certainly aren't and we are going to be doing that... often."

"Let's get you cleaned up," Tanniv commented gently. "But my brother is right, at least in this instance."

I cuddled into Tanniv's chest, a smile curling my lips, my body completely sated. "No complaints here."

"I would think not." Asra's chest puffed up and I laughed at his dramatics.

Tanniv opened a door and then we were outside on deck and I realized it was nighttime, the moon shining down on us in the cool air. Completely at ease, he walked to the back deck that had some privacy and a large bath set up that looked similar to a hot tub. He stepped in carefully and settled down on one of the bench seats and I sighed, realizing it was saltwater, which made sense when I thought of it. Asra slipped under the water and came up, shaking the water out of his face, an underlying tension I hadn't sensed before absent now that he was in the water.

"I didn't realize I slept that long," I bit my lip as I tried to shift off of Tanniv, but he held me firmly on his lap, not letting me give him space.

"You are a lightweight, Ella. Of course you slept that long," Asra joked, a grin on his face until I splashed him with water in retaliation. Asra didn't bother to dodge the water, just kept laughing at me.

"It's not my fault Spencer gave me a shot! I didn't know it was that strong." I tried to defend myself but Tanniv just shook his head.

"Next time go with one of us to help you pace yourself," Tanniv suggested.

"Of course, I don't think Spencer will give you anything that strong again. After all, he is your mate as well," Asra commented. Nerves instantly filled me as I recalled that revelation earlier today and then realized that I was also mated to Hunter... a *cop*. I swallowed hard and a slender finger pushed my chin back so met Tanniv's serious gaze.

"What's wrong? I can understand being mated to so many can be a shock but this seems like more than that."

I chewed on my bottom lip but didn't try to shake free of his hold. "It has nothing to do with *them*. It's just— I don't like cops. Never had a good experience with all my run ins with them."

"You've had a lot of run ins with the police?" Asra and Tanniv asked at the same time, disbelief clear from both of them. "You're quite possibly the bubbliest person I've met."

My face paled as I pulled my chin from Tanniv's hold but I snuggled into him again, hiding my face as I answered in a small voice, a tremor clear even to myself. "My parents would call them to escort me... to the Kensington Mental Health Facility. I can see through the— What did you say it was called?"

"Glamour?" Asra's voice was light.

I nodded against Tanniv's chest as Asra rubbed a hand along my back. "Yeah, that... It's stronger here for some reason, but I could always see supernaturals. Whenever I brought it up they just told me to stop playing around. But when I insisted, they said I was crazy... I've been in and out since I was a kid. Sometimes I fought, so the police got involved to escort me after that. Then I just — I stopped fighting altogether. This last time I ran before they could take me. So every time I see a uniform that's what I think of."

"I'm going to kill them," Asra's voice was dark and I shivered.

"*We* are," Tanniv's voice was soft and somehow more terrifying than Asra's bold declaration.

"You should explain that to Hunter. At least be open about getting to know him. He isn't like those people that did that to you. He genuinely wants to keep our town safe and he takes his role as a protector seriously."

Tanniv nodded at his brother's suggestion before he stiffened and pulled me away from his chest, searching my face closely. "You can see through the glamour... Have you seen—"

"Your form?" I pushed past the uncomfortable topics, happy that he managed to change the subject. "Flashes of it from both of you. And flashes from others in town too. Like I said, it's stronger here than I've seen other places." I shrugged lightly, slipping off Tanniv's lap so I go under the water, rinsing myself off more then came back up to find the twin alphas watching me closely with heated eyes. I held out a hand to stop them, as if that would make a difference. "I don't think so, you two. I doubt I'll be able to walk tomorrow as it is. No way."

"I want to be there when she tells that to Leif." Asra smirked at his brother. "I can't pass up the opportunity to see the shock on his face."

"We both will be." Tanniv reached for me and I pulled back, dodging his hands, and making his eyes narrow.

"Why would Leif care?" I laughed, sinking low enough in the water that I was nice and warm. I needed this in my life.

They both stared at me like I lost my mind.

"I swear you're oblivious." Asra snorted.

"He doesn't just pop in on other tourists and new residents," Tanniv confirmed.

"Something to deal with tomorrow when I have to face a lot of other things, I think." I sighed then let out a squeal of surprise as Asra snatched me, situating me on his lap as he smirked at his glowering brother.

"Don't be a sore loser, brother. It's not my fault you're getting slow in your old age."

"We're the same age," Tanniv grumbled.

"Yes, but I don't let it affect me like you do. Probably all your time up on land," Asra commented, laughing as Tanniv flipped him off.

"Before you are missing a mate," Tanniv focused on me, ignoring his brother completely. "Let's wash up and get back in bed. I have a feeling tomorrow is going to be a big day, especially for you."

"Yeah, that's a good idea," I fell back into Asra's chest and tilted my head back to look up at him. "I could use some help with that. You might even be able to convince me to help you out afterwards."

"Like a blowjob?" Asra joked, a sparkle of amusement in his dark eyes.

"I meant washing your back... but I've never done that before. You'd have to be really good at that to get me to think about it right now," I teased him.

"What if we were both really bad instead?" Tanniv asked heatedly, voice deep and almost distorted as he handed his brother shampoo and he held soap.

"Glad we're on the same page," Asra rumbled.

They proceeded to do a very thorough job cleaning me off then making me dirty all over again. A lot more than my first blowjob happened in that tub before they gently cleaned me off a second time and carried me to bed. I fell asleep again between my two alphas and I knew that I would never be around saltwater and not think of them.

Leif

My cup of tea had just touched my lips when my doorbell rang. Glancing at the clock, I frowned. It was nearly half past nine. But then again, the job of mayor is never quite finished. Especially in this town.

Setting down my mug, I got up and stretched before going to the door. The last person I was expecting was Violet, which had my mind immediately jumping to Ella. Her face was set in a grim line and I ushered her in without hesitation.

"Is this a tea kind of conversation?" I asked warily. She didn't speak, just nodded. "This way." I led her into the kitchen and gestured to the barstools at the breakfast bar before getting the kettle going. As I got her mug and tea ready, I kept glancing at her, my anxiety raising a bit at the sight of her troubled expression. She was trying really damn hard to hide it but wasn't having any luck. I briefly thought of going back to grab my own cup but I didn't want to miss what Violet had to say, it seemed too important.

"I'm sorry," she finally said softly after letting out a soft, long sigh. "I know it's not proper to do a house call on the mayor like this. But it seems Ella isn't human after all."

"I assumed when I saw her run past the cafe while I was grabbing lunch earlier. Not to mention the mate mark incident," I said. Truthfully, the sight of her blonde hair whipping around her in the wind as she ran past was like a beacon of hope for me today. The thought of her leaving with the tourists was killing me slowly. I found myself getting up in the mornings, trying to beat her to the coffee shop. Hell, I risked running into Drystan for her. That beta hated me with every fiber of his being, then again the elves and fae have had a rivalry for millennia.

"You did?" Violet's question was sharp and I cocked an eyebrow at her tone. Violet's eyes glittered with challenge until she took a deep breath. "And you didn't think to share this with the rest of us?"

"What difference would that have made?" I questioned, genuinely curious. "I had no evidence to back up what I thought so there was no use in saying anything."

"Says you."

"Yep. Is that what you came over to tell me?" I tilted my head slightly considering the alpha female across from me.

"That's not all," she said heavily, her shoulders dropping. "I just hate spilling her secrets but I wouldn't do it if I didn't think it was important. I'll let her tell you more details when and *if* she wants to share later. But she had a magic spark out today, like actual electricity on her fingertips."

"What?!" My mouth dropped open slightly, shocked at that.

"She also gained two new mates last night and my guess is she isn't done yet."

"With who?" I growled, but she just kept speaking as if she couldn't hear my outbursts.

"But it triggered her magic to spark out. I figured we should call in Birdie to help Ella figure things out. But apparently, Ella's been able to see through the glamour this whole time. She hid it because of her past. And the storm to cover the evidence of the lawn ornaments coming to life? I think she saw through it. She thinks we all just lied to her, and I mean, we *did*. But we did it to protect our town but she is hurt by it all the same."

"You mean yesterday when she was super angry at the world? That's what was going on?" I asked, wincing at the memory. I'd seen her running off from the Enchanted Mug in a hurry with a grim face and clutching her hand close to her chest. There was little in this town that I missed.

Violet nodded and sipped at the steaming mug of tea I slid her way. "She wasn't doing well after she came back to the inn, but Tanniv and Asra are taking care of her."

"Asra? Tanniv's brother?" I asked, pressing my hands flat on the counter to hide how they were shaking. Jealousy sliced through me like a hot dagger, my chest tightening at the thought of her with anyone else. She was *mine*. Though she wouldn't let me get close to her and I couldn't figure out why. I'd assumed it was my position, but she clearly had no issue with the Harbormaster. *Wait... she can see through the glamour, could it be because I'm fae?*

"Yes, that happened yesterday as well. Don't go getting all territorial. Given how infatuated with her as you are, I guarantee you both have some sort of connection. So you should work past that jealousy because she isn't one to stand for that bullshit," Violet said bluntly as she finished off her tea. After our last few interactions, she'd lost the caution she'd generally shown around me. It was kind of nice. I loved being mayor here, but it was getting really old constantly having only formal conversations and no real social interactions.

"She won't even let me get close." I huffed out a defeated laugh, combing a hand through my hair, and tugging at the ends. "It'd be comical if it wasn't so damn frustrating."

Violet grinned the moment I cursed. "Getting worked up over a cute little omega?" she teased. "Good. You need a life outside of this town." The wisdom in those words was met by a pointed stare and I sighed.

"You're right. It's just not easy. People keep me at arm's length either for being fae or being the mayor. Sometimes I can't win. And after a lifetime of parents with ungodly expectations... well, I didn't stand a chance," I said bitterly.

"Ouch. I feel that one," she mused. "When I left my pack, my father told me I was a disgrace and not to come crawling back. He went into detail about being a rogue wolf and how I was going to go feral... all kinds of bullshit."

"The traditionalist fools of our past generations have no idea how detrimental they are," I commented dryly. "I've seen far too many families separate over it."

"I'd never do that to my pups," she said, eyes flashing as her wolf agreed. She was a powerful alpha and I had no doubt she was right.

"Agreed," I said softly. In my head, I already pictured little blond-haired babies with almond shaped eyes and fae features. A mix of me and Ella. *What the hell, Leif? Getting a bit ahead of yourself.*

"So, we plan on contacting Birdie tomorrow to see if she can help, but if she's sparking from only these mates and a half-finished mate mark? Well, I'd hate to see her when she finds the rest of her mates," Violet said darkly. It wasn't something we saw often in our community, but fated groups as large as hers could cause outbursts of power and instability until the group was fully complete and mated.

"Thanks for letting me know everything that's going on. At least I can help keep an eye out. Birdie is a great plan, there's little that woman can't handle. I'll also let

Opal know that she needs to put a bit of extra power in the town glamour, just in case. Large fluctuations of magic are never good on a large glamour like that," I stated.

"That's exactly what I thought. And Opal already bolsters it a few times a month. But remember what happened when that dragon couple were having issues? They nearly blew us off the map," she said, eyes widening as she relived the memory.

"That was awful." I smiled slightly, but I couldn't stop the huff of laughter at the reminder of the chaos that had erupted. "It took every witch in town to help fix it and shield them." The couple was fighting in the midst of a heat and had nearly let their magic explode. It could be felt clear across town. But one thing we learned was that our emergency magical response team was quick. They had the area shielded and the couple calmed when the heat took over again. But it was a near disaster. And there were only two of them.

"Tomorrow we can deal with it. Just so you know, Ella means a lot to me. I didn't just come here because I knew you had feelings about her. She's my friend and I'm going to help her however I can," she said as she cleaned her mug and put it in the drying rack. Seeing my new friend comfortable was reassuring. Things were changing and I was more than ready to see where it took us all.

"Seems I'm not the only one taken by our newest omega," I joked. She flashed me a fanged smile, the glamour slipping away. It was a bit jarring whenever they faded like that, it usually hung around for a week or so after the spell changed, lingering effects from the tourist season.

"Except I don't want to fuck her, just wrap her in a

blanket, feed her chocolate, and protect her from the big bad world. She deserves it."

"On that, we agree," I said as she opened the door and slipped out. Returning to my usual chair, I gave my tea a burst of heat before sipping it contentedly. My mind was busy with thoughts of Ella and how quickly she'd come in and changed so many lives.

Now if I can just get her to give me a chance.

CHAPTER 13

Ella

"Come on, Ella," Tanniv's voice gently prods me from sleep. I'm so comfortable and warm that I grumble and snuggle further into the human heater in front of me. Asra's rumbling laugh followed my action and Tanniv let out a heavy sigh. "While we'd love nothing more than to keep you on this boat and fuck you senseless for days on end, omega, you have some things to handle today and it's already ten. You have one hour to get ready and get to the Enchanted Mug to meet Birdie."

I groaned at the reminder. No part of me wanted to handle the shitstorm that was brewing on the horizon. The thought of seeing Spencer and Hunter again had me cringing. My memories were no longer hazy and I made an ass out of myself. Some mate introduction that was.

"You can brood later," Asra prompted, getting out of the bed and taking the blankets with him. I let out an exaggerated sigh but followed his lead.

It took every bit of time we had to get all three of us dressed and walk across town. The fact it was at the Enchanted Mug was the only reason I got out of bed. Because dealing with my new mates and magic and the mayor *and* an unfamiliar witch... didn't sound that enticing. I'd take every advantage I could get and that meant coffee, a lot of it.

I noticed the town was much quieter than what I was used to and then I remembered one of the brothers mentioning yesterday that the tourists all left yesterday. They didn't explain why everyone was leaving on the same day, that just seemed weird to me. Could it be magic related? My thoughts snapped back to the present when Tanniv opened the cafe door and motioned me inside. Shooting him a tight smile I rushed past him, ignoring the group of people in the back who watched me closely, to approach Drystan at the counter.

"What would you like today, Ella?" Drystan's eyes were concerned as he studied me, though I caught a hint of what looked like jealousy as his gaze flicked to my two alphas as they left me to order my drink.

"Surprise me?" I asked, giving him a wobbly smile, my nerves getting the better of me. "I'm sorry for yesterday. There was— There was a lot going on in my head. But I shouldn't have snapped at you."

Drystan looked shocked, completely fucking speechless as he stared at me. When I bit my lip unsure if he'd forgive me or not, he smiled gently and held up a finger for me to wait. He moved around the small space gracefully and efficiently, creating a coffee with an extra shot of espresso. Maybe he can read minds because that's exactly what I need for this meeting I won't be able to ignore for much longer.

"Here." He handed over the oversized mug, his hands pressing mine to the hot cup, joking lightly that he wanted to make sure I didn't drop or crush it. A shocked gasp escaped me as I felt my eyes widen to match the surprised expression on Drystan's face. Burning along my ribs immediately alerted me to what was happening. This time I knew this person, at least more than I did Spencer and Hunter, bonus points for not being a cop or anything related to my trauma-filled past.

Looking down, I saw the waning moon appear and his mouth dropped open as he looked down at it too. Then a swirl of purple magic covered both of our hands, tingling along my skin until it suddenly let loose. Lights throughout the store flickered, the electricity sparking as customers cried out with surprise. *What the hell was going on? This was different from the last time.*

"Ella? Are you okay?" Violet called my name and I don't know what I would have answered, but luckily Drystan took care of that for me.

"The shop is closed until I say otherwise. If you aren't here for the meeting, get out." He was the most alpha beta I'd ever met and the entire time he held my gaze as the others in the shop left quickly, as if they could sense the tension building.

"I'm fine," I finally managed to untie my tongue and call out an answer after the last person left.

"Of course you're with us, Elf," Tanniv called out, a thread of amused resignation clear to my ears. "Don't forget two black coffees for Asra and myself though."

"Yeah, we need all the help we can get given we didn't get much sleep last night," Asra's voice was smooth, taunting, making my cheeks heat.

Drystan rolled his eyes, but released me and poured

two large coffees. I remained standing there knowing I should just go and join the others waiting for me, but at the same time, the clean and calming smell of Earl Grey tea comforted me too much to move just yet. It was a safe harbor amongst the storms of my life and I was going to enjoy it for a few moments longer.

Drystan quickly flipped the sign on the door over before leaning into me and bent over enough to whisper near my ear. "You're sitting with me or beside me. I don't care what the others say."

I clenched my hands around the mug I had a death grip on and nodded slightly as he led the way to the table. Sitting there was Asra and Tanniv who both looked satisfied and slightly amused as they both watched us approach. Violet looked shocked and on the verge of laughing hysterically as she looked from Drystan to Leif, the latter's face was completely blank as he glared at the man in front of me. Sitting with them was also Spencer and Hunter, though after a quick glance in their direction I didn't look at them again, too mortified at what happened the last time I saw them. Though I was happy to see Hunter wasn't in uniform.

Among all these people I do know there was one who I didn't. *Birdie.* She was an older woman, though I couldn't guess her age to be honest. Wild, curly, salt and pepper hair surrounded her face in tumultuous waves. Her brown eyes were warm, but sharp, as she considered me as I sat down in an open chair beside Tanniv with Drystan settling down on my other side, his leg pressing against my own.

"So, you're Ella," Birdie's voice was loud and filled with laughter and somehow I felt completely at ease. "I can see why everyone wanted us to meet."

I ducked my head, sipping my coffee, smiling at the taste of pumpkin spice before I answered honestly. "Yeah."

"Well, girl, let's get down to it." Birdie clapped her hands loudly startling me so my gaze snapped up to meet her stare. "You don't feel like a witch, but you obviously are one. Why do you feel human?"

"Oh gods, Birdie," Leif muttered, rubbing a hand over his face. Their reaction told me that this was just her, blunt and a bit chaotic.

"No use wasting time by beating around the bush." Birdie waved a hand at him. "Not with power like this going wild."

"I always thought I was human," I replied quietly. "I've never been able to do magic. Yesterday... yesterday was the first time I've ever seen that spark."

"Ella felt like a human when she arrived here," Leif added calmly. My eyes flickered to his, a soft smile on our faces. He'd been the first face I'd met here and despite the distance, I'd kept from the fae man across the table, it was a nice welcome. It wasn't his fault I couldn't shake those fae lessons from my youth, and the truth was he intrigued me, but I had too much on my plate to get any closer, to let that guard down.

"She felt that way for me too until recently," Tanniv tacked on as well after drinking some of his coffee.

Birdie held out her hand to me across the table and I looked at it, then her, confused about what she wanted me to do. "Let me see if I can sense anything, love. See if I can sort some things out before we all talk out of our ass speculating about what could be going on or not."

I swallowed hard and a warm hand squeezed my thigh reassuringly and I smiled at Drystan, his beta scent wrapping me up to help keep me calm. Putting down my mug I placed a trembling hand in Birdie's and immediately she inhaled sharply, her face paling but she squeezed my hand, not letting me go.

"What's wrong?" Violet asked, pushing her long black hair out of her face.

"Shhh." She waved off the alpha without a care as she focused on something only she could see.

The thought of yanking my hand out of hers crossed my mind, but it was quickly squashed when Tanniv placed a hand on my other thigh. He didn't say anything, but the silent command was clear. *Stay.*

"Oh my, child, what did they do to you?" Her voice was scratchy as she came back to herself a minute later. Tears streamed down her face and I wondered just what she had seen. "Your powers have been bound. *You've* been bound."

"Bound?!" Tanniv, Asra, Leif, and Hunter all growled.

"What does that mean?" I asked, leaning back into Tanniv's side, nuzzling into him, seeking comfort from one of my alphas. Just the feel and scent of him alone did wonders for my confused and worried psyche.

"Someone bound your magic so you couldn't access it and then bound you so no one could even sense that you're a witch. The first thing is never done lightly, it's a very rare thing to do. As for the second..." Birdie shook her head slowly. "I have no idea why anyone would do that. But what I can say is that it seems every fated mate is undoing the bindings, slowly but surely."

"Meaning Ella will have access to her powers for, potentially, the first time ever? As a full-grown witch?" Spencer asked.

The older woman nodded slowly. "It's a good thing Dean and Brooks are coming for the celebration in a week. My son and grandson," she explained to me. "We're going to need all the help we can get to help you learn to control your powers once your mark is complete. How many do you have now?"

"Uhh—" I tried to keep up with her quick talking, but I think I had mental whiplash trying to understand everything.

"Including the one she just found?" Violet asked dryly. "Five, unless you added someone else without me knowing about it."

"Yeah, five, but that design isn't done," I managed to reply.

"How many more spots do you have?" Birdie asked, looking slightly concerned.

"I think... three?" I looked over at Tanniv who nodded slightly.

"Three more..." Birdie looked a bit pale as she swallowed and tried to cover it up quickly with a brave face. "We can do this. Better tell Opal to check those shields at least once a day. I have a feeling things are going to get a bit crazy around here. Soon enough her magic is going to start showing up randomly and we all know how untrained witch magic can be."

"I don't." I raised a hand, but didn't move away from where I was cuddled into Tanniv with Drystan's firm hand still on my thigh. "I don't know anything about all of this."

"But you will," Birdie promised, a spark of determination in her wise gaze. "That much I can promise you. And until then, well, this is the right group to keep things stable." Her confidence actually did help me feel better.

"I'm sorry," I whispered, staring at the table and blinking back tears. "I've dragged you all into my drama and now it's a huge mess."

"No." Birdie's voice was so sharp that even my tears seemed to run away in fear. My head snapped up in surprise and she was leaning so close I nearly screamed. "You don't get to take the blame for whoever decided to make your life hell and bind you. We will help you fix it and for the first time, I would guess, you'll get to really find out who you are. And, my dear Ella, that will be a wonderful thing."

Words were impossible so I just nodded and let her words truly sink in. Because she was right. I'd been through hell, and that was a vast understatement. If my magic was truly locked away, if I was a witch like she was, then this was an exciting new chapter for me. With eight mates total on the table, untrained magic that would break free a little more with each connection, and a few experienced witches for guidance, maybe I would truly find my place in the world. And that... well, it meant everything to me.

Birdie's house was as eccentric and wonderful as the woman herself. It was a small little bungalow, three tiny bedrooms, a bathroom, and an open kitchen and living room. Yet despite its size, it seemed there was always something new to look at. Her walls were covered in art and random decor that should never have logically made sense together, but somehow it fit her and looked cohesive.

"I love this place," I blurted out as I took it all in.

Birdie smiled proudly and looked around like she was getting a new perspective on it.

"It's home," she said simply. "Now. Tell me about the people in your life before you arrived here."

I frowned and her smile turned gentle but she didn't back down. And even just knowing her for less than two hours I knew there was no chance she'd ever let me off easily.

"It was just me and my parents," I answered. "Both humans as far as I've been able to tell."

"And you can see through glamour, right?" she prompted. She's obviously been talking to Violet and I appreciate that my friend handled the messy bits for me. At least the messy bits she knew of.

"The rest of my time I spent in and out of an asylum. There were more supernaturals than I could name. And not one of them acted like I was anything but crazy when I pointed it out. I truly have no clue who could have or would have done it to me." The complete focus with which she was listening to me had me immediately wishing one of my alphas or beta could have come with me. I could use a dose of Drystan's beta energy right about now. My mind was in chaos over the new revelations. The fact someone not only bound my powers but hid them from the world was a punch to the soul. And coming from someone that was raised on trauma, it made it worse.

She seemed to fight for the right words as she watched me process everything. "Look. I'm not one for mincing words but I'm not saying this to be an ass. How sure are you that your parents are actually your parents? Witches don't come from non-witches, or whatever bullshit human TV has made up nowadays. You're born one and if you haven't sensed it all this whole time... it's something to consider."

I laughed bitterly. "As much as I wish that were true. Genetics don't lie. I have my father's eyes and bone structure and my mom's blonde hair. We're undeniably family, even if they never wanted me."

She nodded slowly, genuine pain on her face before she replaced it with what I've already realized was her regular intensity. "Then one of them was a witch. It's the only alternative."

I frowned at that but she seemed ready to move on, clapping her hands and standing up. "Well, we can speculate all we want, but those are the facts and it seems fate refuses to keep you bound. So let's take a look at these powers of yours instead."

"What can we even do about them? They're random or popped up in high emotion situations," I countered. Honestly, I had no real confidence this training would do anything. I mean Birdie seemed to know what she was doing, but I had absolutely no fucking clue.

"I don't disagree, but you'd be surprised what your mind is capable of. And we need to learn a bit of control to get out of those situations before you bring the town crashing down around us," she mused. I didn't bother to argue as I pulled myself out of my downward spiral and forced myself to follow her through the back door.

Her backyard was as chaotic as the woman and house, but gorgeous. She had the entire perimeter covered in raised flower beds, though there was no rhyme or reason to the mix of flowers, herbs, vegetables, and vines. Between it all was a large fire pit surrounded by a rainbow of stones. Crude wooden log benches surrounded it. She walked to the far side of the fire pit and gestured for me to stand on the other side.

"Light the fire." She said the words so casually that I let out a loud, surprised laugh, but it fell away when she crossed her arms and raised an eyebrow in challenge.

Holding back an eye roll, I focused on the neatly stacked firewood in the pit. *But what if she's right, Ella?* That thought had me shaking out my arms and taking a breath, focusing solely on my task instead of doubting myself the entire time. In my head I could hear Asra's attitude telling me to prove him wrong, to claim my heritage. Hell, Drystan would say nearly the same, with less flirting and more of that blunt determination. Tanniv, to his credit, would likely be the encouraging one. Hunter and Spencer... Well, I had no idea what they would say but I set that aside for the moment. *One problem at a time.* Thoughts of my mates was the final push that I needed to break free from my human mindset that was holding me back.

But even if I thought I could, it didn't mean I knew how. I think Birdie skipped a bit of her lesson because just telling me to light a damn fire didn't mean I could just twitch my nose and make it happen. I tried to think hot thoughts, flames, and fires, but not even a spark lit the logs.

High emotions.

That thought struck me. When I was in the coffee shop, I'd claimed another mate and was about to face strangers. In Hunter and Spencer's place, I was freaking out. Maybe it's not confidence I needed, but to focus on the things that fill me with rage, anger, high-intensity emotions. It was as good of a guess as any at this point to be honest.

My mind went straight to the ward so I stared down the log like it was Dr. Sloane, the devil himself. His words that had haunted me for years felt so much more significant than they had before I knew what I was.

These delusions may haunt you forever, you're a very sick girl, Eleanor.

I'm looking right at Nurse Petra, she's as human as you and me. Maybe it's time to change your medication.

Sedate her, she's clearly having an episode.

Each statement I remembered sent a jolt of righteous anger through me. Smoke started first, then a spark, then a fireball shot into the air. Birdie threw her hands out and a shield formed above us, protecting us from my unintentional fireball.

"Good job," she praised, but she looked a bit startled. My anger was still thrumming through my system, refusing to be sated yet. It wanted to burn the world down, the asylum down, and every person that wronged me. The song it sang in my veins was seductive and I felt myself burning up. "Ella. Ella, focus on me." My eyes shifted to hers, but my anger wouldn't calm.

"I can't," I hissed. I left the 'I don't want to' unsaid. I'd fallen down the rabbit hole of my pain, something I knew better than to do, yet I had gone in willingly this time. Years of pent-up pain and volatile indignation and anger were bubbling out as if they had a mind of their own.

"Tanniv, Drystan, Asra, Violet, Spencer, and Hunter. This entire town. You're putting them all in danger, stop this." This time her tone was a sharp command. I had wondered what she was, but now I was seeing the alpha in her coming through. But beyond that, the reminder of my mates struck me, and I realized how out of control the flames had grown. That derailed my thoughts enough to calm the inferno blazing between us, the heat from it covering me in perspiration. "Take a deep breath. Remember something that brings you happiness, your newfound independence. Give yourself the chance to be the witch you were destined to be." The soft words did help soothe me, allowing me to snap the lid back on that darkness that soiled my soul.

Before she could say anything further, a wild-eyed Leif was bursting through the backyard gate, followed by Drystan. *Where had they been waiting?* I thought they had gone back to work when I had left the cafe with Birdie earlier... I guess I was wrong. I knew Asra and Tanniv had to head back to the harbor, and Violet the inn. I wasn't sure about Hunter and Spencer but I'd given them no reason to stick around, a fact that had guilt rising in me until I squashed it down as well.

"What happened?!" Drystan demanded, rushing to my side. He still had his barista apron on and grabbed a rag from one of the pockets, wiping the soot and sweat from my face. The moment he made contact with me, I sagged into him. The comfort his presence gave me was exactly the thing I needed, that scent of tea and warmth like a drug to me at the moment. I breathed him in, letting him wrap me up in a hug. Even his body relaxed into the embrace. It soothed all the jagged pieces of my soul that had been laid bare.

"She's fine," Birdie snapped. "You all are so dramatic. This is why I swore off mates." Her grumbling had Drystan snorting, and I pulled away to look at her.

"Dramatic? I nearly burnt down your garden, Birdie," I pointed out incredulously.

She snorted and gestured at me. "Exactly. If that's not dramatic, I don't know what is. Good, the barista is here.

Let's go make tea." Then the old bat hooked her arm around my mate and forced him to follow her inside, leaving me and Leif behind, speechless and impressed.

Gods, I love this town.

Drystan

What is my life? I automatically went through the motions of preparing and making four cups of tea. Birdie handed me a rose tea mentioning something about it helping to calm my mate before bustling off further into the house. I still couldn't comprehend that Ella was really mine. When Leif and Violet had walked into the cafe with Birdie this morning I had a gut feeling it had something to do with Ella. Hunter and Spencer joining them had confused me, but when Ella had walked in with the twin siren alphas I knew they were all mated. Jealousy had hit me hard but it didn't last long. The way Ella's eyes lit up when she saw me and headed straight toward me before anyone else... Male pride had filled me even as I was cautious after our last encounter.

The kettle hissing yanked me from my thoughts and I grabbed it off the burner, pouring the hot water into the cups waiting on the counter. I stared down at my mate mark on my wrist and recalled the heat between us when the marking had taken place. If only it hadn't happened in the middle of the cafe with all those people waiting for her, things would have ended very differently if that had been the case. I might not be an alpha, but I had been told by quite a few people that I had more than my fair share of stubbornness for a beta. It was always something that had been a negative for most people I had seen in my long life... someone who didn't know his place and not easy-going enough to be a *real* beta. Those are all things I'd heard all my life, even my family had said it behind my back. But none of that mattered now that I had her. Sure, fate thought I should learn to share, but when she looked at me like I hung the moon? Well, that was enough for me.

I put the kettle down and grabbed the tray with all the cups and headed back to the garden, my mind a jumbled mess until I stepped outside. The fire was burning bright and I saw Ella and Leif had both settled down in seats around it, though I didn't miss that they were on different benches. Both of them looked over as I approached and set the tray down on a nearby table. The fact they looked relieved had me biting back laughter. Leif and I had a healthy elf versus fae rivalry going and this was possibly the biggest win for me so far.

"They should be ready in a few minutes," I told them as I moved to settle beside Ella. She shifted closer to me and I lifted my arm so she could snuggle into my side, her eyes still looked a little haunted but she appeared calmer than when I had gone inside with Birdie. "You doing okay?"

"I guess?" Ella answered slowly, letting out a heavy sigh that ended with a slight laugh. "I mean I came here to get away and start over with a nice, *peaceful* life. So far, Mystic Harbor didn't get the message about the peaceful part."

I snorted at her dry tone and smiled down at her. Since she was so close to me I didn't miss how she jerked at Leif's laughter, she looked over at the fae alpha with interest, heat, and hesitancy that intrigued me as much as it irritated me. Leif and I, we have always butted heads and it's been that way since we both got to this town. As much as the alpha got under my skin I wouldn't wish the weight of longing I saw flicker in his gaze as he stared at Ella beside me.

"Where did Birdie go?" Ella asked.

At that same moment, the back door of Birdie's home opened to reveal the older witch. She approached with something in hand. She sat down next to Leif, motioning for him to hand out the cups as she focused on my mate. Leif handed me two cups before grabbing two for himself and Birdie.

"There is a lot we need to work on," Birdie told Ella firmly. "But there are some things only you can sort through. I need to get some things ready before I start trying to train you as your magic is freed. I'll call when I'm ready, but in the meantime, I want you to start working through some things on your own."

She held out an old, worn, leather bound notebook to Ella. My mate blinked and then stared up at the witch, the question clear in her gaze as she slowly took the offered book. "What should I be doing?"

"This is for you to work through some of the emotions you need to utilize for witchcraft. Not everything is emotion based, but it's a good foundation. Write notes about things that happened when you mated and the magic appeared. Anything that's useful to *you*."

"Do I get more instruction next time?" Ella sassed softly, a glitter of amusement in her blue eyes as she stared at the alpha who burst out laughing.

"I like your spunk. Keep that backbone, girlie, you'll need it with eight fated mates." She clicked her tongue as she took the mug from Leif and took a sip. "Wonderful tea as always, Drystan. Oh, Leif, while you're here... Is there going to be a cleanup after that lawn ornament disaster? The town square looks like a complete fucking disaster."

I choked mid-sip and so did Ella, hiding her face into my side as she shook with what I figured was laughter. Leif just shook his head at Birdie and gave her a half smile. "One of my cousins will be here soon to help out. He had a job to finish up first, but he's the best and I wanted him to do it before the town festival."

"Festival?" Ella asked softly, looking up at me as the two alphas got lost in their own conversation on the other side of the fire.

"We celebrate at the end of the tourist season. The glamours on all of us fade, but stay up around the town," I explained to her. "So we all get to be ourselves again without looking like humans."

A huge grin lit up her face at the idea as she pushed some of her blonde hair out of her face making a fresh wave of sweet vanilla and welcoming coffee hit me. "Finally get to be yourself... I'd love that. Besides... it's disconcerting to see double of all of you sometimes."

I pressed a quick kiss to her forehead. "I can't imagine. But you say that now... Wait until you see the real Harold running around complaining about lawn ornaments."

Ella's bright laughter filled me with satisfaction. Now that I'd found her and we were bound together I couldn't imagine my life without her. The reality that I wouldn't be around her most of the time hit me, but I pushed it away for now. Ella still had three more mates to be bound to... then we could figure out the living situation because if I felt like this as a beta, I can't imagine how the alphas were feeling.

CHAPTER 14

Ella

Yesterday had been intense. As if mother nature wanted to give me a break, I woke up to rain pattering on the inn's windows. I rolled out of bed and pushed open the curtains to take in the small New England town covered in a mist of rain. I loved the rain, it always made places seem more alive, yet quieter at the same time. Plus, this weather was the perfect excuse to hide away at the library today and find some books to read. *Not to mention see Maddox whose snowy scent I couldn't get out of my head.*

Showering quickly, I got ready and grabbed my bag, stopping only to grab the new journal Birdie had gifted me yesterday. *If I'm in a good mental headspace maybe I'll start this later.* I waved goodbye to Violet, letting her know I was headed to grab breakfast then was off to the library for the day.

I pulled the hood up of my forest green raincoat and

slowly headed toward the Enchanted Mug. It wasn't raining hard enough for an umbrella and honestly, I didn't mind it one bit unless it was a complete downpour. Drystan handed me a London Fog and a scone, kissing me quickly on the lips before shooing me away to the library so he could focus and work. I laughed at him even as my cheeks heated.

"I'll see you at six?" I asked, making sure I remembered the time we had set up for our date.

"Meet me here," Drystan confirmed over his shoulder as he started the next drink. I called out a quick goodbye and warmed myself by sipping the tea he had made me and hurried to the library.

As I got close to the library entrance someone called my name making me look around to find Spencer not too far behind me. I stopped in the middle of the sidewalk, nerves making my stomach turn into a ball of knots as my tattooed mate approached me. I didn't know him that well. Hell, I didn't really know him at all. I just know that I barreled in like a drunk wrecking ball into his relationship with Hunter... What must they think of me?

"I'm glad I caught you." He smiled gently at me, his hazel eyes cautious as he searched my face. "How are you doing?"

I bit my lower lip as I dragged one of my rainboots along the sidewalk. "Mystic Harbor didn't really turn out to be the quiet small town I was originally looking for. As for everything going on with this mate situation... I guess I'm overwhelmed. I mean... eight?!"

He chuckled lightly, stuffing his hands into his jacket pocket considering me. "That's a lot. Hell, I thought I'd only have one, but fate is funny like that sometimes." My cheeks heated and I stared down at the ground, unsure of what to say to that when I felt a finger under my chin urging me to look back up at him. The comforting scent of citrus and sage intensified as I met his comforting gaze. "To clarify, that's not a complaint, Ella. Just a statement. I know we didn't really have the best introduction, the three of us. Let us take you to dinner and we can try to start over?"

My eyes widened and I almost turned him down, the memory of Hunter in his police uniform holding me from behind making me break out into a cold sweat. But then I thought of him and Hunter laughing together at the town meeting, their looks of absolute devotion to each other I could feel even from far away. I licked my lips as I took a fortifying breath. "Okay. Tomorrow night? I'm meeting with Drystan tonight."

"Works out perfect since that's the night we are both off work." Spencer smiled and it lit up his entire face making me smile back in reflex.

"Can I ask you something?" I ventured, my natural curiosity taking over. Not being able to sense what he was had been bothering me since we met. He nodded, waiting patiently for me to form my question. "I can see through the glamour, even if just in quick flashes... but I can't with you. What are you?"

If the question was too blunt and rude Spencer didn't seem bothered by it. In fact, he seemed slightly amused but nervous. He rubbed his face and just as I was about to backpedal and tell him he didn't need to answer he opened his mouth.

"Griffin. I'm a griffin. There aren't many of us left, but we can maintain a human form and shift similar to shifters."

"But not exactly the same?" I asked, head tilted to the

side absolutely fascinated at this turn of events. I'd heard of griffins before, but only in storybooks so who knew how much of that was actually accurate. *Probably none of it.*

"It's complicated," Spencer answered a bit evasively. "Something to probably pace yourself learning about it to be honest. But tomorrow at six, how about we meet at The Lighthouse, the fancy restaurant? That way you don't feel cornered with us taking you there."

I appreciated the thought and effort he, *they*, had made in making this offer. I knew that they had probably discussed approaching me about dinner and with me not even being able to meet Hunter's gaze yesterday... I felt awful that I couldn't figure out how to push past the uniform to see the man beneath it.

"Sounds good," I agreed. He smiled gently before tucking a loose strand of hair behind my ear.

"Don't sound so terrified. I don't know your story, but I do know Hunter. He won't be in uniform tomorrow night and he really is a great guy," he promised. I swallowed hard, unsure what to say back to that and a bit embarrassed he'd read me so easily. Hunter really must think the worst of me, I couldn't imagine meeting a mate then watching them be absolutely terrified of me. He gave me a quick half smile and wave before walking off, leaving me to my thoughts.

Now that I was thoroughly soaked through, I rushed inside the massive library, happy for the respite. It was empty, even the lobby was silent today which struck me as odd. One thing the gargoyle brothers weren't, was quiet, even I knew that after meeting them just once.

"Hello?" I called out softly. When I got no response I shrugged and walked inside. I didn't feel like reading yet, my head was too preoccupied with all the chaos, so I decided to walk through the library a bit to find a cozy spot to have my breakfast.

The large stone building had a bit of a draft and shivers ran through me, my sweater not drying in the least. It's crazy that I got soaked through my jacket, but with the rain picking up as I talked to Spencer it was bound to happen. It was bad enough that I debated back and forth between running back to my room to change.

"You're freezing," Maddox's voice echoed down the aisle, the scent of snow hitting me just before I turned around.

"I got stopped outside a few times." I shrugged. "I— I'll be okay." Of course, my teeth chattered enough that it came out in a stutter. He snorted and waved for me to follow after him.

"Come back here with me, there's a fire on already," he softly ordered me. I didn't hesitate to follow him at the prospect of actual warmth. His strides were long and I had to jog a bit to keep up, but he led me past the main room and down a hall I'd assumed were offices. He stopped outside of one that was labeled 'employee lounge' and pushed open the door. The warmth hit me and I let out a relieved sigh, moving around him to drop down on the rug directly in front of the fireplace. The heat was a big contrast but I soon let out a happy sigh as the chill was chased from my fingers.

"This is amazing, thank you," I called back to Maddox. He still didn't look satisfied, grabbing the hoodie right off of his back and coming over to drop it in my lap.

"It'll be huge on you, but it's clean, I just put it on. You need to warm up," he insisted. There was a bit of alpha command in his tone but I could easily tell it was unintentional. I wasn't about to turn it down though, ripping off my wet sweater in a quick movement that had him squeaking out a noise of surprise and twisting away from me. I caught the redness on his cheeks and laughed.

"I've got a shirt on underneath," I teased, pulling the hoodie over my head. His cheeks were still tinted red when he came over, grabbing my wet sweater and draping it over the chair nearby so it could properly dry. I snuggled into the warmth of his hoodie, the scent of snow surrounding me enough that I let out a contented sigh. There was just something magical about being surrounded in something so cozy, a fire in front of you, and the scent of a strong alpha all over you. The omega in me was ready to curl up in his lap and I had to remind myself that it might be weird. A little weird? I snorted at myself. *Better to snuggle with one of the three alphas I was already mated to and not one that's just being nice.*

There was a dinging sound and he turned to glance at the door. "It's just me today, I have to go out. Stay as long as you'd like." He gave me one last lingering look of regret before rushing out.

The following silence had me glancing around, but the cozy room was far from disconcerting. The dark walls were complemented by the warm glow of the fire and bright artwork hanging on the walls. Leather couches were shoved against the walls, tables separating them and stacked high with a random assortment of books. There was a kitchenette in the corner, a few baskets of snacks on the counter. Outside of the amount of furniture and things in the room, it was oddly clean and organized chaos. I loved it. I quickly finished off the last of my tea and practically inhaled the scone Drystan had given me as I relaxed in the lounge alone.

Now that I could feel my hands, I pulled out the

leather bound journal that Birdie had gifted me. She had given the least helpful instructions I'd ever heard, so I just turned to the first page and started pouring out my feelings. Page after page filled with my past few weeks, from overhearing my parents' plans, to running, to arriving here at Mystic Harbor, to the chaos that came next and all the flashbacks that had been happening recently. It was like a weight lifted off of my chest, the journal taking on enough of my burden that I could breathe freely now.

It felt like hours later that I glanced away from the pages and shook out my aching hand. The freeing feeling that came from dumping all of my problems on the pages had a smile breaking out across my face and I turned a few pages, the muse finally coming back to me now that I wasn't caught up in my own drama.

Finding my niche in writing had been damn near impossible. Sometimes I had kids stories come to me, others romance, a few times even a good fantasy adventure. But at the moment I found myself using my current location as inspiration. The story unfolded easier than it had ever done before, pages filling with a young woman discovering a secret hallway in an old library, taking her on new adventures with each room she discovered.

Books flew around her in a swirling tornado of musty pages and ink. She grinned as she watched them circle, flashes of their words and pictures flitting across her vision as they flew. It wasn't the same adventure she'd gotten from the last room, but seeing the synchronized dance from the tomes she loved was just as exciting.

The touch of a hand on my shoulder pulled me out of my writing and I jumped, glancing up at Maddox as his cold fingers brushed against an exposed sliver of skin from the hoodie slipping down to one side. The pain in my sternum was immediate and I hissed at the same time as he jerked his hand back. His face paled as he looked at his wrist, surprise clear on his as he stared at what I assumed was a mate mark. *He must have the third-quarter moon design since Drystan had the waning moon. Why are there so many damn phases of the moon?!*

"Mates?" His question was full of vulnerability and awe. I found myself rising to my feet, glancing up at the sweet alpha before me. For once, I wasn't shocked and overwhelmed. I knew I had more coming and I was a bit relieved my new gargoyle friend was among my mates. It shouldn't be a surprise with how much his scent helped calm me today. He stared down at me as I reached up, resting my palm on his cheek.

"Yes, it seems so. Are you okay?" He blinked at the question before a dazzling smile took over his face. It made him even more handsome, his silver eyes lighting up at the thought alone.

"Ecstatic, Ella. I haven't been able to get you out of my head since we met," he admitted. Our eyes locked and my stomach flipped with nerves as he leaned down. All of that fell away at the feel of his full lips slanting over mine. His hand rested on my hip, pulling me close as the gentle kiss turned from sweet to heated. It was clear he wasn't as experienced as my sirens, but it was just as perfect in its own way. He made me feel amazing, like I was the only person in the world who mattered to him, all of his attention on me and making sure I knew it.

When he pulled away, his lips were swollen with our kisses and I was breathless, but happy.

That is until the random stacks of books took flight.

"What the—?" he questioned, pulling me close to shield me with his body. I wiggled around until I could see better, the scene almost identical to the one I just wrote.

"Holy shit," I whispered. Something in my voice must have stood out because he leaned back and looked down at me with confusion. Instead of answering, I pulled out my journal and handed it over, showing him the paragraphs I'd just finished. His jaw dropped as he glanced from me, to the journal, to the books flying around us, then back.

"You did this?" There was no judgment there, only confusion. "I don't think I've ever seen a witch bring words to life, though it's not unheard of. I've read about it."

"I guess?" I shrugged, uncertain and nervous as I took in the swirling books around us. "This is all new to me. And now I need to stop it before it destroys your stuff." The pages were starting to fall out and I panicked. The last thing I needed was to wreck the favorite books of my librarian mate.

Closing my eyes, I took a deep breath and breathed. I wasn't upset this time, but turned on. And so close to adding a mate with magic flowing through me, I knew that was just as volatile. If it hadn't been for Birdie, I might have thought I was going crazy or blame it on something else. *Wait, Maddox just said something about writing... I wrote something and it came to life, does that mean...*

Then I had a realization that had me gasping. My eyes opened to the books swirling even faster, but I barely noticed.

"The lawn ornaments."

"What?" he asked, even more confused now as his brow furrowed trying to follow my jumping thoughts.

"The night of the storm? After all that went down here setting up the battle? I went back to the inn and wrote a short story for fun. It was about lawn ornaments coming to life," I admitted. How I had missed such an obvious clue was astounding, but then again that fake storm and the following day were full of such high emotions it wasn't all that surprising.

"Is your magic strong enough to affect the whole town?" he asked. The way he said it was gentle, like he may offend me, but I waved that off.

"It's so up and down so far, who knows. But I need to write this down. Birdie is definitely going to need to know about this. There has to be some kind of connection, right?" I didn't wait for his answer, writing down every detail I could about that night, then today, including the aftermath. Guilt filled me that everyone was forced to clean up and cover for a mess I'd likely caused. There was no proof that I did, but now that I'd brought the books to life, I was almost completely positive it was on me.

"Hey, it's okay. We'll figure it out," he promised, pulling me in for a hug. With his strong arms holding me tight, the anxiety dropped again, and with it, so did the books finally.

"I hope so. At this rate, this town doesn't stand a chance." Birdie had mentioned fortifying the barrier, and I thought it was just a precaution. But now? Now I knew I was a danger to this entire town. Would I be forced to run away from the only home I'd truly felt I belonged? That thought nearly killed me. Not to mention, I had mates here.

How did I get so far in over my head?!

CHAPTER 15

Ella

My life barely felt like my own anymore. I went from an average human woman to a witch with not just one mate, but eight of them. And fate seems hell-bent on slamming them all at me at once.

But for some reason, mating with Drystan was different than the others. We'd formed a bit of a friendship first, so it was almost a relief. The Enchanted Mug had become a safe space for me, and in turn, Drystan was too. In the uncertainty of my life, his grumpy charm was a constant and he had no idea how important that was.

When we realized we were mated, we fell into step like we'd dated for months, not seconds, and it was a relief after the chaotic mating of the others. Part of me worried that it might cause some jealousy, but so far everyone had been fairly cool about it. I mean it happened this morning with everyone there and I didn't sense any jealousy so I'm going to take it as a win. I guess that was the plus side with fate being involved, none of us got to choose how this all happened and in some ways, we're tied together even before we meet. It feels right, even when other stuff gets in the way... like my issues with Hunter. But tonight that wasn't a problem, my focus was solely on the sexy, stoic beta waiting for me at the coffee shop.

As I approached the front door, I noticed he'd shut down early. It was only about five-thirty yet the closed sign was in place. I knocked gently on the door, jumping when a window above creaked. Stepping back, I tilted my head back and glanced upward, grinning when Drystan poked his head out.

"Hey! The stairs are right back there, meet you at the top," he called down. He pointed to a small alley between his shop and the next. I turned and walked that way, finding a staircase leading to a red door on the second floor. I don't know how I missed it before, but most mornings I was coffee centered, seeking out the caffeine I needed and oblivious to everything outside of that.

"Hey," I greeted awkwardly, giving a small wave as he held open the door for me. He'd dressed up a bit, his hair still wet from a shower and a gray henley that made his eyes pop in contrast. His dark jeans hugged him perfectly and I felt my heart stutter at the sight of him, that or the strong scent of his Earl Grey wrapping around me.

"Come here." He laughed, pulling me close and kissing me. If I had any bits of hesitation they were gone the moment his lips teased over mine. "You hungry?"

"I'm always hungry." I laughed, our fingers tangling together as he led me into the apartment.

The first thing I thought as I walked further inside was how perfectly Drystan it was. The walls were white but that was the only thing devoid of the earthy tones that surrounded him. Plants grew in the windows and filled every open space just like the coffee shop below. The furniture was made up of shades of brown, the couches an inviting, coffee brown leather.

His kitchen was the opposite. It was clean and precise, everything in its place. A large window sat above the counter and he had it open, a cool sea breeze filling the space, mixing with the smell of the food cooking on the stove.

"What are you making?" I asked as he let go and went to the stove. Garlic was strong in the air, but it didn't give away much more than that.

"Garlic parmesan steak and shrimp, potatoes, asparagus, and homemade rolls," he said proudly. "I figured there's something in the mix you'll eat. I wasn't sure how picky you are."

There was a hint of teasing in his voice and I felt myself smiling back, completely at home here already.

"I'm a fan of food... all food," I promised. "As long as I'm not expected to cook it. Otherwise, it's cereal and microwave meals."

He looked appalled at the mere mention of microwaving food.

"Thank the gods you found us. Between me and the others, you'll be well-fed at least," he said, shooting me a look that showed he was less than impressed with my life choices before now.

"To be fair, I didn't have a ton of opportunities to practice." I shrugged, not embarrassed for once. He didn't press for details, simply turning and lifting me to sit on the counter. He pressed a kiss to my forehead before turning back to the stove.

"So what I heard is that you want to learn," he joked

as he flipped the steak on the cast iron, basted it, then shoved it in the oven.

"Wrong." I laughed. "I'm the omega here. You can all feed and pamper me while I look pretty."

He snorted. "Yeah, like you'd ever sit back and let us wait on you. You'd be bored in a weekend of that lifestyle."

"You aren't wrong." I smirked at him, kicking my feet back and forth, unable to sit still for long. "Need help on anything non-cooking related?"

"How about you pour the drinks, this is almost done," he said, pointing to the wine chilling in an ice bucket on the counter. Two glasses were sitting next to it so I poured the uncorked wine and carried the glasses to the table. By the time I'd found plates and silverware he was filling the plates.

On my first bite, I let out a moan. It was phenomenal.

"You really didn't want a kiss after dinner, did you?" I teased. "This is full of garlic."

He frowned. "You don't like it?"

"No, I love it!" I countered, horrified he missed the joke. "I just meant my breath is going to be awful."

"Well, I may have gone to the store and gotten a few necessities," he admitted. His cheeks were red and it was adorable. For such a fierce beta, he really let his walls down around me. I loved that.

"Such as?" I pushed. He groaned and looked down at his plate.

"A toothbrush for you, stuff like that," he mumbled. "Now eat."

The harsh order had me biting back a smile and taking another big bite. I wouldn't argue an order that I was completely on board with. This was so good.

"This really is amazing," I said around a bite of food. We fell into easy conversation as we finished eating, but the entire time I could feel the tension rising. The stolen glances, heated gazes, our scents mixing together. It was all going to come to a head soon and part of me worried he'd try to be a gentleman. *Way to go from virgin to sex addict in the matter of a week... But could I really complain when it involved these men?*

"Do you want dessert?" he asked, he started to go into an explanation but I was over the tension and cut him off.

"I need the bathroom and my toothbrush," I blurted out. He merely raised a hand and pointed to a closed door nearby, startled by my outburst. I stood up and rushed off. The moment I was in the small bathroom, I finally took a breath of non-pheromone tinted air. But it didn't calm my raging libido any.

It only took a few seconds to spot the new things. He'd gotten a bright pink toothbrush for me and a variety of girly scented lotions, shampoos, and soaps. I brushed my teeth quickly before taking a deep breath and stepping out.

Drystan seemed to read my mind. He was standing outside the door. There were no words spoken, we simply came together in a clash of tongues and teeth, greedy hands ripping at clothes. He led me down the tiny hall and through a door, throwing me on the bed.

My breath rushed out of me, but he didn't seem to notice, already pressing soft kisses on my body as he crawled over me. Each one sent a surge of heat through me, only making me wetter. From the deep breath he took as my knees spread wider for him, he approved.

"Gods, you smell like heaven and I bet you taste even better." He gasped before crawling back down to the apex of my thighs. He inhaled again, a move that should have been strange but it just made me feel sexy, desirable. Everything in me was drawn to this man and it made this so much better. He may not have a knot for me, but I knew this would be no less mind-blowing. He's a literal beta in the streets, alpha in the sheets, and fuck if I didn't love that about him.

The first swipe of his tongue over my pussy had me bucking into him. The jolt of pleasure it sent rolling through me had another surge of slick gushing from me and he lapped it up like a man starved. He ate me out with a determination that had me coming more than once, nonsensical babble driveling from my lips as shockwaves of pleasure wracked through me.

"Please, I can't," I begged him but he just chuckled, moving back and swiping a hand over his mouth before moving back up to press a kiss to my lips. I could taste myself on his tongue and it was oddly sexy.

He didn't hesitate to settle between my legs, lining himself up and slamming home. I clung to him, nails clawing at his back as he fucked me relentlessly. Drystan fucked me with no hesitation, no holding back, and I fucking loved it. It was primal and possessive, his scent so strong I was nearly intoxicated on it.

When he came, filling me with his seed, he made sure I came again as well. His fingers teased over my clit and wrung another from my overly sensitive body.

As we came down from the high, I couldn't keep a smile from my face. The evening, the date, the sex, Drystan... it was all perfect.

CHAPTER 16

Ella

"Ella, with all that pacing you might wear a hole in my floor," Violet teased as she opened the door to my bedroom at the inn. I shot her a weak smile, my stomach turning with nerves. She wasn't wrong though, I had been pacing for the last ten minutes going back and forth about going to dinner tonight. Part of me wanted to go, they were my mates after all, but the other half was questioning why I'd *willingly* meet up with a cop. No, not a cop. *Hunter.* I was driving myself insane building this damn date night up that I wasn't sure I'd be able to enjoy it.

"Ella, you need to breathe," Violet commanded, serious as she closed the door. The alpha command in her voice was clear, but my anxiety didn't give a damn about it. She wasn't *my* alpha. "Girl, do not make me call one of your mates to calm you down for a date with someone else tonight."

A broken laugh escaped me as I wrung my hands, forcing myself to still and sit on my bed. Belatedly I realized I was in just a bra and underwear, but that didn't seem to faze my friend as she approached and sat down near me.

"I just—" I swallowed hard. "I don't know how to do this."

I could practically feel the confusion rolling off of the woman beside me. "You weren't this nervous about your date with Drystan last night. You practically ran in here, showered and changed in ten minutes, and skipped out the damn door to meet him yesterday when you got back from the library." Violet sent me a sly smile as I felt my cheeks heat. "Don't think I didn't notice you didn't come back until this morning."

"Vi!" I tried to protest, but she just burst out laughing as I attempted to cover my heated cheeks with my hands. "It's different."

"Why is this so different?"

"It sounds so dumb." I squeezed my eyes shut, trying to stay calm and not let old memories take over. "It's nothing against them, Hunter or Spencer. Hell, I don't even really know them. But... I can't see past the uniform. It shouldn't be this hard."

"I don't know the full story of your past," Violet spoke slowly after being silent for a few minutes. "And you don't need to tell me. But if you've had such bad experiences with the police in the past no one will expect you to just get over them right away. Maybe that's a place to start? Telling Hunter and Spencer that so they understand *why* you left like you did. It might not be easy, but it might be for the best."

"It's not something that's easy to talk about." I chewed my bottom lip.

"Well, you can think it over as you get dressed." Violet stood up. She reached over and pulled me to standing, dragging me toward my closet. "Because there is no way you could show up to dinner as you are. I mean, you could... but I don't think you'd be able to hold Hunter and Spencer responsible for their actions if you did."

"Oh my god, Violet!" I giggled. "No way is that happening."

"You should wear these!" Fabric hit me square in the face, soon followed by more instructions from my friend. It was a super short black dress that didn't even look like it was mine. *Did she bring some of her own stuff up here?!*

"No way." I shook my head, tossing it back at her face. "Way too short."

"That's the best part." Violet rolled her eyes at me before turning back to my closet. She froze for a second then pointed at some of the clothes I had taken from some of my mates already. "You're already stealing clothes?"

I cleared my throat. "They're comfortable." Pushing past her I grabbed the hoodie Maddox had given me, the shirt I had taken from Tanniv's houseboat when I had stayed the night, and the beanie Drystan had shoved on my head before he took me home this morning. Tossing them all on the bed I mock glared at Violet daring her to say anything else about it. When she just quirked an eyebrow, I threw my hands up in the air in defeat. "What?!"

"I think Asra is going to be upset that none of those are his."

"He should make it so his stuff is easier to take," I shot

back, shrugging. "Besides he didn't have anything at Tanniv's to take."

"Bet that's going to change soon," Violet muttered.

"*Anyways*," I turned back to my clothes. I flipped through a few things until I found a flowy navy blue dress that hit just above my knees but had a deep V-neck that managed to give me the illusion of cleavage. I needed all the help I could get in that department.

Trying it on I gave a small twirl for Violet who looked at me with a half smile. "It's perfect, very you."

"Thanks." I ran my hands along the skirt.

"I have some heels you could borrow," Violet offered but I immediately shook my head.

"I'd break my ankle just getting there, but thanks! They are going to have to get the full Ella treatment." I squatted down, rummaging around until I came out with a pair of my favorite two-tone winter duck boots, camel brown and black. They were perfect since there was a chance of rain tonight and there was no heel. I made quick work of putting them up and stood up showing them off proudly.

"Only you could pull that off and look ridiculously adorable." My friend smiled broadly at me. "You just need a jacket cause I don't need all of your men calling me saying I should have made sure you had one."

"Do you think they'd be upset if I used the hoodie?" I gestured to my pile of clothes from the bed. Violet considered me and walked over to the bed, taking the hoodie I had mentioned and Drystan's beanie.

"I think anything that will help calm you will be a good idea." She handed me both and watched as I put them on. "You feeling better?"

I pulled the beanie down, unable to stop the warmth

filling me as I smelled the perfect combination of cool, brisk snow and the warmth of Earl Grey tea surrounding me. Two contrasting scents that smelled like heaven to me. "Yes. Thank you for distracting me and helping me figure out what to wear."

"We're friends." Violet hugged me firmly. "You go at your own pace, Ella, but be open to learning about them. Spence and Hunter are great guys. And with Spencer there... you can trust them completely."

"Why would that matter?" I furrowed my brow, looking up at the wolf alpha in front of me confused. Violet looked at me surprised. "Does this have to do with him being a griffin?"

"How much do you know about griffins?"

"That they exist?" I half-joked. "But really, besides random stories I've read, nothing."

She nodded a few times, clearly thinking over what she was going to tell me. "I'm sure Spence will fill you in on more things as you both get more comfortable with each other. But I think he will be fine with me telling you this, you can't lie around a griffin. It's impossible. So anything they or you say will be the truth and that's something that is a guarantee."

"You can't lie?" Mortification filled me as I groaned. "Oh god, that's what happened at the bar that night. I know I was drunk but he asked me an innocent question and I just—"

"Couldn't stop yourself from telling the complete truth?"

"Yes." I sighed, wishing the floor would just cave in and swallow me whole.

"You aren't the first or last person to do that around him," Violet tried to reassure me. "But my point is, that you can trust everything they both tell you, about anything. You might be surprised by what you hear. If you were looking for a place to start over, a place to fit in, well... they get that. That's all I'm going to say. On that note..." She stepped away from me and clapped her hands. "You need to get going. You're going to be late."

"You've been around Birdie too much if you're clapping like that," I joked as I grabbed my purse off the bed before she pushed me out of the room. "I'm going! I'm going!"

As soon as she let go I whirled around and squeezed her tightly for a moment before running off. "Thank you, for everything. You're like the bigger sister I've always wanted. If they call you, tell them I'm on the way."

I didn't look back as I hurried down the sidewalk trying to remember where The Lighthouse was and hoping I didn't have to call to say I was lost on top of being late. You'd think being in a small town it would be easier not getting lost. I was going to blame it on my nerves. Taking a deep breath I snuggled into the hoodie and grounded myself, this was going to be a great dinner. I was going to work on listening and not reacting... I could do this.

Probably.

Hopefully.

If I make it there.

Spencer

"She should have been here by now," Hunter growled, prowling along the sidewalk in front of the restaurant.

I sighed for the third time, barely restraining my eye roll at his grumbling. Ella was five minutes late. You'd think we had been waiting for an hour given how tense my mate was. As if he could hear my thoughts he shot me an exasperated glare that I met with one of my lazy grins which made him huff and collapse on the bench next to me.

Things had been the same yet different since we'd mated to Ella. We were the same, our connection as strong as ever, stronger even, but it felt like something was missing at the same time. A blonde-haired omega-sized hole was there and she was the definition of skittish around us, not even meeting Hunter's gaze when he looked at her at the cafe. Hunter was stressed and upset that he was the source of her distress. *How can an alpha who loves to fix problems fix that?*

My mate ran his hands over his new blue jeans, uncharacteristically nervous as he met my gaze with a nervous smile. "Sorry."

His amber brown eyes were warm and I shook my head. "No need to apologize. This is a big deal, for everyone."

Hunter nodded a few times, taking a deep breath as he tried to calm down, and rubbed the back of his neck. The new blue jeans and blue and green plaid flannel was Hunter's version of dressed up along with non-scuffed brown boots. His dirty brown hair was newly buzzed and his long beard was cleaned up for tonight. He had pulled out all the stops for her and I hoped that Ella appreciated Hunter and all his rough edges.

Suddenly, Hunter tensed up and looked up. Curious, I followed his gaze to see none other than Ella approaching us talking animatedly with Sterling, the oldest of the gargoyles that ran the local library. The gargoyle smiled at something she was saying and he gestured toward where we were sitting. She looked over at us, her blue eyes lighting up with cautious excitement before she turned back to give Sterling a quick hug. He hugged her back and held up a hand in greeting to us before ambling back towards town.

Both Hunter and Ella had gone for a more laid-back style, though she was a bit more eccentric than the man beside me. Duck boots, a navy blue dress, or at least a skirt, with a black and white hoodie and a black beanie hat. The long strands of her long blonde hair flew into her face with the breeze. It seems I had somehow overdressed with a white button-up shirt and black jeans, though both of them made me feel better about the red chucks I had on.

"Sorry I'm late!" Ella greeted us, though her blue gaze stayed mostly on me. "I realized partway here I didn't know where the restaurant was and I got lost. Then I ran into Sterling. He tried to give me directions but then I got more confused so he just said he'd walk me here himself so he knew I got here and not walked into the ocean instead." She rolled her eyes at that, but she didn't look upset from the other man's dry teasing. Anyone who could handle the gargoyles was impressive in my book. They were equal parts insane, boisterous, proud, loyal, and all-consuming. Yet she didn't seem fazed at all. Though she was still nervous around us given her rambling answer and the way she chewed her bottom lip.

"No worries," I answered with a gentle smile. "We're just glad you're here. Right, Hunter?" I nudged my mate who cleared his throat roughly.

"Yeah," he rumbled, amber eyes focused on Ella with

a guarded but hopeful expression. *A man of many words, not very helpful right now.*

"Shall we?" I stood up and gestured towards the restaurant. Ella took a deep breath and nodded, a wavering grin on her face as she led the way to the host right inside the door. A young teen, Alex, who had just gotten his first job here, looked understandably nervous as we approached. He grabbed three menus as soon as he caught sight of Hunter and I, leading the way through the restaurant to an outside patio. The view was gorgeous and there was just a slight chill outside so it was the perfect temperature to still enjoy.

I thanked Alex as he told us our waiter would be with us soon. Hunter pulled out a chair and gestured for Ella to take the seat. She considered him for a minute before she took the offered assistance. A cautious light lit her face as she murmured her thanks but you would have thought she had offered Hunter the fucking world, happiness filled his face at even that slight show of thawing from her. Hunter could be gruff and blunt, but he was also the biggest fucking teddy bear, which is something I reminded the bear shifter of at every opportunity. He *loved* it. Another reason I requested an outside table was because I had a feeling the ocean would help soothe our anxious omega, remind her of her two siren alphas who she felt safe with, and given the scents I could smell from her clothes I made the right decision. The hint of Earl Grey tea and, surprisingly, snow from none other than one of the gargoyles, had to come from the large hoodie and the hat I recognized as Drystan's.

"Which gargoyle?" I asked, not able to keep my amusement from my voice as Ella jerked to face me with wide blue eyes. "I can tell it's a gargoyle but I swear every time I go by the library it seems like there are more of them. It can't be Sterling or he would have come over to us."

"Maddox," Ella answered, running her hands over the hoodie, giving away what she had gotten from him. "It just happened the other day... I swear I need a drink."

"That is the one thing you don't need," Hunter joked lightly, making Ella choke then burst out laughing. Some of it was nervous energy but she was genuinely amused when she met Hunter's eyes, a twinkle of mischief and flush to her cheeks at his reference to when we all met.

"Alright, I'll give you that one. I don't need alcohol." Right then our waiter came over asking for our drink order. Not looking away from Ella, Hunter ordered drinks and food for all of us, not bothering to ask since he knew what I liked. Our omega tilted her head at Hunter, appraising him as the waiter walked away, but she didn't protest him taking that small bit of control. In fact, I got the feeling she enjoyed it. *Interesting.*

"We wanted to take you out to dinner to try and start over," I spoke up when they just sat there staring at each other silently. Both people turned to look at me and I focused on Ella. "We know we didn't really have the best start between the bar and the next morning... We wanted a chance to get to know you and help you get more comfortable with us."

Ella's smile dropped a bit at that and she turned toward the ocean, breathing in deeply. I could feel Hunter shifting next to me and I placed a calming hand on his thigh, hoping I could help him stay calm as Ella opened up to us at her own pace. It couldn't be easy mating with this many people back to back, much less an established couple like ourselves. Plus, there was just something about Ella that made me think innocent or maybe inexperienced was a better word, though given the men she had collected so far that wasn't going to last long. Alex popped by and dropped off our waters, clearly reading the table and hurrying off before he overstayed his welcome.

"I'm sorry I reacted that way," Ella managed haltingly, still looking out at the ocean then down toward her hands in her lap. "I haven't really had the best experience with the police."

"A big teen rebellion stage?" I teased lightly, making her snort.

"Would you—" Hunter ran a hand over his beard, leaning back in his chair as if offering Ella as much space as he could. "Would you tell us more? Because... I'll be honest, being a cop means a lot to me, it's a part of who I am."

Ella's hand trembled when she reached up to brush hair out of her face but she didn't run away this time. "It's... complicated."

"Why don't we start with stuff about us?" I offered, wanting to make this easier for her. "Then you don't feel on the spot being the only one sharing things."

Both of them turned to stare at me, surprise clear in both their gazes. Hunter also looked concerned and I squeezed his thigh in reassurance. He knew the details of my past and was right to be concerned that I was just offering to talk about it. But there was no way I could watch Ella sit there, vulnerable, and leave her there to open herself up alone.

"I'll start." Hunter wrapped an arm around the back of my chair, pulling me into his side as Ella and I shifted our attention to him. "My sleuth was attacked by humans.

They were claiming land in the Appalachian mountains that had been ours for centuries. By the time they left us alone, I was the only one left." Hunter fell silent for a minute, his expression was faraway as he stared off into space, lost in the past.

"Hunter—" Ella started but he just shook his head.

"I couldn't stay there so I headed up here. I'd heard of Mystic Harbor before, a place of supernaturals only, outside of tourist season of course, to help with money. A sanctuary. I became a cop because I didn't want that to happen to anyone else. No one should have to sit there helpless as their family is slaughtered around them because humans feel entitled to *own* land."

Then Ella did something unexpected, though maybe it shouldn't have been considering we were mated and that I could already see she had a big heart. Ella stood up and rushed over to Hunter. She threw herself into his lap, hugging him tightly as her hair and back leaned into me since he was holding me tight against him. Not hesitating, Hunter wrapped his other hand around her to accept the comfort she was offering him as he buried his face in her neck. *I bet that was fucking intoxicating up close given how heady the smell of vanilla and coffee was just sitting by her.* My heart was full, twistedly happy at this sad moment that Ella caught a glimpse of this amazing man past the uniform that terrified her.

"My parents have been dead for centuries," I spoke softly, moving my hand from Hunter's thigh to rub Ella's back, unable to keep myself from touching her. My beta energy always had a calming effect on my alpha, and I hoped it'd help ease hers too. "Having griffin children is incredibly difficult. Fertility issues, rough pregnancies, hatchlings are few and far between. Plus, we are hunted by humans and supernaturals alike for many reasons. I was here around the time the town was founded and I was promised a safe place to just be, protect the people here and they would protect me. Slowly, I allowed myself to connect to the other supernaturals and I found my family, my place in the world. And I found you both...or you both found me," I added on with mock exasperation. "Eventually."

"It's not my fault—" Hunter pulled back from Ella, though not letting her go, to start in our regular argument that was practically an inside joke now.

"Wait— wait!" Ella cut him off, turning on his lap to face me with a curious expression that I already knew I'd see a lot on our lovely omega. "You're how old?! I thought this place was founded in the 1800s?!"

A slight cough had us all turning to look at the waiter who had just come up with our food. A rack of ribs and fries for Hunter, clam chowder and lobster rolls for myself, and a chicken pot pie for Ella. It smelled delicious but none of us moved to start eating as she kept her gaze on mine, not the least bit distracted as she waited for my answer.

"It was," I answered, smirking slightly once Alex had headed back inside. "And I lost count a while ago but I'm getting close to seven hundred I think... give or take a few decades. Supernaturals can live a long time. And I'd save that shock for your sirens, omega."

"What?" Ella asked, surprise clear as her eyes widened and she glanced over at the ocean below us as if she could sense them or ask them right now.

"Don't you dare try to jump right now," Hunter warned her, making her shiver against him from the low growl in his voice.

"I wouldn't have jumped!" Ella protested, looking at the alpha with an affronted expression. "I can't even swim, but they can bet I'm asking the next time I see them."

"You can't swim?" Hunter's brow furrowed.

"No." Ella shrugged, shifting as if she was going to get off Hunter's lap. She'll learn there was no way that was going to happen. Hunter liked to take care of people and after all the dodging she did, he wouldn't just let her go. I leaned over and grabbed her plate, dragging it to sit between ours. Ella huffed, but didn't protest. *She learns quickly.*

"What about you?" I prodded gently.

Ella took a deep breath and looked at Hunter and myself before looking at the water again. "I can see through the glamour, like I said in the meeting." We both nodded, remembering her saying that. "I've *always* been able to see through it, even when I was a kid. And my parents, well they never believed me when I talked about it. Of course, they thought it was all my imagination when I was really little, but after a while, I didn't stop talking about it. After all, supernaturals aren't real, right?" Her self-deprecating smile twisted my heart and I knew whatever she said next wouldn't be good. "Well, they wanted to 'fix' me because no one in their right mind believed in fairy tales."

"Oh, Ella," Hunter ran a large hand through her hair and Ella looked up at me with blue eyes bright with unshed tears.

"They committed me, a bunch of times over the years, and it made it so much worse because all of the staff there weren't human either. But every time I said something they just upped the medication. So, then I pretended to see nothing and it worked. For a while at least. Then I'd slip up and get tossed back in, hell, sometimes it was just a lingering look or double take that did me in. As I became older they'd call the cops to take me, saying I was fighting back."

Hunter froze and so did I, we shared a quick look and I could see the devastation in his face as it fell. We could both see where this was going. Ella was shaking and Hunter cautiously placed a hand on her hip.

"What happened?" I asked quietly, fighting to keep my instincts from raging. As a beta, I wanted to hunt down every damn person she mentioned and kill them, slowly for hurting my mate. I could only imagine the rage simmering in Hunter right now, the alpha in him fighting between comforting Ella and wanting to tear apart the ones that hurt her.

"They were always rough, mean. They didn't care what I had to say and one of them even hog-tied me and threw me in the back of the patrol car saying I had tried to assault him. I hadn't even moved when he slammed me to the ground. I never escaped those encounters without several days of soreness and several bruises."

A deep growl rumbled in Hunter's chest, so deep that I felt it in my fucking bones. Ella froze and her gaze whipped over to meet the alpha's stare, his amber eyes glowing with the force of his emotions. So slowly she reached out, resting a hand on his face to comfort him before she placed her forehead against his. The rumbling calmed, but it didn't go away. A swift look in my direction promised violence but he was so gentle as he held her. I reached out, my hands finger combing her hair to be able to connect with her right now.

This wasn't how I expected dinner to go tonight. Hell,

I had no idea how I expected things to go, but her curled up with us at the table wasn't even a thought in my mind. Her willingly looking at, much less cuddling Hunter was a huge change. Mating could be weird, pushing past barriers most people thought of when connecting with people. In this moment, as she pulled her face away and reached for me, I knew I'd never let her go.

We'd never let her go.

She was ours.

CHAPTER 17

Ella

For once when I woke up, it wasn't with the weight of the world on my shoulders. In fact, I'd slept great. No nightmares, no stress. The evening I spent with Spencer and Hunter was not at all like I expected. I was insanely nervous going in, but once Hunter told me why he was a cop and about his past, I couldn't just keep my distance. That one story had moved him from scary cop to a real person in my mind and after that, it was just as easy as it was with my other mates.

It wasn't normal to have this many mates, but if fate was being generous, well I wasn't afraid to enjoy it.

After Hunter had tried to hand feed me, which I put a stop to real quick, we ate and talked about lighter things. Like all the things my griffin mate had witnessed in his nearly 700 years and what they did in their downtime.

The reminder of his age had me pulling out my phone, starting a group chat with my two sirens. I had a feeling they'd find it amusing and honestly... I had so many questions. *No wonder Tanniv had so many stories!*

Me: How old are you guys?
Tanniv: Well, good morning to you too.
Asra: Who spilled the age gap?

I could practically see their amused, lazy smiles as they read the message.

Me: Someone old enough to see this town built.
Asra: Ah, the griffin. Should have known.
Me: Stop dodging my question, old man!
Asra: You should respect your elders.
Me: Do you really count as an elder if you make the jokes you do?
Tanniv: Our omega has a point, brother.

Rolling my eyes at their question dodging, I sent a gif of a girl tapping her watch. Of course, Asra had to send one back of Homer Simpson slipping into the bushes.

Tanniv: Don't get upset, little stargazer.
Me: Guys. I'm not a child.
Asra: Welllllllll, compared to us you are.
Tanniv: 1623.
Me: Is that your age or the year you were born?
Asra: Our age. Does that make it better or worse?

I blinked at the age and tried to do the math but then my mind blanked. Some things were better left alone. Mainly math, but also the realization of just how old they

SUKI WILLIAMS & JARICA JAMES

were. How much they must have seen. Yeah, yup.... I wasn't talking ages with my mates again. Any of them.

Me: Let's just never talk about age again since we're all consenting adults. Okay? Okay.
Asra: We broke her, brother.
Tanniv: I know how to fix her.
Me: Not today, sirens. I have to go find a job. Maybe I'll start at Kinkubus.
Tanniv: No.
Me: Good thing you don't make my decisions, alpha. Talk to you later!

As I tucked my phone away, I laughed to myself, knowing damn well I'd given them a bit to think about. I had no intentions of working in a sex shop, but teasing them was too much fun. First, I needed to find coffee, then I could walk around and ask about jobs. Actually, I should ask Violet, she might know of any openings.

Grabbing my winter boots, Maddox's hoodie, and Drystan's hat, I rushed downstairs to find her. It was a bit later than my usual time, but I'd come in late. Nothing had happened between the three of us, except that we talked until closing time. But at least I was at ease with them now.

Hopefully seeing him in uniform again wouldn't change that.

"There she is!" Violet called out as I walked downstairs, startling a guest reading on the couch nearby. I snorted at her reaction and rushed over.

"No big gossip other than we talked... a lot. And it was really nice. I even let Hunter close to me *and* made eye contact," I joked, poking fun at myself. She gasped and clutched her heart.

"What?! That's night and day, it must have been some damn fine conversation," she teased, walking toward the kitchen to give me breakfast. The alpha in her noticed when I missed a meal and she'd made a habit of saving something for me. I took the scone happily and chewed on it while she went on about her girls' night last night. I really couldn't wait to meet Opal and the others, she made the group sound like fun, but I hadn't had a moment to even breathe, let alone meet them. "So, what's today's adventure?"

"Finding a job," I admitted with a frown. "Maybe someone around here needs some help because my funds are quickly fading. I blame Drystan and his magic coffee."

She frowned and I could already see her alpha wheels turning. "Why didn't you say something?"

"It hasn't been an issue. I paid for the room and have been keeping track of my funds, it's just getting low now," I grimaced. "Plus, if I'm going to stay here I have to find something to do with my life. With everything going on I need some normalcy, a job could help with that. My stories aren't going to make me money."

"They could," she said, her eyes lighting up. "You could write and publish through one of the big platforms. People do it all the time."

"Maybe when I'm more confident and less magically volatile." I laughed. "Until then I need to have cash and pay for my room."

"Until one of your mates makes you move out." She sighed. "I really am going to miss you when that happens."

"Ugh, I hadn't considered that," I agreed, finishing off the scone in my hand. "I like it here."

"It won't change anything. If you stop hanging out with me I'll hunt you down. Can't hide from a wolf," she half-joked, half-warned.

"No worries there, you're the only real friend I've ever had," I admitted. She smiled softly and gave me a quick hug. She was more touchy than I was used to, but I actually enjoyed it. Definitely beat all those years of solitude and judgment.

"You'll figure it out. I know it's not very glorious, but I can pay you to help clean around here," she offered.

"You're sweet," I said with a smile. "But I'll look around too. Maybe I'll find my calling today."

"This town is magical, you just might," she grinned at me.

"Want me to bring you back anything while I'm out?" I offered.

"Do I get to give you money for it?" she asked slyly.

"No." I waved her off. "We aren't to that level of desperation yet, Vi."

"Then I'm fine," she huffed.

"So your usual from Drystan's?" I laughed as I walked out of the door, the sound of her laughter trailing behind me.

Mystic Harbor was busy today. People were walking around outside, picking up the last remnants in their yards from the storm. Piles of branches and debris lined the sidewalk and edge of the street but I wasn't sure the plan on getting it completely taken care of yet.

As I walked past each building, I glanced in their windows in hopes of finding some kind of help wanted sign, but unfortunately, today fate wasn't on my side.

"Uh, what are you doing?" Drystan asked, startling me. I hadn't even realized I'd reached his shop yet I was too busy grumbling in my head. He held out a to-go cup and I took it, tilting my face up so he would kiss me. He complied, but raised an eyebrow when we pulled away to let me know he wanted that answer.

"Looking for help wanted signs. I can't exactly build a life here if I'm jobless," I pointed out. His eyes lit up and I held up a hand before he could suggest it. "Look, I enjoy spending time with my mates, but working together is a bad plan."

"I disagree," he grumbled, crossing his arms. He was holding back his arguments though, which I appreciated.

A loud snap from across the square had us both turning. Leif and a group of men were lugging a large branch out of the sidewalks near the town meeting space. A branch had snapped free, knocking one of the men on his ass. When the man next to him turned to help, I caught a glimpse of his face.

"Oh my gods," I gasped, shoving my coffee at Drystan and running directly into the street. A car horn honked but I managed to dodge around it and keep running. "Reed!" His face snapped up, a look of confusion on it until he saw me and recognition sank in. He started to drop the other man when Leif stepped in, saving him from a second fall.

"Eleanor?" He was the only one that name didn't sound like a curse from. Without hesitation, I ran toward my old friend and barely stopped myself from flinging my arms around him. Fae or not, he was an old friend, but it had been so many years I didn't want to freak him out. The scent of spring rain and fresh cut grass surrounded me making me feel at peace, he smelled just like I remembered him and it took all my self-control to not inhale deeply.

"It's Ella," I corrected. He studied me with those pale blue eyes I remembered so well, the flecks of violet shining in the afternoon sun. His hair was long now, the same dirty blond from when we were kids. But it was his smile that got me. Back when we were growing up it was my oasis in a world of cold shoulders and judgment.

"How are you here?" he asked, though his smile told me he was happy to see me as he continued to look at me in confusion. "No, forget that. How have you been?" He stumbled over his words, completely thrown off by my presence.

"You know each other?" Leif's question was almost accusatory and I wasn't sure where his animosity was coming from. I frowned, unsure what to say to him, but Reed stepped in.

"We knew each other as kids. Mom used to be a housekeeper for her family," he explained. Leif's eyebrows raised and Reed chuckled. "You jealous, cousin? That's unlike you."

"Cousin?" I laughed, glancing from the dark-haired man to the blond one, their features nothing alike in the least. Honestly, fae was about all they had in common.

"Yup," Reed said simply. "Now really, how are you here?"

"Well it's a bit of a long story, but apparently, I'm a bound witch and finding fated mates unlocks it bit by bit, I've got a bit to go still," I summarized with a nervous laugh.

"Of course you are." He shook his head, a twinkle of humor shining through his earlier confusion. "I always knew there was more to you than meets the eye. Wait until I tell my mom about this."

"How is she?" I asked. The memory of her smile was enough to give me a good wave of nostalgia.

"She's great, as full of life and mischief as ever," he said fondly. "Now come here." He pulled me in for the hug I'd been hesitant to give and I started to relax in his arms, the full power of his scent of spring rain and grass enough to make my head spin. But then the pain hit. My sternum stinging with a now familiar sensation as yet another marking was added.

"Gods," I muttered, realizing I'd found yet another mate. He hissed and stared down at his wrist as he broke away from the hug, eyes widening at the sight of a waning crescent moon. It was hard to focus on the world around us but I swore I heard someone muttering angrily under their breath.

"Is this—" Reed trailed off, he looked so shocked that I almost burst out laughing. At this point, I think I almost expected that burn every time I touched someone new. At least I knew Reed, or knew him before, it had been years since I'd seen him though.

Self-consciousness hit me right then, my cheeks heating as I dragged my shoes along the grass. "A mate mark? Yes."

"Ella!" Drystan called out, exasperation and a touch of anger clear as he stalked over to where I stood. "You can't just run out into traffic!" Strong arms wrapped around me from behind, pulling my back flush against Drystan's chest. Even with the reprimand clear, his hold on me was gentle and I snuggled back into him, a half smile tugging at his lips as he looked down at me. "You're lucky it was me and not one of your alphas you did that to."

"I think the alphas would have snatched her before she got to the street," Leif commented dryly, his anger clear from how stiffly he held himself.

The workers around us got back to work, working on the gardens and clearing the last of the branches that were piled up. I bit my lip, still inexplicably nervous around the fae mayor. I might have felt comfortable enough around Reed to speak with him casually, the same could not be said of the alpha mayor whose cinnamon scent was strong as he stood next to Reed with a grumpy expression.

"Ella is fast," Drystan retorted to Leif's criticism. He handed me my coffee which I took with a quick thanks and took a big sip as Reed glanced between the two men glaring at each other.

"Just how many mates do you have, Eleanor? Ella," he corrected himself quickly as he wiped at his face. I'd shaken the poor man and tied him to me all in the span of a few minutes. It was a true skill I had.

"Uhhh..." I started doing the math in my head. "With you that makes seven."

Reed froze as Drystan squeezed me closer, pressing a kiss to the top of my head. "Seven? Seven?! Mates... *Fated* mates?" He glanced at his cousin, eyes wide as he studied the man whose grumpiness faded a bit at Reed's facial expression. "The most there has ever been is—"

"Twelve. Yes, I know." Leif grinned.

"Don't you dare wish that fate on me!" I warned them both, unable to keep my filter as I shook my finger. "Birdie thinks I'll end up with eight, that's plenty for me, thanks."

"Eight?!" Reed seemed to still be processing everything we were throwing at him.

"So just one more to help stabilize your power?" Leif asked absently, running a hand through his hair.

"Who are your mates?" Reed asked, curiosity clear as he searched our faces.

I bit my lip and bought myself a moment by taking a large sip of my coffee, but there was no dodging this question. "You, Drystan." I patted the arms still around me. "Tanniv, Asra, Maddox, Hunter, and Spencer."

Reed must have known the names because he threw his head back laughing hard enough I saw tears run down his cheek. "You're mated with four alphas, the most alpha beta I've ever met, and a fucking griffin?"

"And apparently an omega with a good sense of humor," I joked, unable to stop myself from poking fun at him. "A good thing too because we will need it to figure out this dynamic. I'm in a bit over my head here."

"Guess I'll have to talk to mom sooner rather than later to let her know there has been a change of plans." Reed looked around, surveying the land around us. "Where are you all living?"

Drystan froze around me as I just blinked slowly. "Currently, wherever we are living at the moment."

Reed's brow furrowed. "You all haven't figured that out?"

"It's been a long week or so, cousin," Leif came to my defense, his voice soft but firm.

"You've mated with all these people in that short amount of time?!" Reed threw his hands up, amusement still clear on his face. "Okay, I see why it hasn't been figured out yet. Leif, I'll just stay at your place until things are figured out."

"I never invited you to stay that long at my place," Leif grumbled.

Reed just nudged him with a shoulder. "How smart of me to not ask. Don't get scared of Leify over here, Ella, he has always been a grump."

"Leify?" Drystan asked, voice strained as if he was holding back laughter and was about to burst.

Leif, for his part, glared at his cousin though I didn't sense any heat behind it. "I'm cutting your pay."

"How convenient. I charged you more because you're family," Reed sassed back, wiggling his eyebrows as he dodged Leif reaching out to smack him.

A giggle slipped out as I saw another side of the intimidating alpha fae as he and his cousin mock fought. Drystan squeezed me tight before letting me go.

"I need to get back to the cafe. If you change your mind about the job just let me know."

"Thanks." I smiled at him and he kissed me once more before hurrying back across the street.

Leif and Reed were still joking around and I couldn't help the grin that filled my face. It was like I was watching a whole new person as Leif tumbled around with Reed. I thought about sticking around to talk with Reed a bit longer but he was in the middle of a job. I called out that I would see him later and that Leif knew where to find me. Reed winked at me, waving as I walked out of the park area as I forced my mind from my new mate to finding a job. The fact he let me walk away so easily was a good sign. We needed a bit of balance in this group and his laid-back attitude was perfect for that.

Where could I look now?

I walked around town, even checking out Kinkubus despite it being a joke, and found nowhere needed help. A sigh escaped me as I settled on the library steps. What was I going to do? Violet's offer crossed my mind, but I pushed it away. I didn't want to clean rooms, not that there was anything wrong with it, but I didn't know *how* to clean. That was a conversation I didn't really want to have any time soon. A seed of doubt crept into my mind. How could I be with all these put-together people when I didn't even know the basics of being an adult? Hell, I couldn't even find a damn job.

"Ella?" a deep voice called and I smiled as the smell of crisp, cold snow surrounded me as Maddox settled down beside me on the steps. I hadn't seen much of him since we mated, but his moon was clearly displayed on his arm as he placed a hand on my knee. He had muscle on top of muscle with the hint of his natural gray skin tone coming through the glamour as he stared at me, meeting my smile with one of his own. He had on loose dark blue jeans, a Lovecraft T-shirt, and black boots and it suited him.

"Hey." My voice was breathless enough that I felt my blush all the way down my neck. *Damn hormones.*

"That sigh was heavy," he commented, thankfully not teasing me about my tone. "What's wrong?"

I let out another sigh, this time making it extra dramatic as I leaned over and snuggled into his side not bothering to hide as I inhaled his scent deeply. His strong arms squeezed me before picking me up and situating me to sit sideways on his lap. The fact they instinctively knew when I needed this was amazing. It helped me make sense of my tumultuous thoughts. "I'm trying to find a job. I'm running low on the cash I brought with me and nowhere needs help. I asked a few people, but it seems everyone is good now that tourist season is over."

Maddox hummed, the sound gravelly in his chest as he began to rub my back. "A job? What are you looking for?"

"Something that pays?" I half-joked as I shrugged. "I just— I want something that's mine and to find my place here. And just being mated to half the damn town doesn't count. Plus, I don't want a pity job or one that doesn't fit me, you know?"

Maddox cleared his throat and I pulled back to see he was fighting a smile, but his silver eyes were bright with laughter at my statement. "That's fair. Half the town, huh?"

"I just got another one," I mumbled, running my hands up his arms, unable to keep my hands to myself around him. He blushed a bit but didn't complain or move away. My gargoyle seemed to love touch as much as I did.

"Just one more to go then," Maddox rasped, pulling me flush against his chest. We leaned into each other at the same time, completely in sync. He took control of the kiss, his tongue gliding along mine as I whimpered at the taste of him. His answering groan made my toes curl and I nipped at his bottom lip before breaking away from him.

"One more," I confirmed softly. "Which means more than anything I need something that's normal and not mate related."

Maddox cleared his throat, lips swollen from our kiss and his cheeks just as flushed as my own. "I have an idea." Not waiting for my response he stood up, holding me close to his chest even as I let out a surprised gasp and threw my arms around his neck not wanting to be dropped. He grinned, walking us inside.

"Ella, you're back!" Jonah called out cheerfully.

"Are you sure Maddox is the one you want, Ella? There are so many other options," one of the other brothers joked, making Maddox growl in warning as I laughed, burying my face against his neck.

Maddox walked through the hallway he had led me down the last time I was here. In the lounge was Sterling, blond hair bright in the reflection of the fire as he stared at us behind his round glasses.

"Little sister," he greeted me warmly as Maddox finally set me on my feet. "How was dinner?"

"Good." I smiled at the gargoyle who already felt like the big brother I always wanted. "Thanks for helping me get there."

"Of course." He smiled warmly at me before focusing on Maddox. "What's on your mind?"

"Ella wants a job of her own," Maddox stated firmly.

"Do you now?" Sterling cocked an eyebrow, scrutinizing me. I opened my mouth to say I would continue looking, catching onto what Maddox was hinting at. But Sterling beat me to it, "Let me talk to Ella."

Maddox stood still for a minute staring at his brother before his alpha side bowed to the will of his older brother. He bent down and pressed a kiss to the top of my head murmuring to find him before I went back to the inn. I nodded before he turned on his heel and left. It was an interesting dynamic, Sterling and Maddox were both alphas but the deference to Sterling was unquestioned. Sterling was the head of this family and the fact Maddox brought me here showed just how much I was embraced by this group.

"What kind of job are you looking for? Or did my baby brother not ask you that much before carrying you in here?"

A breathless laugh escaped me as I flopped down on the seat across from where he sat on the couch. "He did ask, actually. And I don't know." I shrugged self-consciously. "I've never had a job before but I need money and something that's mine. Walking around town and seeing no one needs help made me realize everyone has their place here. And I want that too."

"You feel like you don't?" Sterling asked gently, propping his chin on his hand as he thought over what I said. I didn't answer that question, my silence was answer enough it seems as Sterling clicked his tongue.

"This is a family run library and has been that way since this town was founded," Sterling spoke gently. "Not all of our family is here, some ventured out of Mystic Harbor for many different reasons. But we all have a claim to this library in some way."

"I love that," I whispered, somehow feeling the loss of something I never really had at the picture he painted.

"You're family now, Ella," Sterling pointed out. "We can find something for you here and you don't have to worry about working for Maddox. You'd be working for *me*. I am the head of this family, which is something you seemed to naturally realize given you asked me for help the other day." Sterling stood up, walking over to hold a hand to me to help me up. "You didn't just get a mate with Maddox, Ella, you got a family. We can work out some of the details later but I saw your face the first day you walked into this place, you'll fit in perfectly."

Tears pricked my eyes and I didn't bother to hide them as I placed a shaky hand in his. "I've always wanted brothers."

Sterling laughed, silver eyes dancing with amusement as he pulled me to standing. "I'll remind you of that when Jonah has another hair-brained idea for a lawn ornament reenactment."

I grinned at him, wiping at my eyes as he led me out of the lounge. "I have some ideas for the next one actually."

He shot me a mock frown which just made me giggle. "Noted, you and Jonah can't work together."

"Don't be that way, Sterling!" Jonah called out as we stepped into the main room. "Ella and I would work perfectly together."

"That would be the issue," Sterling rebuked dryly as he motioned for me to keep following him further into the library. "I have a few ideas of things you can do."

Maddox sent me a huge smile as we passed him and I felt at home in a way I never knew I needed. I didn't want to work with a mate, needing something that was wholly mine, but the prospect of working with all of the gargoyles, around books... It was almost too good to be true. But as the laughter of the brothers filled the air and Sterling started talking about the hours and things I would be helping with I felt completely at ease and at home with them. What should have been an overwhelming moment and conversation felt like second nature, like I instinctively knew this was right.

Maddox had mentioned finding him before I left and I knew Reed would track me down tonight or tomorrow, not to mention the others constantly checking in. My new family was almost complete... Now I just had one more mate to find and my newfound magic to control. Things were finally falling into place.

What could go wrong?

CHAPTER 18

Ella

The streets of Mystic Harbor were silent as I stalked across town. Birdie had insisted on meeting for dinner this time, the sun already falling into the horizon. If any of my alphas knew I was out here alone they'd have a few choice words for me, but for once, I was just enjoying the evening walk in silence. Mystic Harbor was getting ever more familiar to me, this walk even more so since I'd done it several times in the last week or so.

This was the first night I had been mate free in days. Between Drystan claiming breakfast with me most mornings, working days at the library, and then nights with the others, I barely had time to myself these days. That wasn't a complaint, I loved not being lonely anymore, and I'd even seen Reed a few times, usually he came and joined me for lunch at the library since Maddox and him were apparently friends. I felt at ease, comfortable for the first time in ages, but something was still missing. My last fated mate seemed to be MIA and I had no idea how to find them. My magic sometimes flared out at the library and it even happened a few times during sex, which was an embarrassment I didn't want to relive. Birdie had finally reached out and let me know she could help me balance out my magic until I found the last person, but she didn't share many details of *how* she was going to do that.

Birdie's house stood out among the evening light, brightly lit windows and a sparkling, purple smoke coming from the backyard. The sound of music echoed from the open windows and I could already smell a mix of herbs and flowers burning in what I assumed was a spell of some kind. Birdie was truly a witch guru. She dabbled in a bit from all aspects of witchcraft, from spells, charms, herbs, illusions, to shows of power. It was impressive.

"Get your butt in here, girl," Birdie called out impatiently from the now open front door. "This has a few more minutes before it's ruined." She turned and didn't wait so I rushed into the house, closing the door behind me before seeking her out. The back door was also open and the kitchen was in complete disarray, a mix of dried herbs and what looked like actual food loaded on the counters. She took eccentricity to the next level and damn I loved her for that.

"What are you—" My question was waved off and she motioned for me to be quiet before she led me outside.

The fire shifted in a kaleidoscope of colors, the smoke above it switching rapidly with whichever color burned below. It was mesmerizing, but so was she. Birdie stood proud in a flowing black dress. Her hair hung in long loose white waves and her arms were thrown wide as she chanted into the night.

Her words started as an even murmur, the language one I didn't recognize but it was beautiful and melodic. Slowly, she reached a crescendo, the words strong and bold as she practically screamed them into the night. I had a brief thought of her neighbors and their opinion on these rituals but that was forgotten when she finished, one final word punctuating her spell. The fire went out with a pop and I felt a shock wave of magic slam into me, pushing me back on my ass. Birdie stood through it but I was too stunned to question what the hell was going on.

My chest flared with heat from the spot the magic slammed into me, before going straight to my sternum. Panic started to set in and I glanced frantically up to my mentor who looked calm and collected as she stared back.

"Breathe, child. It's fine. I wouldn't curse you, that's too much work and bad for my karma," she protested. A startled laugh escaped but it was cut off as a calm seemed to settle over me. My mind slowed, my body relaxed, and it felt like the next breath was my first in ages.

The next few moments I took stock, making sure the magic was done before getting up and brushing the dirt off of me. I raised an eyebrow in silent question at a now smug Birdie but she was already bustling past me.

"Just a bit of balancing magic, my girl, now get in here and help me finish. We have guests tonight!"

"Who?" I asked as I rushed after her. She started cleaning up her herbs and I'd seen her do it enough to help. She didn't answer me until we were done and I knew better than to push it. Birdie was a woman who did things on her own terms and in her own time.

"My son and grandson. He doesn't like to be in Mystic Harbor for too long, but they always come for the festival, and with me training you, I asked them to come a week early. Remember I mentioned them the last time you were here? He's willing to help train you over the next few days if you have the extra time. I heard you got a new job."

"How the heck did you hear that?" I asked in shock. "It just happened a few days ago."

"You really have to ask that?" she asked with a smirk. I laughed and rolled my eyes but didn't bother to question further. Birdie knew pretty much everything that happened in town.

"Fair enough," I started, but was cut off by a knock at the door.

"Go answer that," she ordered me. I turned and walked through the living room and put a smile in place before opening the door. The man standing there glanced down at me and a flicker of shock and something I couldn't read filled his face, his smile disappeared and he gasped as he stood there frozen.

"Haven?" he whispered, then firmly shook his head. "No, you can't be."

"Who is Haven?" I furrowed my brows, confused as the older man continued to stare at me.

"What is the matter out here? Why is the door still open?" Birdie barked out, coming in then taking in the obvious tension. For the first time, I watched a worried frown take over her aged face. "Dean? What's wrong?"

"Mom, she looks just like *her*." Birdie didn't question who 'her' was, instead, helping her son to the couch. A younger man followed him in, this one closer to my age give or take a few years. He was handsome and something about him held a familiarity I couldn't explain. Both men were obviously related, dark hair, intense vivid blue eyes. Dean's face, though older, held his age well. He was also handsome, with sharp features and a kind smile before I'd somehow ruined that. *These two must be Birdie's son and grandson.*

"I look like who?" I finally asked after he'd had a minute or two to compose himself. "Who is Haven?"

"How old are you?" The random question caught me by surprise and the answer fell out of my mouth before I could stop it. My brain seriously broke in awkward situations and this one was *really* awkward.

"Twenty-one," I hedged. "Why?"

"No," Birdie said, her voice uncharacteristically somber. "You think?"

"Seriously, Mom?" he threw back at her, hands flying up in exasperation. His voice was sharp but the animosity wasn't intended for her and she didn't seem to take offense.

"Dad, what the hell is going on?" the younger man asked as he glanced back and forth between us. He looked just as lost as I did but I was tired of being ignored.

"I'm going to walk out if someone doesn't start talking," I warned. Birdie gave me a small smile and turned to her son.

"Tell her." The command was there and he swallowed hard. It was like he was fighting with a ghost or something, he looked sickly now, skin pale and body covered in a sheen of sweat.

"This'll be easier." He sighed, pulling out his wallet. He reached into the back for a photo before handing it over. My jaw dropped as I looked down at my doppelganger. It was obviously not me, the clothes aged and the feathered hair a dead giveaway, but she had my smile, my eyes, fuck, my hair even. We could have been twins.

"Who is this?" I asked, nearly missing the chair as I

tried to sit without looking away from the picture in my hands. *What the hell is going on right now?*

"Brooks," Dean barked and the younger man reached out to stop me before I fell. At least I had a name now, though I was riddled with confusion.

"Thank fuck for that spell, Birdie," I muttered as Brooks helped me sit on the chair. The old woman cackled and stood.

"It felt like it was needed, now we know why. Now keep talking, Dean."

Dean rubbed a hand over his face, pain clearly etched on there as I looked between him, Birdie, and then Brooks trying to figure out what was going on. Brooks sat down in a chair near mine and he looked just as confused as I did.

"I don't know where to start," the older man mumbled.

"The beginning is always a good choice," Birdie chimed in making Dean glare at his mother as Brooks suspiciously coughed.

"Who is this?" I repeated my question as I returned my gaze to the old picture in my hand.

"I met her years ago. Her name was Haven." A sad smile flickered across Dean's face before he searched my face as if he could find answers there. "Twenty-two years ago, in fact."

"What my not so eloquent and slow son is trying to say is that this woman in the photo," Birdie cut her son off, pointing at the photo in my hand. "I don't know how I missed it, I blame old age. Either way, she was his first love. Disappeared one day and he never heard from her again."

"My parents look nothing like her," I countered, my confusion growing. "I don't have a photo, but they're both brunettes and older. I'm sorry... I don't follow what you're trying to say."

"We were supposed to make a plan to get her away from her crazy family and then poof, she was gone. She took my heart with her to be honest. It took a long time to recover from that, the only exception was Brooks' mom who was equally as wonderful," he said, clapping his son on the back. Brooks gave a weak smile, but seemed to be fighting his own demons as they both focused on me again. "But there's no way she's not your mother, there are just too many similarities. You're her spitting image."

"Dad," Brooks tilted his head as he scrutinized me. It was intense enough I leaned away from him, my heart pounding in my chest. "She looks a bit like you. Is there any chance—"

Dean blinked at his son and focused on me. My anxiety was rising as my vision tunneled and my heart rate increased. Dean and I stared at each other and I saw small things like a similar nose, skin tone, and just something I couldn't quite put into words that reminded me of my own reflection. *What— What was this?*

"You have my nose and skin tone." Now that he said it, I couldn't unsee it. My chest tightened, the need to flee strong but I needed answers more than I needed to run away from this. The stress of the moment made my magic flare. Sparks filled the room making all of us duck. Dean and Brooks stared at me, eyes wide as my magic built up, undeterred by Birdie's earlier spell.

"Ella," Birdie's voice was calm as she held her hands. "You need to take deep breaths. Calm yourself, child."

"Calm?!" I rasped, my voice breaking as the sparks increased around us. "I don't believe you or any of this."

"Ella—" Dean reached for me, but I flinched back from him.

"Don't touch me!"

"Kitchen. Now," Birdie ordered, breaking through the thick silence. We all stood at her alpha command, going to the table and finding our spots, though I hung back picking the seat not beside Dean. She brought over a stew of some kind along with some rolls and an herbed butter. No one moved as she loaded bowls, growing more impatient by the second. "Oh, enough of this. Ella, it's too strong to be merely a coincidence, child. Even you have to admit that much."

"Then who raised me? Where is she? Because this isn't my mom." I challenged her, not willing to just believe this man I'd never met before. I wish my mates were here, any or all of them if I was honest with myself. "I've never seen *her* before in my life." To prove it, I pulled up my father's business site on my phone and clicked around until I found a photo of my parents. "See, *they* are my parents. He always said I had his eyes and he wasn't wrong."

"Haven's parents died young," Dean countered softly, staring at the photo I held up to him. "Her older brother was her guardian. We were just kids back then, so he tried to keep us apart, to control her life. But that's him right there."

My heart sunk and my whole world crashed around me. This couldn't be real, this couldn't be happening. In a sick, twisted way I was relieved, but in another, I refused to see it for the truth. Why would he treat me that way? Where was she then? Why had I never heard of her if that was the case? None of it made sense.

"No," I started, but he cut me off by laying a hand on my own shaking one.

"I'm sorry. But I think you're my daughter," he said gently. My watery eyes raised to meet his, before flickering to Brooks. He looked a bit lost, but almost hopeful. I didn't have the mental capacity to figure it out though. "The timeline fits, though she never hinted that she was pregnant she did say she had big news before we left the night we were supposed to meet up."

"How—"

"Stop, Ella." Birdie cut me off, as they seemed to love to do. "Just mull it over and breathe, you look close to passing out," she urged. "We have ways to test for family bonds, we can do that when you're ready, okay?" I blinked back tears and nodded, not tearing my eyes away from my untouched food. She was right though, my head was spinning. "Then we can all know for sure and then get down to business of helping you."

"Yeah." I roughly cleared my throat. "Yeah, I think that would be for the best. I just— This is a lot."

"We understand that." Birdie patted my shoulder and it took everything in me to not pull away from her touch. Overwhelmed wasn't a strong enough word for what I felt right now. I needed space. I needed to not be around anyone to get my thoughts in order.

I had to leave.

Right now.

"I'm not running away," I started, only looking at Birdie as I stood up from the table. "But I have to get some air. Alone. Alright? I need... time." My eyes begged her to agree, though I'd probably go anyway if she disagreed. She nodded once, sympathy in her gaze but I didn't want it. Not right now.

Without another word I got up and practically ran through the house, going out the front door. I didn't bother to see where I was going, heading for the woods as opposed to the town itself. My mind was too far gone to consider if I'd get lost or not, I just needed distance and needed to process.

My parents aren't my parents.

They tortured me and I wasn't even theirs.

I have a dad... and maybe a mom somewhere?

Each new mindfuck sent me into a spiral of more questions I had no answers for. But the more distance my feet put between me and them, the more I realized it made sense. The resemblances to my parents were minimal, they always had been beside my blue eyes. But she looked just like me, and Dean did have my nose, the shape of it too unique to not notice.

The real issue was, what did it mean for me now? Why did they do this? Because even if I wasn't their daughter, if what Dean said was true, I was their niece.

Though I knew those questions wouldn't get answered. At least, not unless I wanted to go back, to confront them, and I was happy to never make that happen. This was my life and home now and if Dean truly was my dad, then this was exactly the fresh start I needed. Maybe I'd get the full package for a brand new family, not just those from my fated mates.

It was then that I glanced around, the forest almost opaque around me as no light slipped in. Somehow my instincts guided me with the little help from bits of moonlight spilling in here and there. I had no clue where I was and I had zero idea of the time. How long had I been walking? Then there was a tug in my gut, subtle at first then amplifying when I didn't move.

"You're already this far in," I told myself, taking a deep breath and walking further down the path. Now that I was aware I put my hands out, unable to see branches or anything else coming into view until it was too late.

After another ten minutes the trees cleared and I reached a gravel lined road. An old wrought iron gate cut across and I glanced up, taking in the building behind it in shock. The building was what looked like an old barn, the wood worn and weathered in a small clearing. It didn't look inhabited but the feeling pulling at me urged me to approach. The windows looked original and old, the glass warped and in the old frames. Overgrown bushes surrounded the building, but the side door was mysteriously cleared. I swallowed hard and opened the door, unable to stop myself even if I wanted to.

I walked inside and instantly the place lit up. There was a huge stone fireplace on the far wall, fire blazing in the humongous hearth. There were a few brown leather couches, plants hanging everywhere with an industrial style kitchen that looked brand new. Cautiously, I called out to see if anyone was home but the place was empty. The barn turned home was beautiful, huge, and something I would love if I could design my own place. This place felt warm, comforting as if I had arrived... home. It's how I felt the moment I heard about Mystic Harbor.

There was an entire wall of windows offering up a breathtaking view. The barn was right near a cliff, overlooking the ocean waves crashing into the rocks below. I looked over trying to figure out where the town was and was shocked to find the lights far away. *Just how far did I walk?!*

Right then my phone started vibrating in my back

pocket. Reaching for it I was surprised to find text after text coming in along with a few voicemails. I bit my lip realizing that there must have been no signal in the woods and according to my phone I had been walking around in the woods for two hours. I was never going to hear the end of this from my mates... I think even Reed and Spencer would have some choice words for me.

A particularly panicked message from Violet caught my eye and just as I was about to call her and let her know I was fine the door to the barn opened. Whirling around I was shocked to find none other than Leif standing there, confusion and shock clear on his face. From the house or finding me here, I wasn't sure.

"Oh! I didn't know this was your—" I stumbled over my words as I felt my cheeks heat with embarrassment and a touch of fear.

"Ella." He shook his head, emerald green eyes now bright with relief. "This isn't my place. Actually, this is the first time I've seen it in my life. But that's not important right now, are you okay?"

I blinked, searching his face as he hurried past the furniture to stand in front of me. "Yes? I mean, yeah, I'm fine. Birdie's was... things happened. I just needed some time to think."

"Time?" Leif half smiled as he looked me over. "It's been over two hours and there is already a search party out since no one could reach you."

A groan slipped out of me as I dropped down to sit in a nearby armchair that was situated by the wall of windows. My phone clattered to the ground but I ignored it as I looked up apologetically to Leif. "I just got all the notifications. There must have been no signal in the woods. And I don't know how I'd walked that long, it felt like fifteen minutes."

"Mystic Harbor works in mysterious ways," he said ominously.

"Apparently."

Leif hummed thoughtfully as he pulled out his phone and typed out a quick message to someone before slipping it back into his jeans. I started just now realizing that he wasn't in his usual slacks and button-up that I had seen him in so far. Instead, the fae alpha was standing there in jeans, a forest green sweater, and sneakers. Warm cinnamon surrounded me as he bent over and grabbed my phone for me.

"I messaged Hunter to let him know I had found you. He will let everyone else know that you're fine, but I'm sure they are going to be waiting for us to get back to town." He held out my phone and I reached out to take it, my fingers brushing his as our gazes locked.

The world seemed to stop spinning, holding its breath as fiery pain stung my skin and a purple haze surrounded us. The glamour seemed to be ripped away from the fae alpha in front of me, showing me the full iridescent glow of his light skin, pointy ears, and the flecks of gold in his beautiful eyes. He stared at me wide-eyed, a flush on his cheeks as he remained frozen, staring at me then down to his arm where a new moon marking similar to Tanniv's was now etched on his skin.

"Ella?" he whispered my name roughly, making me quiver with need. "Is this what you want?"

"What?" My shock made me break an essential fae rule, I asked him a direct question. "What do you mean?"

"You've been nervous and anxious of me since the moment you stepped off that bus." He licked his lips, his entire body tense as I studied him. "Barely interacting with me... I just want to make sure this is what you want."

"We are fated mates," I pointed out to him.

"That doesn't mean I'll force you." He watched me cautiously as I stepped closer to him and I saw him inhale deeply, savoring my scent.

"I appreciate that," I murmured, reaching out and running my hands over his chest unwilling to not be this close and not touch him. "But I want this."

His face filled with shock, uncertainty clear. "Then why—"

"You're fae," I answered simply, shrugging even as he captured my hands with his own and pulled me closer to him.

He left an inch between us, looking down at my upturned face. "That wasn't an issue with Reed."

"I knew Reed when I was a child," I whispered and smiled ruefully. "His mother taught me all kinds of fae etiquette, along with the need to always remember it."

A rough laugh escaped him as he released my hands to cup my face. "You were so nervous and formal around me because of all those rules my aunt taught you? Well, she did a good job, Ella, but I would really appreciate it if you ignored them from now on."

Before I could form a reply he leaned down, slanting his lips over mine in a searing kiss. I gasped and he took that as an invitation, flicking his tongue against mine as I reached up, wrapping my arms around his neck. I'd found my final fated mate, the fae alpha who I met first was the last person to claim me. A part of me that had always felt empty now was full, an inexplicable feeling of calm rushed over me. We lost ourselves in each other as the heat between us built, the purple mist of magic still lingering around us. We broke apart, our rough breathing the only sound in the empty house.

"I like you better like this." I reached up, tracing a finger along his pointed ear. "The glamours are always so disconcerting. To see double of everyone around me... This suits you better."

"Glad you think so," he growled softly, picking me up suddenly. My body felt like it was on fire against his, desire filled me as I saw his lust-hazed eyes. "If you want to just leave, say so now, Ella. Or we aren't leaving here until every fucking inch of you is mine."

My lips parted, so turned on I felt slick on my thighs and my nipples harden under my shirt. "I want you, Leif. Please."

A rumble vibrated in his chest as he hurried us through the barn and up the stairs to a bedroom with a huge bed. It was big enough I swore that the two of us and the rest of my mates could have slept here and still had room. I expected Leif to toss me onto the bed and get down to it, but he surprised me. He laid me gently on the bed but didn't let go of me. Covering my body with his own he kissed me again, soft and commanding enough that I whimpered as my body arched up into his.

I needed more.

I needed his skin against mine.

As if he could read my mind, Leif pulled back and pulled his sweater over his head to reveal a willowy body with lean muscles. His long fingers pulled at my own clothing until we were both naked against each other. When I tried to kiss him again he pulled away with a playful smile, pushing me gently down on the bed as he kissed his way down my body. Teasing kisses and light bite marks until he pushed my legs apart.

I cried out his name as he swiped his tongue down my center. Quick and light swipes of his tongue were combined with long, slow licks as if he was savoring every drop of my slick. Leif settled in as he sucked my clit into his mouth making my hips jerk against him. My climax was building and I urgently moved against him until he thrust two fingers inside of me making my orgasm crash over me. His name was a harsh cry as my body tensed around him, my thighs tight around his head.

He flipped us so he was on his back with me straddling his face. I reached out, bracing myself on the bed as I looked down at him. Green eyes were mischievous as he met my gaze as he circled his tongue lightly around my clit before pulling back slightly.

"Ride my face, Ella. You aren't ready to take me yet. You made me wait to be your last mate, let's make it worth the wait."

"Leif," I groaned as he licked me again. "I can't—"

"Ella." He gripped my hips tightly. "I want your arousal all over my face, our scents so intertwined that there will be no mistake who we are to each other. I want to wake up tomorrow still tasting you on my fucking lips. So you're going to ride my face until you come so much you can't even speak. Only then will I flip you over and claim you completely, thrusting my cock so far inside of you that you won't remember what it was like without my knot holding you captive."

I cried out, a rush of slick making my arousal impossible to hide as I sat up straight. Slowly, I rolled my hips, riding his face as I felt him start to fuck me with his tongue. Hard hands reached up to cup my small breasts, squeezing and pulling at my nipples until I started riding his face in earnest. When I came the second time I fell completely into it, not letting my self-consciousness ruin the moment as my thighs tightened against him and I ground against his face. Leif didn't complain, if anything his hands got rougher, urging me for more until I came a third and fourth time. The fourth time tears stung my eyes and I flopped to the side as I tried to get away from the overload of sensations.

"Leif," I whimpered, as he pushed my legs further apart.

"You are a fucking goddess, Ella. I could feast on you every damn day and I plan on doing that every day from now on." He slid easily inside of me, bottoming out in one smooth thrust as my back arched. He was so big and thick that even with four orgasms my pussy clenched around him as my legs shook.

He pulled back to thrust back inside slowly, a smooth rhythm taking over as he staked a final claim on me. Every movement ripped away the last of the walls I had up around my heart and between us. I could feel my magic growing and filling me until it looked like my skin was glowing next to his iridescent one. I could feel a fifth orgasm building but I needed more. I needed him. Reaching up I gripped the back of his neck and pulled him down, kissing him and nipping his bottom lip before sucking his tongue into my mouth. His rhythm faltered as I staked my own claim. The taste of myself on his lips made me more aroused and I met him thrust for thrust until he completely lost control and pounded into me. His knot was starting to swell, the slight change just enough to make it almost too much, yet not enough still.

Without breaking the kiss I grunted in almost pain as I came again, his knot swelling and stretching me to my limits. Leif swore, moaning against my lips as he slammed into me once, twice, then I felt him coming inside of me. We fell back onto the bed, not able to move another inch.

"I hope you don't expect me to walk anywhere anytime soon," I rasped. "I don't think I have any bones left in my body."

"You couldn't if you wanted to," he reminded me, grinding his hips into mine, his knot delicious torture that I couldn't escape. My body was on fire, sensitive, and yet he had my pussy quivering like I couldn't get enough.

"You're going to kill me," I whined, my legs wrapping tightly around him to force him to stop torturing me.

A masculine laugh met that statement as he stilled, our eyes locking together. Nothing was said, but it felt like a lifetime passed in mere moments. It was crazy to not know him, yet feel like our souls have known each other forever.

Slowly, his knot went down until he could pull out of me. He didn't leave me though, instead, he laid down beside me. I turned over slightly, cuddling into him and throwing a leg over his to get as close as I possibly could. Leif didn't say anything, just ran his hands over my skin as if he could drink me in by touch alone.

We were silent for so long I had started to drift off when I felt his fingers move around to my sternum. "Your marking is beautiful."

I blinked down at the marking under my breasts. All the phases of the moon under a few decorative swirls. Eight mates. I had eight *fated* mates. My magic felt different but part of it still seemed out of reach, like an essential part of it was missing. But I let that thought go as I heard voices outside.

Panic should have filled me but the voices were

familiar and I just looked at Leif with a soft smile. "Looks like we have company."

"Good thing they're your mates or I'd be really upset," he complained as ran his hands along my sides, not letting me move away from him.

"My clothes are on the ground," I tried to explain as I attempted to move away from him again.

"I'm well aware, I did put them there." Leif smiled as he nipped the top of my breast. "I meant what I said, I want them all to know. So I don't give a shit what they think, they're going to see us here, naked with my cum filling you up and my love bites all over your skin."

"Leif," I breathed.

"You like that," he taunted me softly, running his fingers along my sore pussy. "Good, because they are almost here."

As if he spoke them into existence, my mates burst into the room. Drystan was in the lead, his gaze falling on us before his eyes narrowed.

"You did this on purpose," he growled. The accusation was mellowed by the heat in his tone, eyes trailing over me slowly to take in every mark and I swear I saw his breath catch when it reached my dripping pussy. *Seems like I have more than a few kinky mates.*

"Oh shit," Maddox said, clapping a hand over his eyes. Even with his large hand blocking my view, I could see how red his face was.

"Guys, get out of there, give them privacy, we can talk in the morning," Hunter barked out, his alpha command had my frazzled mates following his lead and leaving us alone. Though I did hear Asra and Tanniv yell out a few points to Leif who just rolled his eyes at their antics as the door closed behind them.

"You're ridiculous," I told Leif with a laugh. He grinned and nibbled at my neck.

"Guilty. But you've been torturing me for weeks unknowingly," he protested. When I opened my mouth to speak he claimed my lips in a kiss. In the back of my mind, I almost felt bad that my other mates were waiting for an explanation, but here in Leif's arms, with his hands on my body, I didn't care.

CHAPTER 19

Ella

The sun streaming through the windows was bright enough that it woke me up. I expected to be sore, but as I stretched my body I realized I felt amazing and even energized. I also noticed that I was alone in the bed.

A small smile crept across my face as I thought about last night and how amazing it was. Leif definitely made up for lost time. A surge of slick had me groaning and I forced myself to get up and out of bed and to the shower before I had to seek out one of my mates for relief. No need setting off a heat just thinking of the man... I don't think he would let any of the others forget it.

It seemed this truly was the house that kept on giving because I found an amazing bathroom attached. The walls and floor were inlaid with stone. A row of shower-heads lined one wall and on the ceiling. Just out of reach of the water was a stone basin sink and a toilet. There was even a row of folded towels on a small shelf in the corner.

All too aware of how gross I was, I turned on the spray and adjusted the temp, stepping into the heavenly rainfall.

Glancing around, I found some generic body wash, shampoo, and conditioner. It smelled like coconut and shea butter and I quickly cleaned myself. Just as I was rinsing out the conditioner, I heard my name echoing through the house. Turning off the spray, I grabbed a towel from the shelf and wrapped it around myself. I did a quick finger brush of my hair before stepping out of the shower. I didn't exactly want to put on dirty clothes, so I tightened the towel and made my way back to the main room.

"Why are you naked still?" Maddox groaned, like he just couldn't take it. The amusement in his voice was roughened by lust. Though I was hardly naked.

"She's in a towel, alpha. Can't handle it?" Reed teased. They were sitting on the large couch, some trash show on the TV.

"I can," he shot back, glaring at the cheeky omega.

"I can take it off if you want?" I offered innocently. Reed burst into laughter and turned toward me, propping his hand under his chin to make a show of giving me his full attention.

"Not if you want me to stay over here," Maddox said. I appreciated his attempt at bravado but I could tell it made him nervous. He must not have had a ton of experience, something before this week I could sympathize with. Just for that, I decided to not tease him further, at least for the moment.

"Where are the others?" I asked, changing the subject.

"Leif got called into town but he said he'd hurry back.

Drystan had to go close the shop for the day. The twins went to get their things and Hunter and Spencer went for supplies. Everyone agreed we should spend the weekend together. Especially since this week will get crazy as we prepare for the festival. Things always get hectic then," Maddox explained.

"That makes sense. I'll need clothes too," I mused. But Reed was already standing and coming toward me with a wolfish grin on his face.

"I don't see why," he laughed, hands toying with the edge of my towel. Just like that a surge of slick hit me as lust filled me. The strong scent of my omega mate wrapped around me and I wanted nothing more than to let him fuck me, right here in front of the fireplace. There was no shyness left in me, in fact, the thought of my other mates watching us had me letting out a small whimper. Reed didn't miss the change in me, his cheeks red and pale blue eyes filled with arousal as he licked his lips. He glanced over at Maddox, a hopeful tone in his voice as he called out to him, "Come on alpha, we have her to ourselves. We should probably take advantage."

"But I..." Maddox trailed off, a bit of panic in his tone. Before I could reassure him, Reed's teasing dropped away.

"It's okay, I'll help," Reed promised. "We can torture and pleasure her together." That had Maddox's eyebrows raising, but he didn't seem opposed and that had me letting out another moan, too turned on at the thought of the two of them fucking me to hold it back. "See, she likes that idea."

"You do?" Maddox asked, standing slowly but his eyes were locked on me. I nodded, pleading with my eyes for him to give me relief.

"Yes," I whispered. And that was all it took for Maddox to come over. The scent of crisp snow and earthy tones contrasted one another, yet somehow worked perfectly together. Reed reached out to take Maddox's hand and pull him closer, both of them gasping and looking down at their wrists. Just below the moon phases was an open book with flowers growing out of it, tying them together as fated mates as well. I thought it was odd when I found Reed as an omega mating an omega, it was nearly unheard of. Now we knew why. "Oh my gods."

"Well, I guess this worked out perfectly then," Reed joked, but his humor was still mixed with shock.

"Mads, you okay?" I asked softly. I reached out instinctively, pulling him close. With all of us touching it was as if our emotions amped up. Maddox's insecurity and shock fell away and his eyes locked on mine. He leaned forward, the kiss far more dominating than I expected from him. Just as quickly as he claimed my lips, he pulled away and turned to Reed. He hesitated, just for a moment, but Reed was having none of it.

"Nah, alpha. You're mine too," he warned, wrapping his hand around Maddox's neck and pulling him down. Watching them kiss was sexier than I could have anticipated, sharp jawlines, muscles, and strong and lean bodies melding together.

"Fuck, that's hot," I whispered accidentally. I hadn't meant to ruin their moment, but I couldn't stop it. They both chuckled, pulling away from each other and turning their gaze on me.

"I think our alpha needs to hear your screams of pleasure, Ella. Come here," Reed urged, taking my hand and leading me to the plush rug in front of the fire. It was silky and soft under my feet and the perfect temperature. He unwrapped the towel and let it fall to the floor before moving in like a wolf stalking its prey. His lips crashed into mine, the kiss bruising and demanding. He guided us to the floor before pulling away. "Come on, alpha. Don't be shy now."

Maddox swallowed hard before stripping out of his clothes. I watched every inch of skin he exposed, his body hard and huge. My eyes widened as his boxers fell to the ground, exposing his very hard, and very large cock. Fuck, this one might hurt, but damn if I wasn't ready to find out.

"That's a monster cock," Reed echoed my thoughts, licking his lips. "Ella can wait." Without hesitation he crawled forward on his knees, wrapping his hand around our alpha's dick. Maddox groaned, one hand going to Reed's head as he leaned forward to tease him with his tongue. His gaze locked onto mine as our omega mate swallowed him down. My hand slowly trailed to my pussy, the need for relief so strong I teased myself as I watched Reed suck off Maddox. They both moaned as he picked up the pace, bobbing his head back and forth, Maddox's hand guiding his movements. Our omega seemed to lack a gag reflex, something Maddox certainly wasn't complaining about.

"Stop, unless you want me to knot that mouth," Maddox warned him. Reed pulled off of him with a smirk.

"Fine, but only because our mate here is feeling left out," he teased, giving me a wink. "But it seems she approved of the show." He leaned back to look at my dripping pussy with a nod of approval.

As I pulled my hand away from my clit, I realized how fucking wet I was. But he was right, I needed some relief.

"Can I taste you?" Maddox asked like a true gentleman. I spread my legs wide in invitation, definitely not about to turn that down. He settled between my thighs, hips shifted to the side to accommodate his hard cock. The first swipe of his tongue was tentative and unsure, then there was no hesitation as he pushed his tongue into my core. He groaned before eating me out like he'd never tasted anything so amazing. Long swipes of his tongue and torturous swirls around my clit had me grinding into him. Refusing to let Reed sit on the sidelines I let my mouth fall open and urged him forward.

"Damn, don't have to ask me twice," he said, moving in front of me and lining himself up. He was gentle as he pushed past my lips, setting a pace that had his head falling back. Since I couldn't move thanks to Maddox pinning me down with strong hands as he tongue fucked me, I hollowed my cheeks and teased Reed with my tongue each time he pulled back to thrust further into my throat.

My orgasm hit me hard and fast, legs tightening around Maddox's head as I gave Reed even more to make it through the onslaught of pleasure that was quaking through me. That was all it took for Reed to spill down my throat and I swallowed down every drop he gave me.

"Damn," he whispered as he pulled away, flopping onto the floor. Maddox also shifted, though only to his knees. "Fuck her first, then you can fuck me, alpha."

Maddox chuckled as he pulled away from my pussy. "Don't think you're going to give me orders forever, omega."

"I'll never be a silent, submissive omega. I've got too much snark for that." He laughed, though I could hear the warning and vulnerability in it.

"I do like a challenge," Maddox said, leaning over me to give Reed a reassuring kiss.

"Besides, you'll need all of that sass when it comes to his brothers," I tacked on, which made Reed and Maddox both laugh.

"Oh gods. I forgot about the brothers!" Reed exclaimed, falling back onto the rug beside me as he let out a dramatic groan.

Maddox shook his head at our antics at the same time he slammed his hips forward, taking me in one move. I cried out, the sting and stretch taking my breath away. He paused to let me adjust but I was too wet for it to take long and I wiggled my hips to get him to move.

Maddox didn't hold back, his movements purposeful as he lifted my hips slightly. Each snap of his hips let him fuck me deeper and I was soon matching him thrust for thrust. It was like I hadn't fucked in months, my omega starving for his knot.

"Fuck, Ella," he breathed out. "You're fucking perfect."

"Then make me come," I begged. He didn't hesitate to tease his fingers over my clit, following the sound of my moans until I was coming around him. His knot swelled in response. He was the biggest of my mates so far and it felt like I was being ripped apart for a moment, but as he started moving gently, it eased, giving way to pleasure. I was breathless and babbling as he came, shoving his knot as deep as he could and holding me to him, whispering breathless praise in my ear. My omega practically purred, being knotted to her alpha and fully sated.

He continued to slowly fuck me through the knot until it finally released me from his hold. We'd just turned to Reed when he threw my towel at me and Maddox's clothes at him.

"Our time is up, mates, but you can rain check this ass for later," he teased our gargoyle with a wink. Maddox choked out a laugh and hastily threw on his clothes. I had just wrapped the towel around me again when the door opened. We glanced over innocently but from Asra and Tanniv's smirks, they knew what we were up to.

"We swung by the bed and breakfast for some clothes for you. Violet picked them out, much to my annoyance." Asra sighed, but couldn't hide his grin.

"I think we interrupted things, brother," Tanniv joked as he shut the door behind them.

"No need to stop on our account." Asra tossed a bag, which I assume had my clothes in them, down on the couch. "We can be team players."

Maddox's cheeks were so red at this point I started to wonder if stone could catch on fire. Reed chuckled, tugging our mate up and dragging him down the hallway toward what I assume were other bedrooms.

"No audiences, sirens. We will meet up with you all later!"

Maddox stumbled after the swift fae and gasped his name before a door slammed shut. Well, it was no secret what they were going to be doing, so much for a rain check. I smiled and let out a small laugh as I sent good luck to Reed's ass because Mads' knot was intense.

"That is something I wasn't expecting," Asra commented lightly as he reached for me. "Always nice to still be surprised. Hello, beautiful."

He kissed me soundly, pulling me tight against him. I wrapped my arms around his neck, not caring as the towel fell to the ground again. Asra groaned as I nipped his bottom lip at the same time. Even more slick wet my thighs, ready to take the two alphas surrounding me as Tanniv came up behind me. I whimpered when Asra broke the kiss and started teasing my neck with small nibbles and Tanniv tilted my head back to claim my lips in a searing kiss. Was this weekend going to be all sex?

If it was I couldn't find it in myself to complain. I had found my mates and this was our oasis from the world. I whimpered into Tanniv's mouth as Asra tweaked my hard nipples. Tanniv pulled away long enough to kick the towel away.

"Bedroom?" Tanniv asked.

"Shower?" I gasped as Asra scooped me up in his arms.

"Perfect." The twins smirked as they leisurely carried me back to the bedroom I slept in and peeled off their clothes as we made our way to the huge shower.

This is perfect.

That was my last coherent thought before the siren alphas claimed me over and over again, eventually collapsing into dreamless sleep.

Chapter 20

Ella

I swear if I *have sex one more time today my vagina will break.* After having sex with Maddox, Reed, *and* the twins my body was so fucking sensitive. I was very aware that I didn't have any heat suppressant medicine here and I wasn't sure where the closest clinic would be to get some. Hell, I don't know if my mates would be good with me taking them. A discussion I wasn't up for just yet.

After a nap with Tanniv and Asra I dug through the bag they brought me and was happy to find my notebooks and pens were in there as well. Slipping into a pair of leggings I snagged Asra's T-shirt off the floor and pulled it on before padding out of the room. I didn't see any of my other mates as I made my way downstairs then outside. I took a deep breath, happiness filling me with the cool fall air and the hint of saltwater in the breeze.

Walking around the barn I found a nice shaded spot over in the far corner of the clearing, under a large pine tree. I wasn't worried about any overprotective alphas freaking out because I was in clear view of the house but I also had a bit of privacy sitting here by myself. Settling on the ground I shifted around a bit until I was comfortable and happy with the combination of Asra's scent of sage and rosewood combined with pine.

I hadn't told the guys about what had sent me on the late night walk in the woods and I wasn't sure how to say it. I mean, how many people outside of books can say they just randomly ran into a man who had a picture of a woman who could be your twin and claims he could be your father? I *had* a family! A shitty one that kept committing me to a mental hospital, but a family nonetheless and the possibility that my parents weren't my parents... it was a thrilling one and it was terrifying.

Biting my lip I opened my notebook and fiddled with one of the pens I had grabbed. Years in and out of a mental institution made journaling a habit of mine and this was the best way to process big changes like this. Plus, Birdie said it could help me with my magic. Briefly, I recalled that my words had a habit of becoming reality but with a shaky breath I decided it was worth the risk. I needed to work through all my thoughts and the best way to do that was to get it out of my head and on paper.

It wasn't long before page after page was filled with a stream of consciousness about everything that had happened since I'd gotten here. Finding a friend in Violet, my supernatural fated mates, finding out I wasn't just an ordinary human omega, and then the rest of my fated mates before the bombshell last night. Some of these brought back memories of my time at the ward and I wrote those down too, jumping from memory to memory until I felt tears stinging my eyes and a cry falling from my lips as a tear fell onto the paper, smearing the black ink.

"Stop crying, girl!" a loud voice barked, making me jolt.

I jerked my head up and I wasn't in the forest anymore. Instead, I found myself in an all too familiar room, a small medical bed under my butt that I was sitting on. A burly and angry security guard of the hospital was standing in the doorway glowering at me and the room that I just now realized was completely wrecked. What the hell had happened?!

He stalked forward and I scrambled backward, or at least tried to until my back hit the wall. My notebook and pen fell from my lap, clattering to the floor. He kicked them away as he grabbed me and threw me against the cold tiles.

"Destroying hospital property." He ground me into the hard linoleum floor. "Resisting me trying to help you."

"I didn't resist!" I tried to protest but he shoved my head into the floor hard enough my ears started to ring.

"Talking back," he growled, pushing me harder into the floor until it was difficult for me to breathe. "Keep going and make my fucking day. I would love to lock you up in a solitary room for a while. I bet you'll be much more humble after that."

I shook like a leaf, squeezing my eyes shut as I tried to shut him out. I kept trying to think of anything at all besides the man who was now hauling me up. I needed help. I needed someone who could rescue me from this asshole.

A flash of a growly, bear shifter, messy dark blond hair, amber eyes, and the smell of crisp wintergreen had me gasping. Then I called out for him over and over until my voice broke.

"Hunter! Hunter, please! Help me!"

A growl filled the air and the man above me didn't react, but I knew that sound. My alpha had heard and was coming for me. Trying to squirm under the man above me I found a renewed source of strength to attempt to get away. A taunting laugh was his only response until he flipped me over and smacked me. Blood filled my mouth as I cried out, shock and pain filled me after he hit me.

No. No, it couldn't be *him*. He was fired. Even the doctor at the hospital had been shocked when they found me. Bruises and handprints clear on my pale skin, the officer had been hauled away as they asked me over and over again what had happened. Luckily he had just hit me, never trying to hurt me worse than that, but I had been shaken. My parents were also angry on my behalf, a rarity to be sure, and Dad had demanded the security officer be fired and he be sent proof.

"Ella!" A strong voice called out my name and I turned to look at the still open door as Hunter appeared. He was in uniform and I immediately froze, but searching his amber eyes I saw only the promise of safety as he prowled forward and yanked the man off of me. The guy swung at Hunter, making my mate stumble back. But the next second he tackled the man onto the ground.

"What is going on?!" Reed called out and his face paled when he caught sight of me from the hallway. He rushed forward but it was too fast and I scrambled back making Reed freeze.

"Oh gods," breathed Spencer as the others all came into view. They all seemed confused and alarmed as they took in the full scene, including me and my split lip that I could feel swelling.

"There are no gods in places like this," Leif murmured, his voice bleak as he looked around the hallway.

Surprisingly it was Maddox who stepped forward as Hunter finally contained my attacker on the floor, pinning him in place but not hurting him. Maddox ignored them and approached me slowly, he kept his focus on me and Reed scooted back giving him room. I swallowed hard as I stared at Mads with wide eyes. Without breaking my stare he reached over and pushed the notebook and pen in my direction.

"Were you writing, Ella?" His voice was so gentle that I felt new tears run down my cheeks. I nodded slowly in silent answer. "Sometimes your words come to life, just like the lawn ornaments. All of this, that's what this is. You aren't here anymore."

"What broke it last time?" Reed asked.

"It played out," Drystan answered after a moment. "And we barely managed to cover the tracks with visiting tourists. Birdie had to help Opal with the glamour because it almost broke under the strain."

"Fuck," Asra cursed.

"We can't just let this play out," Maddox replied.

"I have an idea," Spencer finally spoke and everyone moved out of his way so he could sit down near me. "Hunter, come here." Maddox moved and took Hunter's place to hold down the guy and came to crouch near me, watching the two of us with an intense gaze. "Ella called out to you for help, Hunter. I think you're the only one that can help her fully break this. I might be able to help just by being here."

"I'll contact Birdie, just in case," Tanniv commented before stepping away. He must be calling her, better do it quickly before the nurses come back or he'll be in big trouble. We couldn't have phones here. Or maybe it was just me who couldn't have a phone? I couldn't really remember.

"What have you done!" The familiar sound of my usual night nurse was like a bucket of cold water poured over my head. A whimper escaped and instinct kicked in. I stood and ran before anyone could stop me. There was only one exit so I did the only thing I ever could, crawled under my bed. It was a fifty-fifty shot that they'd leave me without shoving a needle in my arm, but I'd take that chance over one hundred percent. The sedation meds were awful and I didn't like being vulnerable around them. "Who are these people?"

"Stay away from her!" Asra's yell was feral and I heard something crash but couldn't see the outcome from under here.

"Don't get close, Asra!" I pleaded. "She's a vampire and she'll force you immobile."

"This was real?" Reed whispered. "This is what she lived through?" The raw emotion in his tone hit me in my chest and I couldn't hold back my tears any longer. Panic and fear were so overwhelming I could barely breathe. I focused on the broken tile under the bed, looking away from the chaos and begging for a miracle. When the bed was ripped away, I screamed, cowering in the corner. But gentle hands found me, lifting me and placing me in someone's lap. Not someone. The smell of spring rain hit me and I knew Spencer had me. But I was in the hospital. He couldn't be here.

"Oh god. I've gone crazy. They finally broke me," I

whispered around a sob, curling further into myself as if that could hold me together.

"Never," Hunter said vehemently. It was a strong enough growled word that my head snapped up. Amber eyes met mine and he scooted close until his knees were hitting Spencer's and his hands took mine. "Look at me, Ella. You're free of this. You made it out and you made it to us. And I can promise, we'll never let go. We will always find you, always save you."

"It's too real," I said, a moment of clarity kicking in at his words. "It's like two worlds pulling at me and I can't find reality." The admission was full of vulnerability but I didn't know how else to explain it.

"We are the reality. You're in our forest, in Mystic Harbor," he explained. "In fact, we have food waiting for you when we get free of this."

I laughed at that, wiping at my running nose in a moment of true beauty. Honestly, I was a mess and we all knew it. Yet no one seemed to care. This wasn't too much, they weren't running. In fact, I managed to look around and all eight of my mates were here, for me. They'd come for me.

"Of course we came," Tanniv said softly.

"There's nowhere you could drift off to that we wouldn't find you," Reed promised.

Their reassurances helped some of the shadows clinging to my heart recede, but the vision refused to fade.

"Oh dear gods." The sound of Birdie's gasp cut in and for the first time, I looked upon her face that held no confidence and sass, just horror.

"This is where they kept my daughter?" Dean's shock matched Birdie's but his was colored with anger. Guess he was claiming me even before Birdie did the spell to confirm anything. Brooks came in behind them. My mates and maybe family, all here to see my skeletons, that closet door blown to bits now.

"It's calmed significantly, but how do we get rid of it?" Tanniv asked, but Birdie shook her head sadly and looked at me.

"Sweet girl. This is your battle, we can't do it for you. Overcome. Win." The words were gentle but she still said it with fire, urging me to take control.

"Come on," Hunter said, pulling me out of Spencer's lap. I did as he asked, following him to the center of the room despite wanting to run as far and fast as I could. "Look, they're gone. Find the forest."

"I can't," I admitted, shaking even with him still holding my hand. "It's the same four walls I spent far too many years in."

"But they can't hurt you," he explained. "Not anymore. You aren't a lost human, you're a strong witch with a whole town behind her. We've all got your back. And I won't let them hurt you."

"Promise?" I whispered back. He nodded, and even as my eyes took in his whole body, uniform and all, the only thing I felt was strong and safe. He was different from the rest and he was on my side. And damn that felt amazing.

"There you are." The sound of Doctor Sloane's stern voice hit me and panic clawed at my throat. But Hunter's hand tightened in mine.

"Not alone." That was all my bear mate said to me, but it was perfect. Determination filled me and I clenched my free hand into a fist.

"You're not real and you have no power over me. Not anymore!" I screamed. The yell echoed around us and a blast of magic hit my own personal villain. He gasped before falling into a pile of ash. As a breeze blew it off into the wind, the walls around us crumbled, revealing the reality hiding behind it. We were back in the forest and the asylum was gone.

"You did it," Hunter cheered, picking me up in a hug and swinging me around. I couldn't stop the smile on my face and it felt so fucking good that I'd been the one to fight back, to end this. But then reality hit me. I'd conjured this, trapped then exposed myself to them all.

Fuck.

"So, we're going to need to talk this one out," Birdie said, "before I go find this alleged former family of yours and blast them off this earth with glee."

"I'll be there helping you. I can be very fucking creative," Reed murmured, his voice so dark I shuddered and pushed myself closer to Hunter's body.

"We have breakfast inside, let's head back," Spencer suggested. Birdie, Dean, and Brooks led the way, but my mates held back.

"Are you okay?" Drystan asked, coming forward. He'd been quiet so far, but he was practically shaking with anger.

"Yes and no," I admitted with an uncertain shrug, stepping away from Hunter to see if I could stand on my own. "I'm proud of myself, but feel vulnerable and exposed and angry and upset and so many other things."

He stopped my rambling with a hug, holding me tight. "I'm so sorry."

"I'm safe now," I said, needing to hear it myself.

"You are," Hunter agreed. He still has a bit of a growl in his voice and I realized just how shaken my mate was now. I let go of Drystan and walked back over, placing a hand on his cheek so he'd meet my gaze.

"Thank you, Hunter. You really did save me," I said softly before wrapping my arms around him. He held me back tightly enough I didn't feel like I was falling apart any longer. My other mates let us have this moment until Tanniv finally spoke up.

"Birdie and the others are waiting for us," his voice was rough. "But why is Dean calling you his daughter?"

I swallowed hard, realizing that between mating with Leif and then this morning with Maddox and Reed, I hadn't been able to fill them in on what happened yesterday. They had no idea why I had gone on my long hike which ended up with me lost in the woods and finding this place. "They came here early to help me with training. Apparently, I look just like his old flame, Haven. His picture of her could be a picture of me. It was... a lot and—"

"That's what started your late night walk?" Asra finished for me and I nodded in agreement.

"We should go inside," Spencer spoke softly. "They are waiting on us and from the looks of things they aren't going anywhere without answers."

I bit my lip and started making my way towards the barn, Hunter and Spencer on either side of me. The moment we stepped into the house it was like I was on the spot, everyone's eyes going to me and waiting. Spencer guided me to the table, urging me to sit down.

"Where do I start?" I asked quietly. Some of them knew some things, others nothing.

"At the beginning," Dean said softly. My heart clenched at the worry and kindness in his words. Everything the father who raised me was not.

"Buckle in then, it's not a fun one," I grumbled. As if he knew I needed it, Drystan pushed a fresh cup of coffee in front of me while Leif slid me a muffin. They gave each other a suspicious glance, but in light of the tension in the room they backed off. It would be fun to watch them drop their guards over time. Picking at my muffin, I finally started, summarizing my years at the asylum, from the lies to the awful staff. "The three staff members you saw tonight, they were my own personal demons, torturing me every second they could." My fingers brushed over my split lip.

"They allowed violence like that? Or was it an out of hand memory?" I hated to dash Spencer's hope but I couldn't lie. Even if I could, I wouldn't. Not to them.

"They didn't know at first, he was careful. But the last time it was bad enough that he was fired. Even my parents intervened," I admitted. "The only time they ever seemed to care."

"Those monsters were not your parents," Birdie said firmly. Something in her tone had me looking up. "Look, I'm not usually shady, but I was too nosey to not try it. I found a blonde hair you left behind and did the ritual. He's your father, and I'm your grandmother."

"I know," I said softly. "When he showed me the picture, I knew. I could feel it, but I was overwhelmed."

"I'm sorry. I had no idea," Dean said, but I gave him a small reassuring smile.

"If they were involved with me never knowing you, I'm not surprised. But we know now," I reassured him.

"Go on. There is more, Ella. I can sense it," Tanniv urged. I nodded in resignation and continued.

"It went on like that, first it was like a week at a time then it escalated to months. I learned to keep my mouth shut but sometimes I'd get caught off guard and my expression would betray me. In reality, they had to have been trying to find any excuse. I confided in the one person I thought was a friend and walked in on them discussing sending me away. So I got out before they could. I'd been saving for years, every time they handed money over or left it lying around, so I got a ticket and came here. And now here we are."

"And what happened to you there at the hospital?" Reed asked reluctantly.

"Isolation, abuse, medicine that I didn't need," I admitted, looking down to not meet anyone's gaze. "I won't go into the gory details, but you witnessed the worst of it. There weren't really any good times. Even the other patients treated me like a leper to save themselves, but I survived."

"That you did," Dean said proudly. I could tell he had questions but was holding back from asking them. But I wanted a subject change.

"Sorry that I don't know anything about her," I said. "They raised me as 'mother' and 'father' so I didn't know any other family. I've never even heard her name."

"Haven was such a bright soul, but she was so timid. That summer she said it was the first time she felt alive," he said. His expression was wistful and sad. Everyone else slipped quietly away, giving us a moment alone.

"If my 'father' raised her, I get her being timid. I wasn't able to leave alone, to go places, to have a life of any kind," I said softly. "Do you think she's out there somewhere? Do you think she left me there?"

"She never would have left you," he said fiercely, shaking his head in denial. "Which is why I want to say no. But I *know* that she's alive. She's my mate."

"Gods, I'm so sorry," I said. My heart twisted at even the idea of being separated from mine and I just met them. "I couldn't imagine not knowing what's happening to my mates."

"It was awful," he admitted. "I was hurt and confused. Even spent years searching. But she was careful not to reveal too much and we really did live in the moment. We were young."

"How did Brooks come about?" I asked. At the sound of his name, he came back to join us, pouring a mug of coffee before sitting beside me at the table.

"His mother was amazing. She was full of life and one of a kind."

"Was?" I asked, putting a hand instinctively on Brooks' wrist, hating to hear the next part.

"She was killed in a car accident. I barely made it out alive," Brooks answered for him.

"I'm so sorry," I said, leaning over and hugging him. For some reason, I didn't feel the need to hold back and he gave me an awkward half-hug in return.

"Thanks. Sorry about all you dealt with," he said roughly.

"Life sucks sometimes," I said bluntly and we both chuckled a little. When we looked back, Dean was gone. It seems that everyone was just leaving me with different people.

"So, are you a witch too? I didn't know I was so I'm not really sure how supernatural genetics work."

He nodded. "I am. Mom was a half witch, half wolf. I got her heightened senses but no wolf form. My witch side is strongest."

"That's so cool," I said with a smile. "So is having an older brother."

He laughed. "I'm not really used to having siblings, but I'll admit, I'm glad to be back in Mystic Harbor. I've always loved coming to visit here. He hated being here but you gave him a reason to stay."

"Can't blame him. Life hasn't been nice to any of us," I said, both of us glancing at our dad in the other room. He just looked happy to be here, talking animatedly with my mates.

"You're not wrong. He's a great man though," Brooks promised.

"Birdie's great too. Though a bit eccentric," I joked. Brooks laughed at that and nodded.

"You don't know the half of it. One time I got a cold while we were visiting so she gave me a potion to 'cure' me. That shit gave me actual chest hair. I thought it was just an expression, apparently not. I was nine," he said, both of us cracking up. "Dad was so mad but he magicked it away. She wasn't a damn bit sorry. 'Hair is better than hacking out those coughs' she argued."

"That's amazing." I chuckled. "Note to self, avoid Birdie if I'm sick."

"It was one time!" she shouted from across the room. "Remind me some time though, I have pictures." Her evil cackle had us laughing again. It was so nice to let go and laugh after all the heavy shit.

Is this what family is really like?

CHAPTER 21

Ella

It has been an interesting week to say the least. Not only had I found all of my fated mates, I'd discovered my family, and the entire town looked like it was in chaos setting up for the festival. Everyone had something they were doing to get ready for the big event, the town square slowly transforming into the grounds of a festival with Reed cleaning up the last of the mess from the lawn ornament war.

We had all looked into the barn house I had found, but there was no record of such a place ever existing there before. Birdie had just commented about Mystic Harbor choosing people and said it looked like the town had provided for us. We had all talked, trying to figure out what we would be doing for a living situation. It wasn't really a situation where everyone could just drop everything and move in, that would be nice, but it wasn't really realistic. Leif was the mayor so having a place in town made sense. Hunter and Spencer had been living together for years and set up their own place. Drystan lived above his shop. Tanniv and Asra had to be near the ocean, the call of the water a part of them. Maddox... he had always lived with his brothers and close-knit didn't begin to describe his family.

After a big discussion between us we agreed the barndominium would be our big house together, but with others keeping their homes because sometimes we all need our own space, for relationships or necessity. I was sad to be moving out of the inn with Violet, but the prospect of my own home was too thrilling to be down for long. Reed and I moved our stuff in right away with the others bringing things over more slowly and claiming rooms. As the two omegas in our big group, the rest seemed happy to let us set up the place how we liked it.

Smiling, I walked out of the forest and headed toward the Enchanted Mug for some coffee from Drystan. I had off this week from the library, the gargoyles were getting ready for the festival, something about wanting to surprise me with their set up for the event. I think they wanted to give me time to settle into my new place without saying it outright. I chuckled to myself remembering Jonah's stumbling excuses for giving me the week off before he pushed me gently out the doors and Sterling shooed me away with a wink. Maddox had watched it all in amusement, laughing at his brothers' antics.

Walking into the coffee shop I found most of the tables full of people talking, everyone discussing what was coming up this weekend. The glamour flickered and I caught glimpses of their true forms as I got in line. Drystan's dry attitude was clear even from back here, his people skills being tested with so many coming in today to fuel up before preparations. When I got closer though he warmed up a bit, the grouchiness fading away until a small smile tugged at his lips when it was my turn.

"Just coffee today or food as well?"

I tilted my head, considering his question. "Just coffee?"

"Nope." He shook his head, giving me a shrewd look. "Reed already messaged me that you forgot to eat before you left the house."

"I think you just like being the one to cook for me," I joked.

A heated look filled his eyes before he instructed me to go to the back corner and sit down. My brows furrowed as I stepped away until I saw a small paper reserved sign with my name on it. It was the corner table Tanniv and I had sat at the first time we had come here together. Just as I sat down Drystan came over with a hot mug of coffee and a veggie frittata. He placed it down on the table as I leaned toward him and pressed a quick kiss to his cheek. Just as I was about to say thank you, he placed a hand on my chin and tilted my face up to kiss my lips. He grinned against my lips and I hummed at the taste of him and the scent of Earl Grey tea surrounding me.

"Thanks," I said breathlessly as he pulled away.

"Sit and eat every bite," he told me gruffly before pulling away. Dutifully, I grabbed the coffee and took a big sip as he waltzed away toward the counter. Once again my beta mate was acting like an alpha protector. I loved the fact he blew our norms out of the water.

I settled in and ate everything he gave me before finishing off the coffee. The bell above the door sounded and Leif walked in. He spoke to a few people before ordering from Drystan then made his way toward me.

Green eyes looked me over as he smirked and settled down beside me, his hand gripping my upper thigh tightly before rubbing his thumb along my jeans.

"Good morning." My cheeks heated under his attention, the spicy cinnamon scent of Leif surrounding me as he pressed a kiss to my cheek. Just one touch from an alpha and it was like the world stopped around us.

"How's preparing for the festival going?" I asked after clearing my throat.

Leif groaned, head falling back just as Drystan walked over with a cup of tea. Drystan stumbled a bit before catching himself and frowning at the fae. "It's just been one thing after another! I swear if I hear one more thing about the booth placements I'm going to lose it."

"You do realize everyone here can hear you, right?" Drystan scolded him as he put down the cup.

Leif half smiled at Drystan. "I'm hoping they do so I can at least enjoy my tea in peace."

"Are either of you coming to the house tonight?" I asked, looking between the two of them. Both men's expressions fell.

"Sorry. I can't." Leif squeezed my thigh. "I need to help Sterling tonight and it sounds like we will be going until pretty late."

"I'm prepping a bunch of food tonight for the cafe and the festival." Drystan reached out and ran a hand through my hair.

"Oh." I deflated, my shoulders hunching.

"Once the festival is done I'm sure I can make it up to you," Leif hinted, his voice deepened enough that I bit my lip to keep from whimpering.

"I *promise* I can make it up to you," Drystan replied, one-upping Leif with the promise and an arched look.

"Why do you always have to make it a contest, beta?" Leif asked, raising an eyebrow as he questioned Drystan.

"Because I'll win," Drystan snarked back, brown eyes flashing with challenge with a toothy smile. "Afraid of a bit of competition?"

"Never," Leif replied easily. "Sounds like a plan once the festival is finished. One night, all three of us. We can figure out who the clear winner is then."

"Deal."

I looked between the two of them wondering if I should question them talking about me like I'm not here, but honestly, this seemed like a win-win situation for me regardless so I was going to stay quiet. Leaning into Leif's side, I rested my head on his shoulder as someone called out to Drystan to order. He grumbled about annoying customers as he hurried back. Leif rested his head on top of mine, pressing a quick kiss to the top of my head before sitting up and drinking his tea.

We sat there and talked about the festival. I'd never been to one before and my mates were all determined to make it a memorable one for me. Once people realized Leif was there they kept coming over and asking him questions. Whether it was about people coming to town to be there for the festival or about Harold wanting more lawn ornaments set up at his booth. I think my cheeks were on fire as others flat out refused the idea of more flamingos and gnomes being allowed in town. *If the ground would swallow me whole right now that would be great.*

As a crowd started to gather around him I shifted away, overwhelmed by the amount of people and the noise. Leif smiled warmly at me, understanding clear on his face as I gave him a small wave in goodbye and my spot was taken by someone waiting to talk to him. Drystan shot me a quick smile as I left, desperate for some peace and quiet.

I didn't see any of my mates or Violet running around so I made my way to the one place that always promised quiet, the harbor. And the harbor didn't disappoint, no people running around or talking, the only noises were the birds squawking and the waves lapping the shore. I sat down near the end, but not right at the edge. All I needed was to fall in with no one here since I didn't know how to swim, though Asra and Tanniv both promised future lessons next summer. I couldn't wait.

A few deep breaths and my mind settled, happy to be alone until I heard someone approaching. The hint of leather made me grin as I turned to find Tanniv standing beside me.

"What are you up to?" he asked as he settled down next to me.

"I needed some quiet," I replied honestly, scooting over to get closer to him. He grabbed ahold of me to pull me onto his lap. A soft nip, followed by a kiss on my neck made me shiver in his arms.

"I love that you come here for that," he whispered against my skin.

"Am I interrupting?" an amused voice asked from in front of me.

"Yes," Tanniv growled as I giggled.

"Good," Asra commented as I heard hands slap on the dock and I looked up to find Asra pulling himself out of the water.

First I saw his fully webbed hands that were slightly blue with scales. He was shirtless and the blue coloring continued up his muscular chest. Solid charcoal black eyes met mine as he stared at me. He grinned fiercely, noticing my attention fixated on him. His teeth were sharper, more menacing and maybe I should have been afraid but I trembled with excitement as he crawled toward me.

"You like what you see?" he teased.

"Yes." I reached out, cupping his face with one of my hands. Right then I yawned big enough my jaw cracked. I covered my mouth with my other arm, snuggling into Tanniv. "Sorry."

"Long night?"

"Yes." I pulled at Asra to come closer, needing both of them with me. "I've gotten used to not sleeping alone and Reed was with Maddox last night. I couldn't really sleep at all."

"We need to work it out so you don't have to. You're not restricted to the house," Tanniv said absently, his mind already making plans. Just like that my alphas heard an issue and were trying to fix it. Being an omega was kind of awesome. Not that I ever thought so before. Humans used their designations like a badge of honor, so the alphas were dominating, and not in a good way. They chose to use their power against others and force their way. Omegas were seen as tools or trophies. Honestly, humans got a lot wrong about life. A true alpha was dominant, yes, but also protective and sweet, ensuring his family was properly cared for and had what they needed. It wasn't a power trip.

"You always have a place here, call next time," Asra agreed, pulling me out of my thoughts again. I was so tired even my thoughts were rambling. "Nap first, then we can find something fun to do."

"How can a girl resist that?" I joked but another yawn

made the words slur together. Tanniv chuckled and stood with me in his arms like I weighed nothing, before carrying me inside. I was asleep before my head hit the pillow.

The sound of talking outside had me opening my eyes. Hunter's voice mixed with my twin alphas. Before they came back in, Reed's joined the mix. What was going on? Did they all come here looking for me? Yet as I glanced at my phone I realized they hadn't been blowing up my phone, in fact, I'd only slept an hour but somehow I felt refreshed. That tended to happen when I had my mates around, it was like their energy fed into mine. Shifting in the bed I finally noticed that I was naked. I grinned, not the least bit put out that they had undressed me before putting me to bed. I rolled over, enjoying the warmth of the bedsheets from whoever had laid with me.

After throwing on Tanniv's shirt and a pair of Asra's clean boxers, I made my way to the deck. Tanniv and Asra were coming my way with a pile of things in their arms.

"Leif sent out a group text saying you were over-whelmed and exhausted. We said you were here getting some rest, so the rest of your mates all ended up sending stuff. It seems you took a group of badass supes and have them whipped already," Asra teased.

"I prefer to call it getting them in touch with their sweet side," I joked back. "What is it?"

Tanniv gestured for me to head back down so I did. They unloaded the items on the table and I burst out laughing.

"Is it sad or a power move that I can tell who sent what?" I laughed.

"Let's see if you're right," Asra challenged, sitting back.

"Drystan definitely sent the food, which might mean he thinks you can't properly feed me," I joked.

"One right," Tanniv hummed.

"Maddox obviously sent the book and the blanket," I continued, getting another nod of approval. "Reed sent the pillow, it's from my bed and smells like all of you, he'd get the significance of that. Leif sent the chocolate, because he and Drystan can't help but be competitive even subconsciously."

"I'm a little impressed," Asra said. "Now for the hard ones."

"Not hard," I shot back. "Hunter is the jacket, because he's the kind of alpha that would be afraid I'd leave early and get cold. Spencer is the journal, he knows it helps relax me to write."

"Perfect score." Tanniv laughed, opening up the to-go boxes to show a small buffet of my favorite comfort foods, from macaroni and cheese, to fries, to wings. Stuff he normally wouldn't feed me which made it so much more adorable.

Tanniv turned on a ghost hunting show, one of my favorites, and the three of us cuddled together on the couch as I dug into the food. I don't even remember bringing that up to him but I was learning very quickly how observant they were. It was like we were automatically attuned to each other without even having to try and that was more reassuring than anything else. No more pretending, no more being anything other than my authentic self and they seemed to love that version of me. And for once, I was learning to as well.

CHAPTER 22

Ella

The entire town had transformed almost overnight. I'd witnessed the slow progression as they built up the booths and did preparations, but this was a stark difference.

A live band was playing a cheerful song and between that and the sparkling magical lights floating in the air, it was the perfect ambiance. If it looked this great under the afternoon sun, I couldn't wait to see it at night. Leif even promised there'd be a bonfire later, something I was particularly looking forward to. The only ones I'd attended so far have been Birdie's and they always ended in spells and magic, not s'mores.

Everyone running a booth seemed to have an unspoken competition to outdo each other, decorating them to entice customers to come check them out. The bright colors and decor definitely worked on me. I made a mental note to come back to the gorgeous Amazon selling bath bombs and the sweet old wolf who made blankets. My need to collect all things soft was intense these days.

Would it be weird to ask the guys to roll around on it a bit so I have something to wrap myself in that smells like all of my mates?

The smell in the air was magical, a mix of fried foods, sweets, and popcorn. If someone asked what heaven smelled like, I'd refer them back to this very moment.

"Where to first?" Hunter asked, matching my enthusiasm. He was still in his uniform, just in case he was needed, but he was going to spend as much time as possible with us until then. He had a bright smile on his face and it made me wonder how I'd ever held a uniform against him.

"Food." I laughed, grabbing Spencer's hand and dragging him with me toward the popcorn booth. "Holy hell, they can do that to popcorn?"

"There are no laws against making popcorn delicious," the incubus behind the booth joked. His eyes were glowing bright magenta and he looked like he was thriving on the high emotions here today.

"But I want to try it all," I pouted playfully. "You pick."

Spencer laughed before turning to the old incubus. "We'll take a small bag of each," he said, making me gasp.

"Spencer, I was kidding!" I protested but he shook his head.

"Nope. Today we've agreed to indulge and spoil our omega, and I intend to do just that," he said firmly. I bit back a retort but my smile was obvious. Rocking up on my tiptoes I pressed a quick kiss to his cheek to let him know how much I loved the gesture. It was our first kiss and even one so innocent filled my stomach with butterflies.

Spencer's cheeks heated, but I could see the happiness shining in his hazel eyes as he paid. It felt nice to have someone doing something just to make me happy. And I was determined to do the same for my alphas once I was able.

The surprised incubus got to work, putting them in several bags and handing them out to my mates. I snagged the first bag I got and untied it, taking a deep breath at the birthday cake popcorn I'd picked. I munched on that as we continued our procession, checking out everything.

"How do they strengthen the glamour?" I asked as we stopped for a moment for the guys to grab a taste of the popcorn in my hand.

"They let the energy build during the day. This many supernaturals out here always helps. Then the mages all go to Opal and she leads them in bringing the glamour back to life and strengthening it," Leif explained.

"It's actually really cool to watch," Reed said. "I've seen it a handful of times and it's exciting every single time." He was lighting up at the prospect and it was nice to not be the only one losing my mind over all this. They were experiencing it with me and that made it so much more fun.

"We have to take her by my brothers," Maddox chimed in.

"And the games," Hunter added.

"And the mixed drinks," Asra said with a grin.

"No," Hunter and Spencer retorted at the same time, making me laugh at the last time I drank.

"And dancing." Leif smirked. "Don't worry, I can show you how."

"Ella!" Violet's timing was impeccable and I rushed

over to my friend, giving her a hug. I missed seeing her every day. "I was wondering when you'd get here."

"We got... distracted," I said, my cheeks heating as Leif chuckled behind me. He'd ensured that I smelled like him before we left. The others probably didn't think I noticed but they'd all been touching me whenever they could, trying to make sure his scent didn't overpower theirs. Having mates was hilarious sometimes.

"I don't blame them at all," Violet teased, winking at me as she looped an arm through mine. "I'll bring her right back to you, but there are a few people that want to say hello."

There were some lighthearted protests behind me but we paid them no mind as we walked through the crowds toward two women who were standing near one of the park's trees talking and avoiding the general chaos of the party. First, there was Birdie who greeted me with a knowing look and wink before hugging me roughly. Next, there was a beautiful fae, she had long pink hair that had to be hair dye and it was the color of cotton candy. Her eyes were shades of purple from light lavender to a dark plum color. The fae was dressed in a long flowy cream dress that offset her almost glowing tan skin. She was beautiful, more than just fae beauty, there was just something about her that caught and held my attention.

"Ella, this is Opal. Opal, here is the witchling who is putting you to work lately," Violet joked.

Opal's bright laughter made me feel instantly at ease as her eyes danced with amusement. "It is good to be put through my paces. Besides, it's not every day the fae gets to experience something new and you certainly are that."

"It's nice to meet you," I greeted her with a hesitant smile. Even being tied with Leif and Reed didn't put me at complete ease around other fae, but at least I didn't go into full avoidance like I did with Leif.

"I can't wait to see what else you have coming our way." She pulled me into a quick hug. I couldn't help but laugh, her greeting so intense but sweet that I liked her instantly. "Also, I know you're probably worried about the whole fae and asking questions thing," Opal waved her hands. "Don't worry about that with me. Though it was amazing to see the cat and mouse chase with you and Leif."

"Opal!" Violet tried to scold her, but it failed as she didn't quite manage to suppress her laughter.

"What?! It was." Opal winked at me. "I wish I could stay longer, but it looks like they need me for the glamour stuff. I'll see you around though? You need to start coming to our girls' nights because I have so many questions."

I didn't even manage to answer her before she ran off. Violet patted my shoulder. "Opal is a whirlwind of energy."

"Who is a whirlwind of energy?" a male voice asked.

We looked around and there was Dean walking up to us, followed by Brooks who was talking to Hunter and Spencer. Dean and Brooks were both dressed in jeans and T-shirts, both casual and comfortable as they approached. *My dad and brother, not just Dean and Brooks.* It was weird to think of him as my dad, my gut instantly twisting at the title. *Maybe I'll find him a new thing to call him? Pops?* I don't know. Maybe I'll just hold off to make sure it isn't just nerves.

"Dean," Birdie greeted her son with a shrewd look. "I thought you were dressing up."

"I did," he replied, with a lazy smile. "There are no holes in the jeans or my shirt."

"Low standards, boy," Birdie huffed as Brooks and my mates joined us.

"I think I look good. What do you all think?" He turned to face all of us, imploring us to agree with him.

I schooled my features, barely, as I replied innocently, "I'll have to agree with Birdie."

Dean pressed a hand over his heart as he staggered back dramatically. "Betrayed!"

"Smart girl knows who is her mentor and trainer." Birdie grinned conspiratorially at me.

"I'm staying out of it." Brooks held up his hands.

"Probably for the best," Violet commented.

"Ella!" I spun around, a wide grin filling my face as I saw Jonah approaching us. "You have to come see what we set up at the library. Sterling would be heartbroken if you didn't come right now."

"Sterling, huh?" I teased.

"Devastated."

"We can't have that. The dramatics of alphas." I rolled my eyes as I reached for one of Hunter's hands. "Come with me?"

"Mind if I tag along?" Brooks asked, looking between me and my mates.

"Not at all," Spencer waved for him to join us as we told the others we would see them later.

Jonah happily led us toward the library and I gasped as we got closer. It was a spooky house. The library was completely covered in fake spiderwebs and huge spiders on the outside of the windows. I burst out laughing, almost falling over when I noticed the leftover gnomes, whole and in pieces, redecorated as zombie gnomes.

"What do you think?" Jonah looked so proud as we stopped outside of the building.

"Oh my gosh," I managed to reply a few minutes later once I got my laughter under control. "This is amazing!"

"Are those— Are those your brothers up there?" Spencer asked, pointing up and I looked up and shock filled me as I noticed the gargoyles sitting at the top of the library.

They were all sitting and talking to each other, not paying attention to anyone at all until one of them suddenly dive-bombed down, almost hitting someone near us making them scream. He landed right in front of us and my eyes widened when I realized it was Maddox. Cold and snow surrounded me as he grinned at me. His skin was now completely stone gray, muscles literally looked like they were chiseled onto him, and bright silver eyes stared at me as I took him all in. He tucked dark bat-like wings tight to his body as he leaned down to brush a light kiss on my lips.

"I'll meet up with you and the others once my shift here is over."

"Okay." I kissed him back before he stepped back and flew back up to the roof.

"Guess we really don't have to worry about the glamour coming down and scaring you off," Jonah joked, but I heard an undercurrent of nerves and relief in his statement.

"I could see through it beforehand."

"That's different than seeing us as we are twenty-four seven," he pointed out. "Besides, not all of us look mostly human until we want to shift."

"Most of my sisters' mates don't look human," Brooks interjected.

"True." The gargoyle's shrewd gaze shifted to my

brother. "Looks like you're collecting yourself a big family, little sister. All kinds of trouble we can get into."

"I heard that!" a gravelly voice called out.

"Heard what, oh great brother of mine?" Jonah asked innocently as I grabbed Hunter's hand and led the way into the library.

"You both are going to keep Sterling on his toes," Hunter commented.

"We have already been separated at work. How much trouble can we get into?"

"I don't want to know the answer to that question," Spencer joked, coming up on my other side as Brooks trailed behind us.

"Please tell me there aren't any clowns in this thing," Brooks muttered as he stayed close.

"You can borrow Hunter if you're scared," I told him sweetly as Spencer chuckled.

"I can see you both fell into the sibling roles easily," Hunter muttered as Brooks flipped me off. I grinned, knowing he was right. For some reason, Brooks and I skipped right over that initial awkwardness to a mutual understanding, then straight siblings. Joking and teasing seemed like it would be our natural fallback and I was here for it.

It was an amazing haunted house. Each room of the place was expertly set up and I instantly thought of ways to add to it next year. There was no way they could keep me from helping next year, but I loved that they surprised me with it. I loved spooky stuff! But it didn't look like Brooks had the same taste because as soon as we got out he looked a bit shaken and said he would catch up with us later.

"Think he's okay?" I asked, trying to look back at him.

"Yeah, just needs a few minutes to get himself together," Hunter reassured me.

"Hey, Hunter!" a cool voice called. We all stopped and looked over, there was an unfamiliar man there. Short brown hair fell across his face and yellow eyes gleamed with a toothy smile. *Werewolf.* "Looks like there is a fight breaking out at the bar tent. Leif asked me to track you down."

Hunter heaved a resigned sigh. "I'll be right there." The stranger nodded and left us with a small wave. Hunter pulled me into a tight hug, pressing a kiss to the top of my head. "Well, this lasted longer than I thought it would."

"They must have waited to pull out the dwarven brews." Spencer gave Hunter a soft smile as the alpha pulled him over to kiss him soundly. "You can catch up with us later."

"Love you," Hunter told Spencer who said it back with another quick kiss.

I felt safe and at home between the two of them, wintergreen, citrus, and sage making me feel so cozy and at peace. Their love for each other just added another level to that. I didn't grow up around people who loved me and to see it between two people I cared about... Well, what more could I want for them? I shivered between them and Hunter felt it. He took off his black beanie and stuck it on my head before walking off to get to work.

"If you're cold we could hit up one of the food tents." Spencer grabbed my hand, threading his fingers through mine. He tugged at my hand but I didn't move to follow. "Is something wrong?"

I shook my head, trying to find the words for what I was feeling. Spencer turned to face me fully, concern clear in his eyes. Wrapping my arms around his waist I held him tightly, burying my face in his chest as I felt tears prick my eyes.

"Are you crying?"

"Happy tears," I whispered as he hugged me back. "I just— I didn't think I'd be this happy. I want you to know that I'm happy. Happy here with all of you. With you and Hunter."

He squeezed me tighter. "Me too. I'll be honest, you weren't something we were expecting. I think that's safe to say for everyone. But honestly, I don't think we would have it any other way. I know Hunter and I feel that way."

"You do?" I asked, uncertainty making my voice so small I don't think he would have heard me if he wasn't supernatural.

"You are an addition to what we have together." Spencer pulled back and gently cupped my face, forcing me to meet his fierce gaze. "You changed us, yes, but not in a bad way. You created this space that's just for you with us."

I sniffed, searching his face, trying to detect the lie. When there was nothing but patient honesty staring back at me, I leaned forward, capturing his lips in a timid kiss. Spencer moaned, his hands tensing on my face as he tilted me to deepen the kiss as his tongue teased my lips so I would let him in. The hint of beer and apple pie on his lips made me hungry as I felt slick wet my pussy. Gods, I wish we were anywhere besides this damn festival. Then it really hit me. This was our first kiss. A wave of chaotic emotions hit me, throwing me off balance.

As if he could read my thoughts Spencer broke the kiss, pressing his forehead to mine. "Hunter is going to be annoyed with that drunk guy that he wasn't here for this."

I laughed roughly. "I think we could reenact it. If he asks nicely."

"Big talk, Ella. Wait until you have a bear chasing you."

"I like a challenge," I murmured and I could feel his answering smirk as I kissed him again.

"Be careful what you wish for." He chuckled before another person I didn't recognize walked up to us.

"Hey, Hunter sent me to find you, he needs help with something," the short man said, his hands weaving nervously through his beard.

"The bear beckons," Spencer joked. "Want me to walk you somewhere first?" It was sweet to offer, but I was still feeling a bit off either from the kiss or everything going on.

"I'll just head back to the others," I promised. He bent down and gave me one more kiss before rushing off, but even that small touch from my mate had more slick flooding between my thighs and I was so hot I was about to strip right here in the middle of town.

What the hell is going on?

Wiping at my still damp cheeks, I went for the closest bench, sitting down for a second. A cool breeze filled the street and I let my head fall back, just trying to calm the overwhelming heat hitting me.

Then it hit me.

The dull ache. The hot flash. The slick response to my mates.

I was in heat.

"Shit," I cursed, thinking back on if I had any heat suppressants with me in town. I didn't have a huge supply when I left and I'd been so distracted I'd lost track of time. Either way, I'd have to find a mate and head home before every alpha in the area lost it. We were a long way from the old days where alphas would simply lose their minds at an omega in heat, but that didn't mean that it didn't make the wrong kind of alpha aggressive if he happened upon me alone like this.

My mind fogged and I tried to stand, wishing I could find my phone. As my hand fumbled around my bag to find it, someone sat next to me.

"I thought I smelled the vanilla tainted tears of a sad, broken little omega," a familiar voice said. It was like ice was thrown over me, shocking my overheated system. Was I hallucinating? But one look to my left and I knew that my nightmare had followed me here.

"What are you doing here?" I gasped, standing and nearly falling. "Maddox!" He was my closest mate and I was panicking. A jolt of magic escaped me, chaotic in my desperation to save myself. Before I could yell again, he grabbed me and slapped a hand over my mouth and the prick of a needle in my neck had my heart stopping. There wasn't even time to react before blackness overtook me and I fell back in my former father's clutches.

EPILOGUE
MADDOX

The wind carried the sound of Ella's voice to me, followed by an odd jolt of magic that slammed into me like a lightning bolt. It wasn't painful, instead, it filled me with panic. When I glanced in the direction I heard it from, she was nowhere to be seen. At first, I was going to write it off as our bond and her chaotic magic, but that settled when she found Leif. Then it hit me.

Something's wrong. I could feel that down to my soul and it pushed me into action.

"I have to find Ella," I called out to my brothers. The panic in my voice had them all on alert, glancing down at the grounds below but I was already flying off. I could hear them behind me and I was relieved to have support.

Ella's scent was strong here and so was the scent of her heat, but the scent accompanying hers was foreign to me. It was bitter and smokey, like dark magic and Spencer's was so faint that I knew they weren't together anymore.

"That scent isn't from anyone in this town," Sterling commented darkly.

Ella said she was running away from her life to start over. I saw enough from the asylum coming to life that the people who raised her were fucking garbage. But abusers, they don't like to let people just walk away from them. They must have come after her.

"Someone has her. Get Birdie, get the others!" I screamed as I flew off, following her scent like a bloodhound. Moments later I could smell something acrid, her scent tainted and I knew she was drugged. It was just about the only thing that could mask and change a scent like this.

"What's going on?" Violet's voice growled next to me. She was half in wolf form but keeping as human as possible to communicate. "Oh gods... this scent. She lost it soon after, but this scent is familiar. She reeked of it when she first got here."

"Then they found her," I said, confirming my earlier thoughts and my worst fear. That thought was terrifying, almost more terrifying than if it was some stupid alpha in a rut. We could have gotten him in time, but this was a calculated move, prepped down to the point of stealing her away and being gone before we could follow.

As we approached the glamour shield, we froze. We'd have to bolster our own before following and from the burn of tires on the road, she was already on her way back home.

We were too late.

"We have no idea where she's from," I growled, helplessness and rage filling me. "This is going to be a near impossible hunt."

"Hey, don't break down on me now, alpha. She has a human ID with her address. We need to find it. It has her real name as well so maybe with Hunter's connections, we can track them down too. After that, we can find where they are keeping her," Violet reasoned. Her logic was sound and the only reason I didn't cross the line to start hunting her down myself. Not to mention, the others deserved to know. *Plus, we will all need to be looking for her to find her.*

By the time we reached the center of town, the festival had literally paused. Over half the town was here waiting for answers, worried looks on almost everyone's face. The other half seemed to be searching for her.

"Where is she?" Dean approached, eyes wild with his son, Brooks, right behind him.

"From the scents... It looks like she was drugged and kidnapped by her former family," I admitted in defeat. "We have to get our girl back."

"And we will. We made a promise, that no one could ever take her away, we'd always find her," Leif said firmly before barking out orders to all of us. Once it was just our group and Violet, she started explaining her side of things.

"That's not all," I added heavily. They all froze, not expecting this to get worse. "She's in heat."

"Fuck, find her info, now!" Tanniv yelled, losing his generally calm demeanor. We turned and sprinted to the barndominium in hopes of tracking that information down. Hunter went back to the sheriff's office to start setting up a missing person's report, and as soon as we had the info, a kidnapping alert on her father's car. He was just waiting on the full name and information to submit it.

"Got it!" Violet yelled, holding up the ID, the contents of Ella's suitcase emptied on the bed. A hollow eyed Ella stared back from the plastic card, and the thought of her back in that life nearly broke me.

We're coming, Ella.

WANT MORE?

Power of Fate is the first book in the Mystic Harbor Trilogy, if you love Ella and her men, check out book two, here: https://geni.us/maskedbychaos

---

For updates and info on Suki's work, make sure you join her reader group and stalk... I mean follow, her on social media!

https://linktr.ee/SukiWilliams

Reader Group
Suki's House

Newsletter Sign Up

For updates and info on Jarica's work, make sure you join her reader group and stalk... I mean follow, her on social media!

The Reaper Realm:

Bookbub:

Instagram:

Website/Newsletter:

ALSO BY SUKI WILLIAMS

ALSO BY JARICA JAMES

Paranormal Reads

Obsidian Cove Supernatural Academy series: (6 book series)

Call of the Siren: http://geni.us/cots

Path of the Bear: http://geni.us/potb

Trial of the Vampire: http://geni.us/totv

Mark of the Psychic: https://geni.us/motp

Power of the Mage: https://geni.us/POTM

Vigil of the Gargoyle: http://geni.us/votg

The Spirit Vlog series: (Ghost hunters, each book is a new case) (completed)

Haunts and Hotels: http://geni.us/handh

Parks and Poltergeists: http://geni.us/pandp

Haunt Sweet Home: https://geni.us/hauntsweethome

Mines and Manifestations: https://geni.us/mandm

***

The Forgotten: (Co-write with Suki Williams) (Dystopian PNR Demigods) (Completed)

Nexus: https://geni.us/fpnexus

Broken:https://geni.us/fpbroken

Memory: https://geni.us/fpmemory

Reset: https://geni.us/fpreset

***

Not Your Basic Witch series cowrite with A.J. Macey: (completed)

Witch, Please: http://geni.us/NYBW1

Resting Witch Face: http://geni.us/NYBW2

Witches be Crazy: http://geni.us/NYBW3

Born to be Witchy: http://geni.us/NYBWnovella

***

Academy of the Elite series cowrite with Rowan Thalia: (3 Book Series)

Juniper's Sight: http://geni.us/juniper

Juniper's Peril: http://geni.us/juniper2

Juniper's Trial: (in progress)

***

Pinch of Sass cowrite with Chloe Gunter:

http://geni.us/pinch (Standalone)

Scifi Reads

Chosen by the Stars: https://geni.us/SOSChosen

***

Check out Saved by the Stars and Healed by the Stars here:

https://geni.us/sosshareduniverse

Dark Reads

Cruel Crimes: (Dark Mafia RH Romance Duet)

Damaged goods: https://geni.us/Damaged

Wicked Games: https://geni.us/ccwicked

Twisted: (Bully BDSM Standalone)
https://geni.us/twistedmmf

Young Adult/New Adult Reverse Harem Reads

Broken Silence: http://geni.us/brokens (YA)

Battered Voices: *https://geni.us/batteredv* (NA)

Contemporary Romcoms

Besties & Booze series of standalones-shared universe:
Faked by A.J. Macey: http://geni.us/faked

Arranged by Jarica James: http://geni.us/arranged

Performed by Suki Williams: http://geni.us/performed

Played by Elyssa Dawn: http://geni.us/played

MF
Once Upon A Pineapple: https://geni.us/ouap (Standalone MF as Jarica Riley)